W9-ALN-605

DISCARD

DOUBLE MURDER

DOUBLE MURDER

BARBARA TAYLOR McCAFFERTY
and BEVERLY TAYLOR HERALD

Kensington Books

KENSINGTON BOOKS are published by

Kensington Publishing Corp.
850 Third Avenue
New York, NY 10022

Library of Congress Card Catalog Number: 96-076490
ISBN 1-57566-084-9

First Printing: September, 1996
10 9 8 7 6 5 4 3 2 1

Printed in the United States of America

To Bill Herald,
and to our double sets of children:
Paul and Beth Young, and Patrick Young Herald;
and Geoffrey, Christopher and Rachael Taylor

Acknowledgments:

Special thanks to Bill Love, a thirty-year veteran of radio, now with WKDQ-FM, Evansville, Indiana, for sharing his expertise and advice.

Chapter 1

●

BERT

What happened wasn't all that out of the ordinary.

I tried to make that clear to the police later. I told them, when you're a twin, it happens to you all the time. Some guy you've never met before just walks up to you one day and starts talking as if you and he were old friends.

And what do you do? Well, if you have a twin sister like mine, you smile and act friendly. Right away. Without hesitation.

I know. I know. Every female in the world has, no doubt, been warned over and over again *not* to talk to strangers. *I* have been warned. My sister, Nan, has been warned. As a matter of fact, when we were in junior high, I remember quite clearly our mother taking a certain grim satisfaction out of directing Nan's and my horrified attention to the latest blood-splashed cover of *True Crime Stories* in the magazine rack at the local drugstore. As our identical eyes widened, Mom went on and on. "Nan, do you see that?" she said. "Bert, do you?"

That's right. Nan and Bert. Our mother actually named us after the older pair of twins in all those Bobbsey Twin books. The Bobbsey twins had been boy and girl twins, but Mom had not let a little thing like that stop her. Oh, no, when her own babies had turned out to be two identical *girls* instead of the boy and girl twins she'd planned on, Mom had simply lengthened one of the names she'd already picked out—from Bert to *Bertrice.*

And then, of course, everybody had immediately started calling me Bert, for short. Thank God, I might add.

As I recall, I complained to Mom about my name just once, when I was around thirteen and pretty much complaining about everything else in my life at the same time. Mom's response had been to remind me quietly that she could've named me after the girl in the younger pair of Bobbseys: *Flossy.*

Mom always knew how to make a point.

Like with that *True Crime Stories* cover I just mentioned. By the time Mom finished with us that day in the drugstore, Nan and I had been convinced that the horrors depicted on that magazine's lurid cover would never have occurred if only the woman in the photograph had simply refrained from speaking to a man she didn't know.

So, all right already, to give Mom her due, I admit it. I know better than to strike up a conversation with some stranger on the street. Unfortunately, however, I also know that my sister Nan can work herself up into a real snit if she finds out that I've inadvertently snubbed some potential date she's been cultivating for months.

That's why I made up my mind a long time ago that the chances of my being approached on the street in Louisville, Kentucky, by a possible bloodthirsty *True Crime Stories* killer was a lot less likely than my running into a possible Mr. Right of Nan's.

I also made up my mind a long time ago that I'd *much*

rather deal with a bloodthirsty killer than deal with Nan when she's in a bad mood.

I mention all this so that you'll understand why—when the total stranger in the gray overcoat came up to me right after I'd walked out of the Citizens Plaza Building around noon on that clear, sunlit Thursday in October—I actually stood there and talked to him.

I wasn't the least bit afraid.

"Why, hello, there," he said, gliding up beside me.

By the time he spoke, I was standing at the crosswalk just outside the Plaza's front door, waiting for the traffic light to change. My eyes were on the light across the street, and several people had collected around me, so for a moment, I wasn't exactly sure who'd spoken.

When the guy added, "It's great to see you again," I realized it was the bearded stranger at my elbow. Who was looking straight at me with eyes so blue they might've made Paul Newman envious.

Before I said anything back to him, I gave the guy a good long look. First, to make sure I really didn't know him.

I didn't.

And, second, to make sure I could accurately describe him later to Nan. That's how convinced I was right from the first that this guy had mistaken me for her.

Nan and I had already made plans to have dinner at her place that night. That is, if you'd call what we planned to have, *dinner.* Neither of us wanted to cook, so I was supposed to stop by McDonald's on the way home. I knew very well that if I couldn't give Nan a clear picture of whoever this was, she might slip something lethal into my Quarter Pounder.

I stared at him, trying to think of a movie star he reminded me of. Other than his eyes being bluer than Paul Newman's, I couldn't think of anybody. This was too bad, believe me. Because Nan is one of those people who has spent far too much of her life in a movie theater or in front of a television screen. And she always describes everybody she meets in terms of how much they look like some actor or actress. Really. To hear Nan talk, you'd think her entire world was peopled with movie star look-alikes.

Unable to come up with an actor this guy resembled, I tried to fix him firmly in my mind. Let me see. He was about six two with dark brown hair, broad shoulders, and the aforementioned unbelievably blue eyes. He had a deep tan, a neatly clipped beard, and crow's feet around his eyes. Which meant he could've been a twenty-five-year-old who hadn't withstood the sun too well—or a forty-year-old who'd somehow managed to keep his physique amazingly trim and muscular.

Or he could've been any age in between. With that beard concealing most of his face, it was hard to tell.

Other than the gray overcoat, the guy was wearing gray flannel slacks, a pale blue shirt that went very well with his eyes, a navy blue blazer and a red tie with navy diagonal stripes.

My first impression was that he had to be a banker.

A banker who could easily make my list of Top Ten Handsomest Men I'd Never Met.

This particular list, incidentally, is headed by Mel Gibson.

"Oh," I said uncertainly. "Hi."

"I've been hoping we'd run into each other again," Top Ten said.

I blinked once before I put a smile on my face.

Oh my yes, Top Ten had me confused with Nan, all right. No doubt about it. Because he didn't look even slightly familiar. And I knew, if I personally had ever laid eyes on this particular guy before, I would've remembered him.

Much like I would've remembered Mel.

If I hadn't been in such a hurry, I probably would've taken the time to tell Top Ten that I wasn't who he thought I was. That I had an identical twin sister who, guess what, looks exactly like me.

I knew from experience, however, how this particular conversation usually went. As soon as I mention the word *twin*, whoever it is who's just mistaken me for Nan starts peering into my face, studying my features like something strange they've just spotted under a microscope. All the while they're invading my space, they're telling me, in appalling detail, exactly where—in their opinion—Nan and I differ.

Let me tell you, it's a real treat to discuss such things as moles, freckles and blemishes with a complete stranger.

It also takes up quite a bit of time. Have I mentioned, I was on my lunch hour? Have I also mentioned that, according to one of the other women in my office, Bacon's Department Store in the Galleria shopping center downtown had only just this morning put up little signs all over *both* floors that said TAKE AN EXTRA 30% OFF THE LOWEST MARKED PRICE? I was more than a little anxious to join the feeding frenzy, so all I said to the stranger was, "Oh, really?"

Sort of noncommittal.

From the guy's reaction, you'd have thought I'd swooned at his feet.

He gave me a grin that told me he was well aware how good-looking he was. "You know," he said, moving even closer, "I think you get more beautiful every time I see you."

This time I didn't even blink. Nan and I are not beautiful. We don't look bad for two women who have only ten months to go until they're forty, but beautiful—let's face it—we ain't. Our brown hair is shoulder length and naturally curly, so it's always out of control. Our brown eyes are probably our best feature, but Nan and I are both extremely near-sighted. On days we can't wear our contacts for one reason or another, our so-called best feature is hidden behind thick lenses. *And,* although we could be described as slender, we could also be described as bony. Our elbows should be registered as lethal weapons.

Given all this as fact, however, I still didn't particularly want to argue with a good-looking man who was insisting that I was good-looking, too. So I just said, "Thanks," and smiled at him. I hoped, knowingly.

What I knew, of course, was that all of Nan's potentials are like this. Not only extremely good-looking, but extremely smooth-talking. "I think the night we met you must've put some kind of spell on me." Top Ten was now going on. "I haven't been able to get you out of my mind. It seems to me as if—"

The traffic light changed then, and everybody around us started to move forward. I would've liked to follow, but it seemed rude to just walk off when Top Ten was in the middle of a compliment.

He must've thought I might be inclined to be rude, though, because he reached out and took my elbow. He wasn't really preventing me from leaving, but then again, I couldn't exactly ignore the pressure of his hand on my arm. "—ever since that night, everywhere I turn, I see your face."

If he was seeing my face at that moment, he was seeing a look of total skepticism. Evidently, he picked up on it, too. He quickly added, "Look, I know you think I probably say these things to every woman I meet, but I really am telling you the truth. You've been on my mind for weeks."

I stood there, resisting the urge to pull away. I really hate to have somebody hanging onto me. My ex-husband Jake used to grip my elbow like this whenever he had anything at all he wanted to say to me. He would position himself right in front of my face, take hold of my arm, and drone on and on. It had been his way of making sure he had my complete attention.

It had also been his way of making sure he was a complete pain in the neck.

Now, to keep from abruptly wrenching my arm out of Top Ten's grasp, I had to remind myself that I wasn't being me right then. I was being Nan. And if *Nan* was acquainted with Top Ten here, she would most certainly let him take her elbow. She would also most certainly want me to find out exactly where she and this guy had met.

So I cleared my throat and said, "Weeks? I've been on your mind for *weeks?*" I was hoping Top Ten would take the cue and elaborate a little.

I was also hoping—not to belabor the point—that he'd let go of my arm.

He didn't.

On both counts.

"*Weeks,*" he repeated. "In fact, I've been trying to get up the courage to give you a call for some time now."

I blinked. This is the kind of effect Nan has on good-looking men. Me, I'm lucky if they remember my name. Nan makes them shake in their shoes.

Of course, the way Nan seems to draw men like a magnet might have something to do with her job. Nan is the afternoon deejay on WCKI, Country Kentucky Indiana, a country music station in Louisville. Everybody we meet—men and women alike—seem pretty impressed when they find out what Nan does for a living.

I guess I'm pretty impressed myself. Around Louisville, Nan Tatum is what is known as a local personality.

I, on the other hand, happen to be what is known as a local nobody. Far from having an interesting job that impresses people, for the last year or so—ever since my divorce was final—I'd been working as an office temporary and wondering what I'm going to be when I grow up.

I think I've made up my mind that what I'm going to be is irritable. I was now resisting another urge—to ask Top Ten, "You haven't called in weeks because you've been too scared? Then, what you're trying to tell me is that I'm *frightening?* Gosh, *thanks.*"

I was pretty sure, however, that Nan would never say something this antagonistic to a man this good-looking. I was also pretty sure that she'd be batting her eyelashes at him by this time. So I tried to do the same.

I probably looked as if one of my contacts had slipped, and I was trying to blink it back into place.

Top Ten's grin widened. "You know, you look stunning in that navy blue suit. That's got to be one of your colors. You ought to wear it all the time."

I just looked at him for a second, and then I began to smile in earnest. The suit I had on was a very nice, wool Liz Claiborne but I really didn't think the outfit warranted applause or anything. What's more, did this guy actually make a habit of walking up to women on the street and giving them fashion tips? I couldn't help wondering what kind of success rate Top Ten could possibly have with an approach like this.

"Thanks again," I said, starting to step off the curb.

Top Ten's hand tightened on my arm. "So, what do you say? Do you think there's a chance that you and I could go out sometime?"

My goodness, he didn't waste any time, did he? I swallowed once before I answered. Back when we were in junior high, when we'd first started dating, Nan and I had discussed exactly what each of us could do when we were being the other one. We'd decided: As Nan, I could flirt outrageously. As Nan, I could give some guy my phone number. And, yes, as Nan, I could shamelessly encourage some guy to call me. It was, however, at this point that Nan and I drew the line.

As Nan, I could *not* accept an actual date.

Not since that time back in the ninth grade when, as Nan, I'd agreed to go out with Lester Jeffries. It had been an honest mistake. I'd thought the reason Nan always turned so pale whenever Lester was around was that she'd liked him.

As it turned out, Lester's presence had made her nauseous.

Now, staring into Top Ten's stunningly blue eyes, I was almost sure Nan would drop to her knees and thank the dear Lord that this guy was interested in dating her, but you never could tell. There *was* a chance, albeit slim, that Top Ten here was a Lester Jeffries, extremely well disguised.

So all I said was, "Why don't you give me a call, and we'll talk about it. OK?"

As I spoke, I turned to give Top Ten an encouraging smile, but oddly enough, right then he was no longer looking at me. He was staring across the street. The light had changed again, and a small crowd had gathered over there, waiting to cross. Much like the small crowd now gathering in back of us on this side of the street.

Top Ten's gaze, directed straight across from us, was so intense I thought for a second that he'd caught sight of someone else over there that he thought he knew.

I followed his gaze, but I couldn't tell who he was looking at. Or if, for certain, he really was looking at somebody.

I gave the opposite side an intense stare of my own, but it was useless. Either whoever it was who'd caught Top Ten's eye had already melted back into the crowd. Or else there had never really been anybody there in the first place.

Top Ten's blue eyes were now again riveted on mine. "OK, then, it's settled, I'll call you this afternoon," he said. The traffic light changed once again right then, and this time when I started to move across the street with the rest of the crowd, Top Ten let go of my elbow and fell into step beside me. "Are you headed toward the Galleria? Because that's where I'm going, and I'll keep you company if you don't mind—"

It's funny, but even now—even after everything that's happened—it is this part of the entire encounter that still stands out clearest in my mind.

I suppose that's because it was at this particular point that I could so easily have agreed to walk to the Galleria with him. After all, the Galleria was indeed exactly where I was headed. What's more, the prospect of spending a few more moments with somebody who looked like Top Ten did have a certain appeal.

I opened my mouth, pretty much intending to say, "Fine," and then, for several reasons, I reconsidered. The Galleria shopping mall *was* several blocks away, a good ten minute walk from where we were at that moment. And, it occurred to me, I still didn't even know this guy's name. So far, I'd managed to pull off being Nan, but sooner or later, I was bound to slip up. If Top Ten should start talking about specifics, mentioning anything at all that I should remember about the night Nan and he had met, I'd be dead.

Oh yes, I distinctly remember thinking those actual words.

I'd be dead.

The longer I spent with this guy, the more likely it was that I might reveal that I didn't have the slightest idea who he was. If that were to happen—and I were to spoil Nan's chances with this guy—there was every possibility that Nan might be even angrier with me than she'd been over the Lester Jeffries episode.

All this flashed through my mind just as Top Ten and I were about to pass a drugstore on my right. I stopped abruptly and indicated the store with a nod of my head. "No," I lied, "I'm not going to the Galleria. I was just on my way to this drugstore. To, uh, pick up a prescription. For a friend."

Top Ten stopped abruptly, too, and then just stood there, looking disappointed. "Oh," he said. "Well, then."

That, I believe, is an exact quote. *Well, then.* Standing there on the street, I had no idea what exactly he meant by that.

After Top Ten said, *Well, then,* though, he did something that my ex-husband Jake had not done in nineteen entire years of marriage. Top Ten walked over and opened the door to the drugstore. What's more, he actually continued to hold it open until I stepped through it.

My mouth almost dropped open.

Top Ten gave me a warm smile, his blue eyes intense, as I moved past him. "I *will* be calling you this afternoon," he said.

I nodded, returning his smile.

It was an effort to smile, believe me, because I was suddenly feeling extremely sharp twinges of something that here lately, I'd been trying very hard *not* to feel.

That something being Nan-envy, of course.

And yet, how could I keep from envying her? I would've liked to have believed that things were going just as great for me as they seemed to be going for Nan, but if I really thought such a thing, I'd have to be out of my mind.

Nan seemed to have all the men she wanted, and today, no surprise, she had apparently added an extremely good-looking guy with Paul Newman eyes to her extensive collection.

I, on the other hand, could count on one hand the number of dates I'd had since my divorce was final.

All her life Nan has had just herself to spend her money on, so today her MasterCard was paid off and she owned a very nice brick duplex on Napoleon Boulevard in the High-lands neighborhood in Louisville. Me, I was scraping along trying to live on a salary that wasn't even a third of what Jake used to bring home, and—because there was no way I could afford to keep it—I'd had to sell Jake my half of the house I'd lived in ever since our first child was born.

I knew I should consider myself lucky that Nan had offered me the other half of her duplex at a very reasonable rent. My half of the building was a two-story townhouse with a fireplace in the living room and an updated kitchen, virtually identical to Nan's. I had my own separate entrance facing the street, and there wasn't a reason in the world that I shouldn't be tickled pink with the whole deal.

And yet, every time I wrote Nan a check, I wanted to wince.

I mean, my landlord was a woman I was ten minutes *older* than, for God's sake.

Apparently, I had not made the best use of those ten minutes.

At the age of 39, Nan had a great career, and her life was full. At the age of 39 and ten entire minutes, I had a crummy job, and my life—with my son, Brian, away at Indiana University and my daughter, Ellie, away at the University of Kentucky—well, my life was running on empty.

Now, as Top Ten continued to smile at me, it was all I could do to keep my own smile from wobbling.

"Talk to you soon," he said softly.

I just looked at him. I *wish*, I thought.

If I really had been Nan, I would've, no doubt, been able to think of something terribly clever to say, but all I could do was smile at him weakly and head on into the drugstore.

Top Ten gave my elbow one final squeeze as I went by him. Then he closed the door in back of me, gave me a quick wave, and walked off in the direction of the Galleria.

I returned his wave, and then, feeling like an idiot, I walked around in that stupid drugstore for five more minutes, just to make sure he'd gotten completely out of sight before I came out.

After that, I walked to Bacon's Department Store. Alone.

Where I spent more than I should, on things I didn't really need, in an effort to cheer myself up.

Which didn't work.

Even so, I had a much better afternoon than Top Ten.

Chapter 2

•

NAN

The way I see it, it was Bert's fault. If she'd been in a better mood that Thursday night, I might never have turned on the TV. And if I hadn't turned on the TV, neither one of us would've ended up at the police station.

True, some of the other stuff would've eventually happened anyway, but that first trip to the police station, it mainly came down to Bert and her crappy attitude.

The second I saw her face, I knew she was in one of her moods.

She was smiling as she walked in my apartment door, carrying a large shopping bag from Bacon's in one hand and a Mc-Donald's bag in the other, but that smile didn't fool me. When you know somebody's face as well as your own—because, in fact, it *is* your own—you can read it like a billboard.

Bert's billboard said, *I'm pissed.*

Actually, now that I think of it, Bert's billboard would never say the word *piss*. Not when she's constantly after me to watch my language. I've tried to explain to her that, for disc jockeys, having a potty mouth is an occupational hazard. When you spend five hours a day in front of a microphone, making damn sure you don't say any curse words over the air, you've got a shit load of them saved up.

Bert, though, has never been at all understanding on the subject. Doing a pretty good imitation of our mother, Bert recently told me in all seriousness, "Southern ladies with college educations don't need to *stoop* to using curse words to express themselves."

My immediate response to that little news flash had been, of course, "Where the hell did you get that shitty idea?"

Bert's response to my response had been to stomp out of the room.

What can I say? Obviously, thirty-nine years ago when Bert and I were splitting up things between us, I must've gotten the entire profanity gene by mistake. Bearing all this in mind, however, I suppose—rather than *I'm pissed*—Bert's billboard would be saying instead, loud and clear, *I'm miffed.*

"Nan!" Bert said, "Hi!"

I was sitting on my couch, going through the day's mail, but Bert's tone got my attention. I stopped in the middle of looking over this month's telephone bill, and stared at her. Ever since her divorce, Bert has not exactly been a happy camper. And yet, right this minute she sounded only slightly less cheery than a Welcome Wagon lady.

So what exactly was up?

"Hiya, Bert," I said warily.

I didn't really mean to, but I couldn't stop my eyes from wandering to the Bacon's bag that Bert was carrying. I was pretty sure Santa didn't carry sacks crammed this full.

It looked like Bert had been indulging in a little Feel-Good Shopping. Not that I begrudged her pampering herself a little. Hell, the way she'd been moping around lately, she could use some cheering up.

On the other hand, I also couldn't help noting that this Feel-Good Shopping was being done by a woman who had yet to pay me this month's rent. And here it was already the fifteenth of the month.

All of which didn't exactly make *me* feel good. It also didn't make me feel good to have to come right out and ask Bert for the money. Like I'd been doing every damn month since she'd become my tenant.

What, in fact, it made me feel like was a damn dog begging for a damn handout at the damn table.

A thing like this could actually make a person think that offering to let Bert rent the other half of my duplex was not the brightest idea I'd ever had.

At the time, though, it had seemed like the answer to a prayer. Particularly if the prayer went something like, *Please God, send me a tenant who's sane for a change.*

When I bought this duplex five years ago, I knew that, in order to make the mortgage payment every month, I'd have to rent out the other half. What I didn't know is that perfectly normal-looking people with good references could end up getting busted for growing marijuana in big, metal tubs in an upstairs bedroom.

Or that perfectly normal-looking people with good references could actually prefer to let their trash accumulate in large piles on the front porch rather than to get off their dead butts and haul it out back to the damn garbage cans.

Or that perfectly normal-looking people with good references could be prone to walking around in the backyard, stark naked.

Mr. and Mrs. Nude America had been my last tenants. The two little old ladies who live on either side of me had nearly worn out my phone, calling me about those two. It might not have been so bad, but Mr. and Mrs. Nude America were in their late fifties and had the kind of flabby, overweight bodies that made you want to yell at them, *"Please! Put some damn clothes on, for God's sake!"*

A thing, as I recall, I did actually end up yelling at them.

The Nude Americas' lease had expired the same week Bert filed for divorce, and when Bert first agreed to move in next door, I'd actually had to *try* to make myself look sad that Bert's marriage had failed. I mean, I knew it was hard on her and the kids. I couldn't say, however, that it was the worst thing in the world that had ever happened to *me*.

Back then I'd been planning on offering Bert half of this building to buy herself, since she'd ended up having to sell Jake her half of the house that she and Jake had owned together.

That was, however, before I found out just how prompt Bert is at paying her rent.

And how prone she seems to have become here lately to spending money with wild abandon when she's depressed.

Bert noticed my eyes wandering to her Bacon's bag, too, because she immediately dropped it out of sight behind the blue upholstered chair to the right of my front door.

"So," Bert said. Her tone was still inordinately cheery.

I braced myself.

"Did that guy call you?" she asked.

I believe I came up with the obvious question. "What guy?"

Bert may have hidden the Bacon's bag, but she still had the McDonald's bag out in plain sight. She carried it over to the coffee table where I was sitting and plopped it down on top of a stack of magazines. "The guy," she said, sitting down on the other end of my sofa. "You know, the *guy*."

"What's his name?"

Bert's mouth tightened. "He didn't give me his name, but you can't possibly have forgotten *him*."

Her tone implied that if I'd forgotten *this* guy, I must've sustained severe brain damage during our birth.

I believe I showed real restraint at this juncture by not saying anything.

My silence must've encouraged Bert to immediately launch into a long, involved story about how some turkey had tried to pick her up during her lunch hour. To hear Bert tell it, he'd been a Greek Adonis. A Greek Adonis with a beard, a gray overcoat, and Paul Newman eyes.

I wasn't surprised to hear the part about Paul Newman. Bert, I believe, has watched far too many movies and television shows in her life. She almost always compares the people she meets with famous actors or actresses.

I put my bills to one side, and reached for the Mickey D's sack. Like I said, I wasn't surprised about Paul Newman, but the Greek Adonis part was something new. I hated to break it to Bert, but I hadn't run into too many Greek Adonises lately. Believe me, I would've noticed.

"This guy doesn't sound familiar." As I said this, I was taking two Cokes out of the sack, handing one to Bert and putting one on the table in front of me. After the Cokes, I took out two large boxes of fries and two Quarter Pounders. Handing both boxes of fries to Bert, I started unwrapping the hamburgers, lifting the top bun of each, and removing the pickles.

Bert and I are sometimes like two old married people. We know each other so well, we don't have to ask questions anymore. Like now, for instance. I knew Bert didn't want pickles. Just like I didn't want them.

While I was de-pickling our burgers, Bert was opening a package of ketchup and squirting its entire contents into the corner of one of the containers of fries. She did the same thing with another ketchup package and the other container of fries.

Bert and I don't agree on all foods, but every time we stop at McDonald's, we get fresh evidence that at one time we swam in the same gene pool. We always order exactly the same thing—a Quarter Pounder, large fries, and a medium Coke—and when we get our order, we always do the same thing. We depickle our hamburgers, and we pour our ketchup in a little pool in one corner of our fries. Neither of us like our ketchup dribbled all over. It's too messy.

Bert and I know each other so well, that earlier today when Bert had offered to stop by Mickey D's on the way home, she hadn't even asked what I wanted.

"What do you mean, this guy doesn't sound familiar?" Bert was now saying. "You've *got* to know him. He told me he was going to call you this afternoon."

I handed one Quarter Pounder to Bert, and kept one for myself. "No guys called me today," I said. "The only calls I got were from people wanting to dedicate a song to some-body—or from people wanting me to play more Garth Brooks." I reached for a french fry just as Bert was doing the exact same thing. Naturally, we bumped elbows.

Without speaking, we automatically rose and switched sides on the sofa.

Bert and I are what is known as "mirror twins." Meaning that she and I are supposed to be the mirror image of each other. We're still identical twins and all, but I guess you'd call us a sub-type. While regular identical twins are supposed to happen about four times out of every one thousand births, mirror twins occur in only about a quarter of those. So—if I'm remembering correctly all the statistics I've read about twins over the years—what I've always suspected is true. Bert and I are odd.

Of course, what being mirror twins mainly means to me and Bert has nothing to do with statistics. What it means to us is that Bert is right-handed, and I'm left-handed. It's as simple as that. Oh, there are a lot of other things, like Bert's natural hair part being on the opposite side of mine, and her dominant eye being the right one while mine is the left one, things like that. Mostly, however, what being mirror twins means to us is that if Bert is sitting on my left, she and I won't be able to eat without knocking elbows. *Bony* elbows.

Bert was still rubbing her elbow as she sat down again. "I can't believe you don't remember this guy," she said. "He was a real dreamboat."

Really. That's what she said. *Dreamboat.* A word I don't believe anybody else in America has said since Eisenhower was in office.

I just looked at her. I wouldn't ever say this to her face, but sometimes I get the feeling that Bert got out of her marriage just in time. A little while longer, never getting out of that house, and she might not just *sound* like June Cleaver, she might've actually *been* June Cleaver. One afternoon I'd have gone over to Bert's house and found a truly pathetic sight—Bert wearing a full-skirted dress, high heels and pearls, vacuuming her living room.

"He knew you, Nan," Bert was going on. Rubbing her elbow had evidently reminded her of something. "Why, he even squeezed my elbow."

I picked up another french fry. "The men I know squeeze other parts," I said.

Bert let that one pass. "He said you two met a few weeks ago."

I dipped the fry into my ketchup pool, took a bite, and said, "Oh? Where?"

This last was apparently the wrong question to ask, because Bert frowned again. "He didn't exactly say where you'd met." She actually sounded a little put out that I'd even asked such a thing. "He just said, you know, the usual. That he couldn't get you out of his mind."

I stopped eating french fries, and just looked at her again. *The usual?* Oh, for God's sake. Bert sometimes makes me so tired. She seems to be under the idiotic notion that I have so many men in my life, I have to keep track of them with a score card.

Bert has *got* to be kidding.

True, I have had more boyfriends than Bert has had. But, I do believe, having a husband for nineteen years might've cut into Bert's average.

What's more, I'm not at all sure that having a lot of boyfriends is anything to brag about. I mean, I think you could read the word *boyfriends* as *failed relationships*.

I have had a shit load of those.

I've tried to tell Bert that there is something about being on the radio that seems to attract the sort of man least likely to ever make a commitment. I personally don't know what it is, but a couple of the other female disc jockeys in town have told me that they think they've got it figured out. They've decided it's a bad idea to start off a relationship where a man knows for certain that there's a knob somewhere to turn you off.

There could be something to this particular theory. Because in every relationship I've had so far, the guy has eventually reached for that knob.

Like I said, I've told Bert all this, but for some odd reason, Bert actually seems to think that being on the radio is a wonderful thing. That no one has ever heard of me outside of the Louisville/Jefferson County TSA—that's the Total Survey Area for our ratings—doesn't seem to matter to her. That those particular ratings currently indicate that most of our TSA is listening to other stations besides WCKI during my midday 10 to 3 time slot also doesn't seem to make much of an impact. *And* that a lot of the people who work at WCKI call it the SICKIE station in private also seems to go right over Bert's head.

"Bert," I said, and my tone was, I admit, a bit clipped. "The way it sounds to me, this guy was trying to pick you up. And he was just saying he knew me. So *you'd* talk to him."

Bert was shaking her head before I'd even finished. "Oh, sure," she said. "Like a guy who looked like *him* would ever be interested in an ex-housewife with two grown kids."

I'd just put another french fry in my mouth when she said that, and I almost choked. To begin with, Bert wasn't making sense. Had she actually told this guy, *Oh, by the way, I used to be a housewife? And, oh yes, I've got two kids?*

Somehow, I doubted it.

So, correct me if I'm wrong here, but wasn't Bert just bringing up shit that really didn't have anything to do with anything? Just so she could feel sorry for herself?

Before anybody starts thinking I'm an unfeeling clod, I'd like to point out that, at the time of this little conversation with Bert, I'd already been making allowances for months. *Months*, I repeat.

Hey, nobody had to spell it out for me. I knew very well that Bert's self-esteem had taken a real beating when Jake had left her for that blond bimbo. Or rather, that blond bimbette, as Bert calls her. According to Bert, this chick was too young to be a bimbo. Bimbette was the most she could hope for. So, OK, already, it wasn't exactly a stretch to see how angry Bert was. I knew very well that having your husband decide to move in with his twenty-two-year-old receptionist had to be a real bummer.

But, let's get real here, there were worst things that could happen. And if Bert would only look outside herself for five seconds, she might realize that there were other people in the world who had not been fortunate enough to have the "two grown kids" she was now talking about in a tone that might give you the idea that they were albatrosses hanging around her neck.

Hell, if she took only a minute, Bert might actually realize that there were women her age—her *exact* age, in fact, give or take ten minutes—who were worrying, at this very moment, if they were going to sleep right through the alarm of their biological clock.

Believe me, the idea that I might always be just *Aunt Nan*, but never *Mommy*, was something I still hadn't come to terms with.

The way I saw it, Bert had been privileged to raise two wonderful kids, both of whom had made it to college. The only thing I'd raised over the years were radio ratings, and lately even those had slipped.

Not to mention, when you're fast approaching the Big Four-O, you can't help wondering if such a youth-oriented medium as radio will permit you to grow old gracefully. Gracefully, defined in this instance as *employed*.

I'd been supporting myself ever since I was nineteen—oddly enough, the exact same age Bert was when Jake and she got married. That's right, the exact same age Bert was when Jake had started supporting the two of them.

I could sympathize some with Bert being rattled about being thrust into the employment arena after all this time, but hey, Bert, here's a reality check: The rest of us have been slugging away out here *all* our lives.

"No, Bert," I now said through my teeth, "I did NOT get a phone call from this guy today, so he *must* have been interested in you."

Bert's response was another frown. "Nan, the guy—," she started to say, her tone even more clipped than mine, but by then I'd located the remote control for the TV. It was under a magazine on the coffee table in front of me. I reached for the thing, hitting the power and volume buttons in rapid succession.

When the TV came on, what do you know, it drowned out every word Bert was saying. "—are investigating a homicide which occurred in the Galleria this afternoon," the TV blared.

At least, I thought for a moment the TV had drowned Bert out. Actually, what had happened was that her words had abruptly stopped, like a faucet suddenly turned off.

I turned to look at her.

Bert's eyes were huge, and glued to the TV screen.

I turned to look at the TV myself.

In back of the blond anchorwoman, a small square showed a dark-haired man. Tanned, with a square jaw and a neatly clipped beard, he had definitely been handsome at one time.

He was, however, definitely dead at the moment.

The photo must've been taken with this guy flat on his back on the morgue table. His mouth was slightly open, his tanned skin looked slack, and his closed eyes looked sort of sunken. The photo was cropped an inch or so below the guy's chin, but you could still see a faint streak of crimson along the very bottom of the picture.

My first thought was that Channel 7 had finally come up with something surefire to boost their ratings. With the fall season upon us, Louisville was in the midst of television sweeps, and Channel 7 was going with the grisly format. Hey, showing dead bodies on the six o'clock news could possibly beat out showing OJ's Ford Bronco traveling down an interstate.

I think the Channel 7 anchorwoman knew it, too, because she couldn't quite keep the glee out of her voice as she continued. "The police at this time have not yet identified the victim, and they have no witnesses to the brutal slaying—"

The camera left the anchorwoman's eager face, and zoomed in to get an even better view of the dead man. I turned to look at Bert.

Well-known among our immediate family as the twin who'd fainted during *Nightmare on Elm Street,* she continued to stare at the television. I cleared my throat, still staring at her. Why the hell was Bert, of all people, watching this with such fascination?

"Bert?" I said.

I halfway expected her not to answer me. She looked so stunned. But after a long moment, she whispered, "It's him."

"Him?" I said.

"The guy I was just telling you about. The guy who knew—" Bert turned toward me, eyes widening. "There," she said, pointing at the screen. *"There.* Now tell me you don't know him."

I turned to look back at the TV screen. *This* was the guy Bert had talked to on the corner today? *This* was the guy who was supposed to phone me?

Evidently, I should not hold my breath on that one.

"Bert," I said, "I don't know him." I looked back over at her. "This guy's a total stranger." The stubborn tone I sometimes have to use with Bert had crept into my voice.

"He can't be," Bert said. "You've *got* to know him." The whining tone she sometimes used with me had crept into *her* voice.

The photograph of the guy was still on the TV screen, while the voice-over continued, "—unidentified male was found in a men's restroom, stabbed in the throat. The coroner has fixed the time of death between one and three."

Bert's hand went to *her* throat. "Ohmigod. I almost walked with him to the Galleria," she whispered. "I might've been with him."

Not in the men's room, I thought. I didn't say it, though. Bert might've thought that I wasn't taking this whole thing seriously.

And nothing could be farther from the truth.

Now, across the TV screen, a long line of type and a telephone number scrolled under the dead guy's chin. "Anyone having any information should contact the City of Louisville Homicide Division," the message read.

I pointed at Bert. "That's you," I said.

Bert acted as if I hadn't even spoken. Her eyes were still glued to the TV screen even though the evening news had just cut to a pizza commercial. "You always think that violence is something that happens to somebody you don't know," she said. Her voice was actually shaking a little. "I mean, before now, the one time I can remember that I knew somebody who'd been—you know—was *that* time."

Those were Bert's exact words. I knew immediately, however, what she was talking about. I suppose that's one of the ups of being a twin. After a lifetime of shared memories, you can talk in shorthand.

That time was the summer she and I had turned fifteen. That summer a couple down the street by the name of Sandersen had been murdered. We hadn't known the Sandersens well—in fact, the two of us had only baby-sat for them a couple times (back then, Bert and I had considered baby-sitting a group project), but the deaths of the Sandersens had been an unbelievable shock.

When you're fifteen, you don't really believe people can actually *die.*

Bert's eyes seemed to fill her face as she looked over at me. "But, Nan, I *talked* to this guy. I thought he had Paul Newman eyes."

I was going to have to take her word on this. In the TV photo, it had been sort of hard to tell.

I picked up the remote, turned off the TV, and said, "Bert, you've got to go to the police. You may have been the last person to see this guy alive."

Bert shook her head. "The last person to see him alive killed him," she said.

I had to admit she had a point.

"Bert," I said, "you might've seen something. Some trivial something that could help them catch who did this."

I thought I saw something flicker in Bert's eyes for a split second, but she continued to shake her head. "I don't know anything worth talking to the police about," she insisted. "I mean, all I know is that the guy seemed awfully fresh."

I just stared at her for a long moment. Bert may very well be the only person left on the planet who still uses the word "fresh" when talking about something other than fruit and vegetables.

"Bert, the television asked for anyone with information to come forward."

Bert just gave me a stubborn stare. "Don't give me that. You just want to go talk to the police because you think it'll be fun. It's just like that time all over again, isn't it?"

For a second, I was speechless. Can you believe that, after all these years, Bert would still remember that I'd wanted to do a little Nancy Drewing when the Sandersen couple was killed? I mean, for God's sake, of *course* I'd wanted to solve the murder mystery down the road. What else could happen that's even close to that exciting when you're only fifteen?

To be honest, as I recall, the only thing that had finally stopped me from doing a teenage impression of Nancy Drew back then was that the murder mystery had turned out not to be all that much of a mystery. In fact, the police had known practically from day one that the guy who'd killed the Sandersens had been Mrs. Sandersen's lover. It hadn't been hard to reach that conclusion—the lover had skipped town the day the crime was committed.

Now, staring back at Bert, I tried to look indignant. "Bert, this is not at all like that time. I just think you ought to do your civic duty." I reached over and got another french fry. "Too many people don't want to get involved these days. No wonder crime is getting worse and worse." I was bullshitting her rather well, I thought.

Evidently, however, my bullshitting skills needed work, because it took me fifteen more minutes of laying it on thick to finally talk Bert into going downtown. I even had to agree to change into a clean pair of blue jeans before we went.

Still, I got her to go. What's more, I got her to do it without having to tell her the real reason I wanted her to talk to the police.

Which was, simply, this: I wanted somebody in charge to know that the dead guy had indeed talked to Bert shortly before he died.

The fact was, I really wanted to believe that this guy had just made an innocent mistake. And yet, was it likely that he'd confused Bert with yet another somebody who looked like the two of us? True, they say everybody is supposed to have a double somewhere—but a *triple?*

Like I said, I *wanted* to believe that this guy thought Bert was somebody else, and then, shortly thereafter, he'd gone off and gotten himself murdered.

No connection.

But, to be honest, the whole thing sounded fishy to me.

I would never tell Bert this straight out, but—let's face it—she was something of a babe in the woods. This *was*, after all, the very same woman who'd actually sent twenty bucks to Oral Roberts awhile back. It had been during that time when old Oral was asking for extra donations so that God wouldn't call him immediately to heaven. I'd told Bert that she shouldn't send Oral anything because having God call the guy to heaven would, no doubt, convince non-believers faster than anything else Oral could ever do. Not to mention, heaven *was* exactly the place Oral wanted to end up.

Bert had not seen it my way. She'd apparently been convinced that not sending Oral any money would put the poor man's number on God's speed dial.

Given Bert's gullibility, it could very well be that things were not quite as she'd thought. What if the guy on the street had been a total stranger to Bert, *and* a total stranger to me, and yet, he'd tried to make Bert think otherwise for some reason? Like maybe, so that she would be so kind as to accompany him to what was going to turn out to be his own murder?

The very idea gave me chills.

"You want to drive?" I asked, handing Bert her car keys.

Chapter 3

●

BERT

A police station is not a nice place to visit.

I think I knew this even before Nan dragged me down there. In fact, I believe this is something you can pretty much assume about any place where there exists even the slightest possibility that you could be strip searched.

From the excited look on Nan's face, however, the second she and I walked through the front door of police headquarters in downtown Louisville, you'd have thought we'd just arrived at Club Med.

Nan's eyes were darting all around, and I could tell it was taking a real effort on her part to keep from grinning from ear to ear. Nan even looked tickled pink to see the X-ray contraption just inside the front entrance.

This X-ray thing looked a lot like the ones they always have in airports. You know the ones—with the little conveyor belts where you put your carry-on bags? And the arches you have to walk through to make sure everybody knows you left all your bombs and guns at home?

As Nan moved on ahead of me into the police station, it didn't seem to occur to her that there could be anything at all ominous about this X-ray thing being located in what was, in essence, this place's lobby. Judging from the expression on

Nan's face, I believe she considered having a thing like this in your lobby to be a sort of status symbol.

I, on the other hand, took one quick look around the station—at the cold gray walls, at the gray linoleum floor yellowed from too many waxings, at the grim faces of the uniformed policemen standing around—and, unlike Nan, I didn't feel the least bit inclined to grin.

What I felt like doing, I immediately did. I stopped dead in my tracks, did an about-face, and started to head right back toward the entrance. I fully intended to sail back through the door and take off at a full gallop for my car.

I'd been able to find an empty parking space less than a block away from the station's front door. This was a truly remarkable feat, believe me, considering that all the really good parking spaces were, no doubt, taken all day long by thieves, drug pushers, and murderers being turned in by family members.

I probably could've made it to my Ford Festiva in less than a minute, except that Nan can move amazingly fast when she wants to. I hadn't even gotten to the front door when Nan caught up with me. Grabbing my arm, she said, "Oh, no, you don't." Spinning me around, she steered me back toward the X-ray thing.

"LET GO OF ME!" I hissed at Nan through my teeth. "I've changed my mind. I want to go home. NOW!"

Nan totally ignored me. She didn't release my arm until I'd put my purse next to hers on the little conveyor belt, and we were both headed through the X-ray arch.

After that little scene, there suddenly seemed to be quite a few pairs of police eyes directed at the two of us. I wanted to believe that all these cops were now staring at us simply because they'd just noticed that we were twins. I wasn't sure they would've noticed this all that quickly, though, since Nan and I weren't dressed the least bit alike. She, of course, was wearing her usual—a tee-shirt, scruffy jeans jacket and a pair of jeans with the knees worn paper thin. I, on the other hand, was still wearing the navy blue Liz Claiborne wool suit I'd worn to work.

If they weren't watching us because we were twins, I was afraid the police were watching us for another reason. They all probably thought that Nan—obviously, one of my own family members—was bringing *me* to justice. No doubt, considering the way she was dressed, she was desperate for cash, and she was turning me in for the bounty on my head.

What Nan did next made this last scenario even more believable. As soon as we'd retrieved our purses, Nan gripped my arm and pulled me toward a door marked *Homicide*.

If it hadn't been for all those police eyes directed our way, I would've tried to break Nan's grip and make another bolt for the door. Unfortunately, however, it now seemed likely that if Nan started after me again, a half-dozen cops might join the pursuit. Fugitive that I was.

So I contented myself with glaring at Nan and saying, "I mean it, Nan. I don't want to do this."

Nan apparently didn't hear me. Maybe because, right about then, she was speaking to the heavy-set guy in the tan suit seated at the gray metal desk just inside the Homicide door. "Excuse me, uh—" Here Nan paused as she glanced at the name plate on Heavy Set's desk. It read *Detective Hank Goetzmann*. "—Detective Goetzmann? My sister here talked to that guy who was murdered in the Galleria today, and she wants to make a statement."

I turned to stare at Nan. *Make a statement?* The official surroundings must've gotten to her. In another second, Nan would be using words like *perp* and *M O*. Before that happened, I jumped in. "I saw on the news that anybody who'd seen this guy should contact the police, so—"

Goodness. If I'd thought Nan was excited, she had nothing on Detective Goetzmann. He'd been filling out some kind of form, his pen scratching rapidly over the surface, but as soon as I spoke, he sort of jerked to attention, immediately getting to his feet. "*Glad* you came in," he said, interrupting me. "You did the right thing. You really did. We appreciate it when citizens get involved."

I just looked at him. For a minute there I'd thought he was going to leap over his desk and give me a big hug.

It was a scary thought. Getting hugged by Detective Goetzmann could be life-threatening. The guy looked to be about the same age as Nan and me, but he had to be at least six foot three, and he had to weigh at least two hundred thirty pounds. Not to mention, with that thick neck, that square jaw, and that Marine haircut, Goetzmann didn't look to me to be terribly cuddly.

Fortunately, I didn't have to worry very long about getting a hug from him. Goetzmann's excitement certainly didn't last. As a matter of fact, his excitement had died down completely by the time we'd all sat down, I'd introduced myself and Nan, and answered just two questions.

The first was one Nan and I have answered, oh, about a million times. "Are you two twins?"

The second was a bit more difficult.

"What was the victim's name?"

After Detective Goetzmann had resumed his seat, he'd taken out another form. Now he held his pen poised expectantly in mid-air while he waited for my answer. Several of the other cops at other desks around the room seemed at that moment to be leaning toward us a little, all looking terribly interested in what I was about to say.

I swallowed. "I don't know his name."

Goetzmann's square face fell, but undaunted, he immediately turned to Nan. "*You* knew him then?"

Nan shook her head.

As she did so, she did not glance in my direction for even an instant.

Which was good planning on Nan's part. Believe me. Because, if looks could kill, I might have been taken into custody right then.

Detective Goetzmann's face fell even more, but he resolutely turned back to me. "Did the victim mention anything about being scared? Or that he thought somebody could be following him? Or anything like that?"

I shook my head. No. No. And, *No.*

Goetzmann's face had apparently fallen all it could. Now it was working on a look of faint irritation. "Maybe you'd better tell me exactly what the victim *did* say to you. Word for word."

So I told him. By the time I'd finished repeating the entire conversation I'd had with Top Ten, Goetzmann was no longer looking *faintly* irritated. He was looking *extremely* irritated.

"Let me get this straight," the detective said, giving the form in his hand a little shake. "Are you trying to tell me that the victim—a total stranger—walked up to you on the street earlier today and pointed out that you look good in navy blue?"

I blinked. I wouldn't have put it exactly like that, but that did seem to be the gist. "That's right," I said.

Goetzmann's response was to turn and look at the other

cops in the room. While making this really disgusting noise in the back of his throat. A noise that said, *See what I've got to deal with?*

When Goetzmann turned to face me and Nan again, his thick eyebrows had plowed a furrow in his forehead. His voice, though, was still pleasant. Excessively pleasant. So excessively pleasant that both Nan and I began to squirm a little in our metal chairs.

"Ladies," Goetzmann asked, leaning back in his own metal chair, "do you know what I hate?"

He didn't seem to expect an answer.

We didn't give him one.

"I hate it when the higher-ups decide to do these crime stopper segments on the evening news. Showing crime victims or missing persons or whatever." Goetzmann went on. "Because all of a sudden everybody from every podunk county in Kentucky is sure that he—or she—has seen the poor devil. Along with *Elvis* at the Burger King."

Goetzmann did not smile when he said this, but a couple of the other cops in the room snickered.

"Then, whaddya know, every one of these witnesses who've seen this guy *and* Elvis all come trooping in here to tell me about it. And *then* I've got all these reports to fill out—" At this point he rattled the form again. "—and not a thing to show for it." Goetzmann got to his feet. "Ladies, thank you for coming in, but I'm kind of busy—"

"Now just a darn minute—"

Uh oh. I was following Goetzmann's lead and getting to my feet, preparing to make my escape. Beside me, Nan, too, was doing the same. Except for one thing. As she started moving, she started talking. "—I don't know who you think you're dealing with here, but—"

I turned to stare at Nan. I'd known she was mad even be-fore I saw the muscle jumping in her jaw. Nan only says *darn* when the word she really wants to say is totally out of the question.

"—my sister and I have gone to a lot of trouble to make this long drive all the way in here—"

I blinked. It had been a ten-minute drive. Nan was mak-ing it sound as if it had been ten days. By wagon train.

"—to do our civic duty, and *this* is how we're treated? Why, this—this is a *darn* outrage—"

I know I probably should've been admiring Nan's nerve at this point, but to be honest, I was watching Goetzmann's face. And wishing that Nan would just shut her mouth.

She didn't, though. And while Nan was ranting and rav-ing about civic duty, it gave Goetzmann plenty of time to study her, his blue eyes getting narrower and narrower.

Nan was saying something about "crime running ram-pant through the streets" when Goetzmann cut her off. "Just a minute," he said, "haven't I seen you on TV or"—Goetz-mann ran his hand over his short-cropped, light brown hair and then snapped his fingers—"yeah, that's it. You're on the radio. That's right, isn't it?"

For an answer, Nan fished out one of her business cards from the leather knapsack she calls a purse, and handed the card over.

With a little flourish.

There have been times over the years when having Nan produce a business card in my presence was enough to make me depressed for days. I know. I know. How petty can you get? And yet, when you've been a housewife your whole adult life, you can actually come to believe that having a job that requires a business card is a pretty big deal.

Right then, in fact, was the first time in recent memory when I actually felt a little *glad* that I didn't have a business card of my own. Business card-less, I could just stand there, quietly watching Goetzmann stare holes through the card Nan had given him.

"WCKI, huh?" Goetzmann said, his blue eyes going a darker shade as he said the word. "Isn't CKI the station that does all those screwy promotions?"

Nan's chin went up at that. "Screwy? Detective, I don't think I would call them screwy."

I didn't say a word.

Three months ago CKI had made Nan ride an elephant—that's right, an *elephant*—down the middle of Louisville's Main Street in order to advertise that a certain car dealership's prices were peanuts.

A few months before that they'd had her climb a flagpole, and sit up there until the station's ratings improved.

And on St. Patty's Day earlier this year, they'd made her paint herself green.

Goetzmann had now lifted his eyes from Nan's card to Nan herself. "You wouldn't call them screwy, huh?" he said. "Then what *would* you call some radio station jerking me around for a little publicity for one of its deejays? What would you call that?" Goetzmann leaned forward, his eyes still on Nan. "You know what I'd call it? I'd call it a waste of my time."

I swallowed uneasily. I didn't know about Nan, but I was certainly ready to leave. I opened my mouth to make this little suggestion, but Nan started blabbering again. "Look, Detective," Nan said, her voice rising, "CKI has nothing to do with this. Nothing whatsoever. My *sister*—not me—talked to a *darn* murder victim today, and the television said that the *darn* police wanted any information, no matter how *darn* trivial, to help identify this man, so we—"

"The television lied," Goetzmann snapped. "Anything else?"

I personally had nothing else. Not for Goetzmann, anyway.

Once Nan and I had made our way out of the police station, and we were back in my Festiva, traveling back to Nan's duplex, I did, however, have quite a few things to tell her.

In a very loud voice, I might add.

"I have never been so humiliated. NEVER." Actually, the moment the words were out of my mouth, it did occur to me that having my ex-husband Jake leave me for that blond in his office had probably been a little more humiliating. But this came in a close second.

Nan was shaking her head in disgust. "That damn Goetzmann was the biggest jerk I have ever—"

I cut her off. "I have never felt like such a fool. NEVER." Actually, the second I said this, it also occurred to me that having Jake leave me for that blond had made me feel significantly more of a fool. Once again, however, this came in an extremely close second.

Nan was still shaking her head. "I can't believe that damn detective acted as if we were a couple of—of *murder* groupies—"

I gave the car a little more gas. Nan was not getting what I was saying. I was not blaming Detective Goetzmann. I was blaming *her*. I cut her off again. "I knew this was a bad idea, Nan. I knew it! But did you listen to me? No! You just dragged me in there! You're always talking me into doing the dumbest things!"

We were almost home, and I kept my eyes on the road ahead. "I mean, *really*, Nan, I didn't even know who that guy on the street was. I didn't know *anything*. But, oh no, *you* had to make me go talk to the police! You had to embarrass me to death!"

Nan didn't say anything.

I glared at her. "No doubt," I went on, "it was just a co-incidence that I happened to talk to that guy today, and then a little later he happened to have gotten himself murdered."

Nan shrugged. "All right, already, so you're right. So your meeting this guy and his getting killed were two completely unrelated things."

I hate it when she does this. She was obviously agreeing with me just so I'd shut up.

I was pulling into the driveway of Nan's duplex at that moment, and I had no intention of ending our little chat. As a matter of fact, right then I had every intention of following Nan into her apartment, and really giving her a piece of my mind. Unfortunately, as I put on the brakes and glanced into my rearview mirror, I saw something that for a moment wiped my mind clean.

My mouth was still open, still ready to continue telling Nan exactly what I thought of her dragging me downtown, and yet, nothing came out. All I could do was just sit there, gripping the steering wheel of my Festiva and staring into the mirror. No doubt, looking every bit as horror-stricken as Meryl Streep on the poster for that movie, *Silkwood*.

Pulling into the driveway in back of us, as cool as you please, just as if he belonged there, was Jake.

The man who, if you'll recall, had come in first in the Humiliating-Me-and-Making-Me-Feel-like-a-Fool contest.

I stiffened. "What in the world is he doing here?"

I gave Nan a quick, sideways look as she, too, turned and looked out the back window.

Nan immediately picked up on the significance of my look. "Hey," she said, holding up her hands in a gesture of innocence. "Don't look at me. I haven't talked to him in *months.*"

I might not have believed her. Nan *had* been telling me lately that Jake was going to show up at my doorstep one day. As a matter of fact, she'd been telling me this ever since she'd heard on the grapevine that Jake and Bimbette were on the rocks. Word was, according to Nan, that Bimbette had kicked Jake out, and taken up with some guy who was even older. And, not incidentally, wealthier.

I, of course, would believe it when I heard it from either Jake or the kids. Not that it mattered, one way or the other.

Nan, however, seemed to think it did matter. In fact, she'd actually been saying things about forgiving and forgetting. Really. Once, she'd actually referred to Jake's infidelity as a fling.

Can you believe that? A *fling?* Excuse me, but I don't think so. *Fling*, to me, was what I wanted to do with Jake's clothes—right out our bedroom window—when I'd found out that he'd been carrying on with Bimbette for months. *Months*, mind you.

Like I said, I might've thought Nan had put Jake up to this, except for one thing. Her mouth dropped open just like mine did, the second we both got out of the car and got a good look at him.

Jake—the man who, for all the twenty-plus years that I'd known him, had refused to wear colors, stubbornly insisting on wearing white dress shirts even with jeans—was now walking toward us in a red plaid, cowboy shirt, with a tan leather sport coat with fringe, no less, slung over one shoulder. Not only that, but he was also wearing blue jeans so tight there was every possibility he had no feeling whatsoever left in his feet, snakeskin boots, a string tie, and a silver belt buckle.

I couldn't seem to pull my eyes away. During those last years that we were married, I'd secretly thought that Jake looked like Sam Shephard, the actor. Of course, Jake was more of a buttoned-down collar version of Sam Shephard, but still, I'd been convinced that my tall, lanky husband looked enough like Sam Shephard to be *his* twin, believe it or not.

Now I took a deep breath, as I continued to stare. Evidently, in a matter of months, Jake had gone from Sam Shephard to Tex Ritter.

Old Tex was wearing his hair pulled back into a scruffy ponytail, he had a tan too deep to get anywhere this time of year but in a tanning salon, and both legs of his jeans sported ragged tears. I cleared my throat. *This* was the man who'd insisted that I iron a crease in his jeans every time they came out of the laundry?

Then again, maybe that's what had happened to his jeans. Maybe Bimbette had tried to iron in a crease and had burned right through the denim—*twice.* That might explain why their relationship was on the rocks.

Jake began talking very fast as soon as he was within earshot. "Hi there!" he said. His jovial voice was the one he generally reserved for new clients. "I was just in the neighborhood, and I happened to see you two pass me on the road. So I thought, hey, I ought to drop by and say hello."

Think again, immediately crossed my mind.

I might've said it, too, but Nan jumped in. "Well, hi, Jake," she said. Her voice actually sounded warm. "How are you doing? You're—"

Jake had gotten up to us by that time. Nan must've noticed at that moment the exact same thing that I noticed, because her voice momentarily faltered.

In Jake's right earlobe, there was now a silver hoop. Dangling from that hoop was a white feather.

Nan's eyes were fixed on Jake's feather as she continued. "—you're looking good." Her voice was uncertain.

"Thanks, thanks," Jake said. His eyes sort of drifted over to me.

If he expected to hear me say, "ditto," Jake was going to be waiting a long time. I just stood there, staring back at him, unblinking. Finally, Jake said, his voice soft, "How are you doing, Bert?"

I'd been pretty much focusing on the feather, but now I stared straight into his eyes. Well, now, let me see, other than having my husband dump me for a woman twenty years younger than me, and other than my having to find employment with absolutely no work experience whatsoever, and other than my longing to yank that stupid earring right out of your ear, I'd say there could really be only one answer to that question. "Peachy," I said.

Nan jumped in again. "We're *both* doing just fine, Jake."

Jake took a step toward me. Naturally, seeing him coming, I turned and immediately started moving toward my door. As I went, I began fishing around in my purse for my keys.

"Well, now, that's good to hear." Jake was answering Nan, but oddly enough, he kept right on following *me* up to my door.

"You know, Bert," he said to my back, "I talked to Ellie and Brian just last night. Those two sure seem to be doing fine."

I was still rummaging for my keys, and I didn't even look up. Jake was right, though. Ellie and Brian *were* doing great. Ellie at eighteen was a fair-haired, fair-skinned beauty who didn't look at all like me, and tall, lanky Brian at nineteen was—wouldn't you know it—a carbon copy of his dad at that age. Both of them had grades high enough to qualify for reduced rates on car insurance, and both of them had managed to keep up those grades while holding down part-time jobs to help out with their college expenses.

The fact was—and, yes, I realize I wasn't being totally logical here—the kids were both doing so well, it almost hurt my feelings. Both Ellie and Brian seemed to have adjusted to the divorce far better than I had.

Jake was going on. "I guess, when it comes to our kids, we did something right, didn't we?"

I'd found my keys, but this last brought me up short. I turned and gave Jake a surprised glance. This was a first. Jake complimenting the kids, and then going on to actually include *me* as one of their parents? Usually, if Jake had something good to say about the kids, my name never came up. It generally only came up if he had something to criticize about Ellie and Brian. Then you'd have thought I'd raised them on a desert island somewhere, all by myself.

Glancing in Jake's direction was a mistake. Jake immediately moved to my side. "You always were a wonderful mother, Bert, I sure hope you know how much I appreciate—"

After that, I'm not sure what the man said. Whatever it was, I knew I didn't want to hear it. I suddenly got real busy trying to get my stupid door key in my stupid lock, so that I could get my stupid door open.

And then shut it in Jake's stupid face.

Nan was now hurrying over to her own doorway. I turned toward her, to give her a *Don't-you-dare-leave-me-alone-with-him* look, but Nan must've been anticipating it. She didn't glance my way once.

"I guess I better head on inside," she said over her shoulder. "Jake, it's nice to see you again—"

It was so obvious that Nan was hurrying inside in order to give me and Jake some time alone that even Jake sounded a little ill-at-ease when he answered her. "Uh, nice seeing you again, Nan. I mean it, it was *real* nice."

By then I'd finally gotten my key in my door lock, but wouldn't you know, I was having trouble turning the thing.

I couldn't believe it. I'd unlocked and opened this door a zillion times, and I'd never had any trouble. Of course, I hadn't had Jake at my elbow, either. And, as much as I wanted to act as if he didn't affect me in the least, I couldn't exactly ignore how badly my hands had started shaking.

It didn't help any to have Jake move up behind me, reach out and take the key out of my hand. "Here," he said softly, "let me help."

I turned to look up at him, and that evidently was the exact moment when Nan, across the way, got her own door open.

Because she did exactly what I'd been wanting to do ever since I first saw Jake walking up the driveway toward us.

Nan let go with a bloodcurdling scream.

Chapter 4

•

NAN

I can not believe people actually do this primal screaming stuff for therapy, of all things. It sure wasn't therapy for me. In fact, I didn't feel even a little bit better after I'd finished.

Of course, one reason for this could've been that, after I'd gotten finished screaming my head off, my apartment still looked exactly the way it had before I'd opened my mouth.

Totally trashed.

A wall-to-wall disaster.

Somewhere, off in the distance, I could hear Jake and Bert's footsteps hurrying my way, but to tell you the truth, all I could seem to focus on was my apartment.

I walked into my living room, and I could hardly believe my eyes. Every drawer had been pulled out and dumped on the floor. Every sofa pillow and chair cushion had been tossed. Every closet door was standing wide open, so that anybody could plainly see that there was nothing left inside but a few empty hangers.

My entire first floor, in fact, was a jumble of dresses, boots, blankets, luggage, tennis rackets needing repair, coats I hadn't worn in years—you get the picture. The Wreck of the Hesperus had nothing on my apartment.

As I stood there in the middle of my living room, taking

it all in, it didn't even occur to me to be afraid. What it occurred to me to be was angry. Eyeboiling, hair-pulling, teeth-spitting *angry*.

I was so angry, it surprised me. Because, before this, I would've told you that my meager accumulation of possessions wasn't important to me. It was just stuff. That's all. Nice to have, but certainly not anything to get in an uproar about.

In fact, I'd always prided myself on not getting too attached to things. Material possessions could always be replaced. Unlike the really important things in life—like time, loved ones, or slim thighs.

Now, walking around my apartment, my eyes prickling with unshed tears, I realized that my stuff meant more to me than I'd ever thought. Hell, I *liked* all this crap. I liked the oriental rug I'd found dirt cheap at the Salvation Army store, I liked the English country print sofa I'd given myself for Christmas last year, and I liked every one of my books, dating all the way back to high school, for God's sake. It made my skin crawl to think that some lowlife scum bag had actually walked around in here, putting his filthy hands all over everything, no doubt trying to make up his mind what to steal.

The question was, what had he taken? I stopped and took a long, speculative look around.

In back of me, I heard a sharp intake of breath. Even without turning around, I knew it was Bert.

"Oh, dear." The words sounded as if whoever was saying them was choking at the same time.

Oh, yeah, that was Bert, all right.

I turned to see her standing there, just inside my front door, her eyes about the size of hubcaps, as she stared at the landfill that had been my living room.

Jake appeared in back of Bert. "Holy shit," he said.

My sentiments exactly.

"Are you all right?" Bert's hubcaps were now directed at me.

"I've been better," I said.

Jake moved past Bert and on into my living room. "What the hell happened?"

I just looked at him. I've known Jake for almost twenty-three years. That includes the almost-twenty years he and Bert were married, the year they'd been divorced, and the two years they'd dated before they tied the knot. During all that time the man has never failed, during times of stress, to come up with the dumbest question you've ever heard.

Like, for example, the time when Bert fell on the ice in front of their house and broke her arm? She couldn't reach Jake at work, so I'd ended up taking her to the emergency room. When I drove Bert home that night, Jake did a double take when he saw the cast stretching from her wrist to her elbow. "Did you do something to your arm?" he'd asked.

Then there was the time Bert's water broke while all three of us were standing in the checkout line at the Winn Dixie Supermarket. Bert must've been, oh, *twelve* months' pregnant, at least—she certainly looked like a balloon ready to burst. That's exactly what happened, too. She burst, all right. True to form, Jake had taken one look at the puddle rapidly growing around poor Bert's feet and demanded, "*What* do you think you're doing?"

Oh, my yes, old Jake had a gift, no doubt about it. Now, as he continued to survey my living room, his eyes getting more like Bert's hubcaps by the moment, he must've decided his first question was such a good one, it bore repeating. "What the hell happened?"

There had been a time when Bert used to shake her head and laugh when Jake asked one of his idiot questions. Those times, however, were clearly over. Now Bert pulled her hubcap eyes away from the mess in my apartment, and fixed Jake with a look. "Even a *moron* could see," Bert said dryly, "that Nan's apartment has been broken into."

I closed my eyes. *This* I did not need on top of everything else.

Jake evidently didn't need it any more than I did. He sort of caught his breath, and then said, "Well, it seems to me that only an *idiot* would immediately assume that—"

Oh, brother. Before Jake and Bert got into a protracted discussion regarding the level of intelligence required to figure out exactly what had happened here tonight, I interrupted. "You know what's odd?" I looked first at Bert and then over at Jake. "It doesn't look as if anything's been taken."

I didn't have to spell it out for anybody. Out in plain sight was my VCR, my color television, my stereo, not to mention various pieces of jewelry lying in a jumble in the middle of my coffee table. These last were pieces I'd worn in the last month or so, and let me hasten to add—before anybody starts wondering if maybe I'm a slob—that, yes, as a matter of fact, I *am* a slob. I'd had every intention of returning this stuff to the jewelry box I keep on the triple dresser in my bedroom, but so far, it had not exactly been a high priority item.

Besides, it wasn't as if any of my jewelry was wildly expensive or anything. There *was*, however, now that I really looked at the pieces lying there, an 18K gold necklace and a couple bracelets that were 10K gold. Had my burglar been so choosy, he'd pass these things up?

Or was my taste in jewelry so bad, even a burglar wouldn't take the stuff?

"Of course," I went on, "I can't be absolutely sure that nothing is missing. My jewelry box *is* up in my bedroom." I started to move toward the stairs. "Let me go up and—"

That's all I got out before I felt Jake's hand on my arm. "Just a minute, Nan," he said. "Let me go up there first."

I turned to look at him, and that's when I saw it in his eyes. Good Lord.

Jake actually thought that whoever had done this to my apartment might *still* be here.

I couldn't help it. I took a quick glance over at my stairs, and actually shivered. Was it really possible that the intruder was still *around?* Maybe waiting upstairs, to do God-knows-what to anybody who came looking for him?

Once that little thought went through my mind, my heart started going triple time. Jake immediately moved to the bottom of my stairs where he stood for a moment, his head cocked to one side, obviously listening.

Unfortunately, with his head tilted like that, you couldn't miss that white feather dangling from his ear.

Bert, for sure, couldn't miss it. When I glanced over at her, she was staring pointedly at the thing, her mouth pinched with distaste.

"You two wait right here," Jake said. "Let me do a little looking around, OK?"

Bert was obviously moved by Jake's kind and courageous offer.

She looked over at me and rolled her eyes.

I just stared right back at her. They say twins are supposed to be more intuitive than the regular population, and maybe they're right. Because as soon as my eyes met Bert's, there wasn't a doubt in my mind what Bert wanted me to do. She wanted me to throw Jake out. She wanted me to show him once and for all that we single women can do just fine, thank you very much, without some cowboy riding in and rescuing us.

Can you believe, Bert managed to put all this in the one level look she directed my way?

I, on the other hand, managed to put quite a lot in the look I fired right back at her. *Let me get this straight—you want me to go upstairs and maybe get attacked by an intruder? Even though your ex-husband is standing right here, volunteering to go upstairs and maybe get attacked himself?*

Uh huh. Sure. You can take that one to the bank.

I turned back toward Jake. "This is so nice of you, Jake," I said. "I really do appreciate your checking upstairs for me."

Jake, unbelievably, looked as if I were doing *him* a big favor. Apparently, the opportunity to run into a burglar who just might be in a murderous mood was Jake's idea of a good time. He all but beamed at me. "No problem at all," he said heartily. "*Glad* to do it."

I'd never thought Jake was particularly attractive, but at that moment—in his eagerness to help—he actually looked appealingly boyish. In fact, I think if he hadn't immediately gone on to hitch up his belt and square his shoulders resolutely—much like Gary Cooper on his way to meet those gunslingers in that old black and white classic *High Noon*—Jake might've actually gotten out of the room without Bert rolling her eyes again. She also tossed her head, and said the second Jake was out of sight, "That man just *loves* playing the hero, doesn't he?"

This seemed a particularly unkind thing to say about somebody who'd just headed upstairs perhaps to be attacked on my behalf. I cleared my throat. "Bert," I said, and yes, I'll admit, my voice was a little clipped, "look on the bright side. Maybe an intruder really *is* waiting for him up there."

Oddly enough, Bert's response was not what you might've suspected. She glanced toward the stairs, her eyes starting to look like hubcaps again. "Oh dear," she said again.

Uh huh. And Bert kept saying she didn't care if Jake lived or died. *Right.*

Bert looked so concerned, in fact, that I reached out and touched her arm. "Look. I know Jake said for us to wait right here, but I'm going to go ahead and call the cops." I headed for my kitchen and a phone. The 911 call took only minutes to make. They were minutes, however, during which Jake did not return.

When *I* returned, Bert had climbed two steps up my stairs, and was leaning forward, looking up. "I don't hear a thing, do you?" she said. Her voice sounded almost casual, but every bit of the color seemed to have drained from her face.

There seemed to be only one thing to do. I stepped forward, put my hand to my mouth, and yelled, "Jake! Hey, JAKE?"

There was no answer. I wouldn't have thought it possible, but Bert went even paler. "Oh, dear," she said again.

"Maybe Jake didn't hear me," I said. I didn't mention that I really didn't understand how he could *not* have heard me—unless, of course, he were unconscious, or worse. I also didn't mention that it would be just like Jake to have heard me and not answered on purpose. As I recalled, the man just loved drama. This *was* the guy, after all, who'd proposed to Bert in front of the entire family one Thanksgiving.

Our parents' house had been full of uncles, aunts, cousins, both sets of grandparents, and various and sundry relatives some of whom Bert and I didn't even recognize, and yet, this had not stopped old Jake. He'd dropped to his knees in the middle of all that chaos, and proposed to Bert in rhyme. Really. Six stanzas of iambic pentameter. How do I love thee, let me count the ways, let me count them, and count them, and count them while everybody else waits to sit down to dinner. By the time Jake was finished, several of the dinner guests had drifted into the dining room to sneak a biscuit or two off the table.

At the time, of course, I thought Jake's proposal awfully romantic. But then again, at the time I was eighteen. Now, thinking back on it, I wonder if it hadn't been a dirty trick. I mean, Bert had to accept him, didn't she? What was she going to do, spoil everybody's Thanksgiving? Not to mention, let some of our relatives starve?

Beside me now, Bert was chewing on her left thumbnail. She tells everybody that, unlike me, she's never bitten her fingernails, but she seems to be under the impression that thumbnails don't count. "Nan, you don't think anything could've happened to Jake up there, do you?"

I immediately shook my head. "Of course not." It did seem unlikely. For one thing, if an intruder had attacked Jake, wouldn't he have made some noise doing it? Still, I probably would've been a little more convincing if I hadn't immediately gone over and gotten the poker from the fireplace.

Bert gave me a startled look. "Don't you think it would be better just to wait for the police to get here?"

I nodded. "Probably." On the other hand, if some extremely quiet criminal really was doing something awful to Jake at this very moment, would I ever be able to forgive myself for just standing around down here, doing nothing?

Bert was nodding now, also. "I think we should wait, too,"

she said. Then she went over and picked up the only other thing in sight that could remotely be called a weapon—an umbrella, lying in the middle of a pile of books.

Bert and I exchanged a long look, and then we both started up the carpeted stairs—me in front, Mary Poppins bringing up the rear.

On the way up, I idly wondered if Bert and I weren't doing one of the stupid things that victims always seem to be doing in horror movies. You know, like going to check on that growling noise? Only, in this case, we were going to check on the absolutely-no-noise-whatsoever. Talk about *stupid*.

When we got to the landing, I glanced back at Bert. In response, she brandished the umbrella menacingly. Oh yeah, *that* made me feel better. While I poked an attacker to death, Bert could keep us all out of the rain. *Indoors.*

I took another deep breath, turned, and then started moving as soundlessly as I could down my carpeted hallway. My bedroom was at the end of the hall, and the door was standing a little ajar. I moved so that I was standing right next to it, but with the thing almost closed, I couldn't get a good view inside. I took another deep breath, tightened my grip on the poker, and I nudged the door open with my foot. Very slowly, I eased myself inside.

What I saw then made me want to scream all over again.

My bedroom looked like my living room downstairs. The contents of all my dresser drawers, the Lane chest at the foot of my bed, and both my closets were strewn all over the floor. In fact, my bedroom floor was a virtual sea of shirts, skirts, shorts, bed linens, and—oh yes—*underwear.*

Oh God. This was worse than downstairs. It looked as if every single one of my bras and panties—from the nice ones I spent too much money on at Victoria's Secret to the discolored ones with the elastic all stretched out that I only wore when it was unlikely anybody else would see them—were lying all over the floor. In full view.

On the up side, there was also something else in the room in full view.

Jake.

He was standing off to my left, at the foot of my Jenny Lind bed, not five feet away. His back was to me, but from where I stood, he didn't look as if he'd sustained any injuries in the last few minutes.

Although I wasn't sure I could say the same thing for the next few minutes.

Behind me Bert had spotted Jake a split second after I did. "Jake?" she said, punctuating the word by waving her umbrella. "Why in the world didn't you answer us?" As scared as she'd looked moments earlier, she looked just as angry now.

The second Bert spoke, Jake jumped as if he'd been shot. He made a kind of odd movement with his arms, and then he whirled around to face me and Bert. He looked a little taken aback when he saw the poker in my hand. And a little puzzled when he saw the umbrella in Bert's.

"I didn't hear you," he said, moving away from my bed and putting some distance between himself and Bert's umbrella. "I *was* kind of busy, you know. Checking this place out."

I leaned my poker against the wall, and stared at him. Jake had been checking this place out, had he? I glanced back over toward my bed.

Now that he'd moved away from it, I could see through the spindles of my foot board what was now lying on top of the quilt. Two pieces of my lingerie were lying there, in a heap, as if they'd just been tossed there.

So *that* was it. Suddenly, I knew exactly what old Jake had been doing when he'd made that odd movement with his arms. Right after Bert had called his name.

He'd been getting rid of what he'd been holding in his hands. Which was, of course, these two pieces of lingerie— my black silk teddy and my peach lace one. I'd ordered both these little garments out of the—yes, I'll shamelessly admit it—Frederick's catalogue several months ago when things were still going hot and heavy between me and Tab, the construction worker.

Now, of course, I realize that I should've known that the relationship was doomed from the start—that I could never really be serious about anybody named *Tab*. Or, for that matter, anybody who had not read a book since 1963.

At the time, however—it being quite a few months since I'd had any kind of relationship, serious or otherwise—I'd been wildly enthusiastic. And, let's face it, madly in lust.

As was evidenced by the two teddies now lying on top of my quilt. These two teddies had one tiny, little detail in common. Or rather, they had the *absence* of one thing in common. To put it bluntly, neither one of these teddies had a crotch.

"I wanted to make sure there was nobody hiding up here," Jake was now telling Bert.

I glanced back over at Jake, and then back over at my teddies. Maybe Jake hadn't had time to examine them very closely. Maybe he hadn't noticed they were missing a little something.

Bert was now waving her umbrella in the air again, looking disgusted. "You didn't hear Nan when she yelled for you at the bottom of the stairs? How could you not hear her? Are you deaf?"

Jake had not looked over at me once since I came in the

room, but at this point, he gave me a quick, sideways glance.

The second his eyes met mine, I knew. Oh, brother. He'd noticed, all right. If that wasn't the beginnings of a leer on that man's face, I'd never seen one.

I cleared my throat again, and looked away. Well, now, *this* was embarrassing. If I ever got my hands on that damn intruder, I might actually have to kill him.

I would've jumped all over Jake for fingering my lingerie except that, let's face it, my lingerie was all over the place. You couldn't get through the room without stepping over one of my bras or panties.

Jake had turned back to Bert. "I was *preoccupied*," he said.

I stared at him, wondering what the chances were that Jake would believe me if I told him that the only reason I happened to have those particular teddies was that I'd gotten them unbelievably cheap. Because of what was obviously a manufacturer's error.

Uh huh. *Right.*

Bert was waving that damn umbrella one more time. I stepped away from her before she put my eye out. *"Preoccupied?"* she said. "Jake, how can you be so preoccupied, it affects your hearing? Tell me that."

Jake mumbled something or another, sounding defensive, but to tell you the truth, I'd stopped listening. Instead, I moved across my bedroom to my jewelry box. Once again, just like downstairs, nothing seemed to be missing.

I moved around the room, taking a good look. My Minolta single lens reflex camera was still sitting on top of my triple dresser, my five inch color television was still on my night stand, and my cordless telephone was sitting right beside it. It seemed to me that these were things that no self-respecting burglar would pass up. So the story up here was the same as downstairs. The entire room had obviously been tossed, but nothing had been stolen.

Then, what exactly had my intruder been up to? If robbery had not been his motive, then what had it been?

The doorbell rang just as all this was going through my mind. It was also just as Jake was saying to Bert, "Look, I'm sorry, all right? I just didn't hear—"

Oddly enough, for a man who hadn't heard *me* screaming, Jake managed to hear the doorbell on the first ring. He was off, running down the stairs, in a split-second.

Bert stared after him, and then, finally lowering that damn umbrella—thank *God*, I might add—she turned to me. "Nan, you're not going to let Jake answer your door, are you?" She made it sound as if I were letting him steal my car.

"I sure am," I said.

"That's the *police*, you know," Bert said.

I just looked at her. I knew, already. Actually, that was the main reason I was happy to let Jake answer my door. Had Bert forgotten already how much fun it had been to talk to the police earlier? Jake could have my part of it as much as he wanted. In fact, if this was the sort of treat Jake enjoyed, I'd be glad to let him stand in for me the next time I got a speeding ticket.

"It's just like Jake to waltz in here and take over," Bert grumbled.

"Bert," I said, "If Jake wants to take over dealing with the cops, more power to him."

I did not add that I wasn't so sure Jake liked talking to police so much as he would've preferred to talk to the Gestapo than continue the conversation he'd been having with her. I mean, I knew Bert was just using the present situation to vent some of the anger she had toward Jake over everything, but even I had gotten a little tired of hearing her berate him.

Oh, no, I wasn't about to mention any of this. Bert looked angry enough, as it was. Her mood did not improve when we got downstairs and found that Jake had already ushered in two policemen.

I never did get their names. Clod One and Clod Two is pretty much how I've always thought of them. The two cops were both standing at the foot of the stairs when Bert and I came down. Clod One was flipping open a small notebook the way Captain Kirk opens his Enterprise communicator.

"This the apartment with the break-in?" he asked.

I blinked at that one. It could very well be that Jake wasn't the only person in the room with a gift for stupid questions. Before I could answer, Jake jumped right in. "That's right, Officer," Jake said, nodding his head so emphatically, the feather dangling from his ear bounced wildly.

The two patrolmen glanced around my destroyed apartment without the slightest change on their faces. They could've been looking at the set of a play.

"Names?" Clod One said. His tone was bored.

Jake jumped in this time, too. "Jake Powell. I'm a, uh, friend of the family."

That summed it up nicely, I thought.

Jake hurried on, indicating Bert with a careless wave of his hand. "And this is—"

Before Jake could finish introducing her, Bert jumped in, "Bert Tatum."

When Bert said that, Jake actually winced. I guess, up to then, it hadn't really hit him that Bert had taken back her maiden name after the divorce.

I stepped forward, and introduced myself. "I'm the one who phoned. This is my apartment."

Clod Two was nodding. "You're the one on CKI, aren't you? The station that does all those screwy promotions?"

I just looked at him. Where had I heard that little phrase before?

I knew then, of course. Before they'd headed out here to answer my 911 call, Clod One and Clod Two had obviously had a little talk with the Clod of all Clods, Detective Goetzmann. Apparently, all the Clods had decided that trashing my apartment was yet another publicity stunt for the radio station.

My stomach was starting to hurt. "Exactly what does my being on the radio have to do with anything?" I demanded.

Clod One shrugged. "Nothing. Not really." He looked me straight in the eye. "So. Is anything missing?"

I really hated to answer that one.

I also hated to watch the Clod brothers go through my apartment. It was obvious that they were just going through the motions. In what seemed like five minutes tops, the Clods were again standing at my front door, making final scratches in their little notebooks. "OK, that's just about it," Clod One said. "There's a broken window in your kitchen. Above the sink." He exchanged a look with Clod Two. "That might've been how whoever did this got in."

It was clear he didn't believe a word he was saying.

"We'll file a report," Clod Two said. His tone was even more bored than Clod One's. "If we need any more information, we'll—"

I didn't hear the last part because he was already out the door, with Clod One at his heels.

"Well now, that went well," Bert said. She and Jake were standing right behind me, watching the Clod Brothers drive off. Bert patted me on the shoulder. "Now, don't you worry, Nan, they'll find out who did this—"

I was already shaking my head, as I turned to face her. "Bert," I said, "they're not going to find out a damn thing. They think I staged this on my own."

Bert now shook *her* head. "Oh, no—" Her tone was disbelieving.

"Oh, *yes*," I said. "It's obvious they've talked to the same detective we talked to earlier."

Jake interrupted. "Detective? What detective?"

So we had to tell him. We all trooped into my living room, put the cushions back on my couch, and sat down. Then we filled Jake in on everything that had happened from the moment Bert talked to the dead guy at lunch. Once again, Jake didn't fail us. The master of the stupid question managed to come up with another one. "Do you think this break-in could have anything to do with that murder?"

I frowned. "But how could that be? How can they be connected when it was Bert who ran into the guy on the street? And it was *my* apartment that got broken into?"

Jake blinked once, ran his hand through his sandy-brown hair, and then abruptly turned to Bert. "God, Bert," he said, "what a thing to happen."

I stared at him. One thing about Jake, he was quick on his feet. If somebody blew holes in his argument, he didn't waste any time changing the subject. Now he was actually looking upset. As if hearing all about what had happened to Bert, and how she'd been nearly lured to a murder scene, had shaken him badly. His voice even broke a little as he added, his eyes on Bert's face, "I mean, think about it—you . . . you—"

Could have been killed, I willed him to say. Could be dead now. It looked to me as if this would be an ideal opportunity for Jake to get back in Bert's good graces. Tell her you could've lost her forever. Tell her you'd be devastated, you pea brain.

"—you've got to be more careful, Bert," Jake finished. "NEVER talk to strangers!"

Oh for God's sake. No wonder these two didn't get along.

Bert stiffened. She took a deep breath, no doubt getting ready to tell Jake just how much she appreciated his instructions. Jake, however, must've picked up on the gist of what Bert was about to say because he immediately cut her off.

"What I mean to say is—*what* an awful thing for you to go through." He reached over and touched her cheek.

Bert, amazingly enough, did not flinch.

"You must be exhausted," Jake went on, his tone concerned.

Inwardly, I was smiling. Things were looking up. At this point, it seemed to me that I was the one turning us into a crowd. I got to my feet, but Jake stopped me. "Don't go, Nan," he said. "You're going to need some help getting this place cleaned up. And Bert here looks done in. Let me help you put everything away."

I now stared at him, openmouthed. Like I said earlier, I'd known Jake for years. In all that time, I'd never known him to volunteer for work.

"Why don't I walk Bert to her door," Jake went smoothly on. "And then I'll be right back, and we'll get this place spic and span again."

Even Bert was looking surprised now. "Why, Jake," she said, "this is so nice of you."

Jake just shrugged his big shoulders. "Hey," he said, "I

don't mind. And you have to work tomorrow. Come on, I'll walk you next door."

Jake was back in about ten minutes, and true to his word, he stayed until my entire apartment was cleaned up. The only room I didn't let him help me with was, no surprise, my bedroom. I closed the door to that one, telling him, "I'll do this one myself."

Jake just looked at me, a smile playing about his mouth. "Whatever you say," he said softly.

With Jake helping me it went a lot faster than I would've ever expected. It was only a little after two when, my apartment close to being back the way it was, I walked Jake to my front door. "You know, Nan," Jake said, holding his coat, "if you're feeling a little nervous, I'd be glad to stay overnight."

I shook my head. "That's sweet of you, Jake, but I'm fine. Don't worry about me."

He just stood there, staring at me for a minute.

"You know, I can tell you're the youngest twin," Jake said.

I lifted an eyebrow. He could tell I was youngest by ten entire minutes?

"I mean, you look like Bert, of course," Jake went on, "but you're a lot more open-minded about things."

Could this train of thought, by any wild notion, have something to do with my crotchless underwear?

"I mean, Bert's kind of stodgy, you know, kind of set in her ways," Jake said. "She's a wonderful woman, of course, but she's a little old-fashioned."

Uh huh.

"Well, thanks for your help, Jake," I said, and started to reach for the doorknob.

Before I knew what was happening, Jake leaned toward me to give me a kiss. I thought it was going to be one of his usual brotherly pecks on the cheek, but Jake missed his aim a little. His lips brushed the side of my mouth.

I took a quick step backward, and stared at him.

Now what was that?

"Put the chain on," Jake said, putting on his coat. "And call me if you hear any strange noises, OK?"

I nodded, breathing a little easier. Jake was just being a brother, that was all. Obviously, Brother Jake was trying to cozy up to me so he could get next to Sister Bert.

Sure. That was it.

Chapter 5

●

BERT

I wish I could say I was so upset about what had happened to Nan's apartment that I tossed and turned all night. Or that I was feeling so sad about what had happened to Top Ten that I couldn't sleep. The truth was, I did toss and turn, all right, but it wasn't because of the mess over at Nan's. Or because of Top Ten.

It was seeing Jake again.

I don't think I would've been so rattled if Jake had acted terrible. But, no, I had to admit, he'd been sweet. His offering to help Nan clean up her apartment had actually been thoughtful. I mean, this *was* the man who'd never even so much as unloaded the dishwasher during all the years we were married.

Lord. Could it really be that, in the months we'd been apart, he had changed?

And, as much as I'd complained last night, I had to admit it had even been considerate of Jake to deal with the police for us, instead of Nan and me having to go through that ordeal again.

As I went through the motions of getting ready for work, I actually found myself smiling every once in a while. Just thinking about Jake, and the way he'd acted the night before.

Every time it happened, though, I wiped that smile right off my face. Instead, I tried to focus on what it had been like that final afternoon. How it had felt to get that terrible phone call. It had been Friday, my day to clean the first floor. I'd already mopped and waxed the kitchen, and I was in the middle of doing the dining room. I still had the bottle of Pledge and the dust cloth in my hand when I answered the phone.

"Mrs. Powell? You don't know me, but there's something I think you ought to know." The voice had been smug. And young. Afterwards, I wondered if Bimbette had not gotten one of her friends to do it.

"Your husband has been carrying on with Heather Dixson, his receptionist, for ten months now."

My mouth went dry. The name meant little to me. I vaguely remembered a young blond woman at the front desk, but I couldn't even recall her face. I could recall, however, that she had to be at least fifteen years younger than me.

The smug voice hurried on. "The whole office is talking about it. And, well, I just thought I'd do you a favor."

The dial tone sounded in my ear. Leaving me, of course, standing there in my dining room, staring at a spray can of furniture polish.

I had not done any more cleaning that day. My reasoning, of course, went along these lines—I'd rather be boiled in oil as to spend one more minute cleaning the home of a philanderer. Instead, I'd sat on my living room couch, and I'd quietly waited. I'd confronted Jake the minute he'd walked in the door.

I'd expected embarrassment, shame, maybe even pleas for forgiveness. Instead, Jake acted almost relieved to have everything out in the open. He had his things packed and was gone in a matter of minutes. I was amazed. If the man had been competing in an Olympic event called Leaving Your Wife, Jake would've won the gold. The entire time he was getting his things together, he hadn't met my eyes once.

After his car pulled out of the driveway, I practically collapsed into one of my dining room chairs, and I cried until I realized that my tears were making little white circles on the gleaming surface I'd just polished earlier that day. I stared at those little circles, and I realized I was no longer cleaning the home of a philanderer. I was just cleaning mine.

Now, after inflicting that kind of pain, did Jake really think he could make things all better by being nice, for a change?

And yet, I couldn't deny that seeing him had upset me. A lot.

Did that mean I still cared about him?

With all this going through my head, I guess I was pretty distracted as I finished putting on my makeup, got my car keys off the ring in the kitchen, and started to head outside.

When I got to my front door, I could already hear Nan starting her Neon next door. So I just stood there, waiting. Nan usually leaves at the same time I do, but we almost never ride together. Mainly because, even though Kentuckiana Temps often has me working in downtown Louisville, only blocks from Nan's radio station, Nan's hours vary so much.

This morning I just didn't want to see her. Not right away, anyway. I didn't want to give her the chance to ask me any questions about Jake that I didn't feel ready to answer. And I sure didn't want to give her the chance to give me answers to questions I was not ready to ask. She does that, you know. I realize her intentions are good, but I could just hear her now. The woman could give Alex Trebek a run for his money.

"And the answer is, *A husband worth forgiving.*" The question? *Who is, Jake, of course.*

I was still thinking about Jake as I walked into the law office on the twenty-second floor of the Citizens Plaza building. This week I was filling in as a temporary receptionist for a woman taking her summer vacation. It was a testament to the generosity of the firm that she had not been permitted to take time off during the summer, and had to wait until every one of the attorneys in the office had already taken their vacation. The poor thing probably had to take her Christmas holiday in July.

Wouldn't you know it, I'd just stashed my purse under the front desk, and sat down when the phone started ringing. I answered just like I'd been told to do. "Farley. Nevin. And Woods."

The firm's name was Farley, Nevin, and Woods, but each of the partners had made a special trip into my office to tell me that I was to answer the phone, putting special emphasis on the commas. Apparently, even in their name, these three wanted as little as possible to do with each other. Of course, after I'd met all of them, I could certainly understand their viewpoints. "May I help you?" I went on.

The voice on the phone was a hoarse whisper. "Where is he?"

"Excuse me?" I said. The caller evidently had a bad case of laryngitis. I could barely make out what he was saying.

"WHERE IS HE?" Now the voice seemed to sound more female than male, but I couldn't be sure. The laryngitis had not improved. *"WHERE?"*

I believe I asked the obvious question. "Where is who?" If the caller wanted one of the partners, they never got in before eleven. The only people in the office this early in the morning were their secretaries.

"Don't play stupid with me," the hoarse voice on the phone said. "You know damn well who I'm talking about, bitch."

I caught my breath. Apparently, the caller's illness had made him testy. I, on the other hand, tried to keep my cool and remain professional. "I'm sorry, but I do believe you've dialed a wrong number."

The voice got lower and even more hoarse. It was like talking to Darth Vader. "Look. They told me what they were going to do, and I know you're in on it."

I was getting ready to hang up on this nut case. "I think if you'll check the number you dialed, you'll—"

Darth interrupted me. "I don't need to check anything, you asshole. I know exactly who I'm talking to. You're one of the twins, aren't you?"

My heart started to pound. *What?* Up to that very moment I'd been so sure that this had to be a wrong number, I actually felt a little dizzy.

Darth had more to say. "And you might as well stop trying to get me to say something over the phone. I'm not anybody's fool, you know. I know there's ways you can record this, bitch."

Darth was not making any sense. It seemed highly unlikely I'd want to record somebody calling me names. Speaking of which— "Who is this?"

"Somebody who's saving your life," Darth said. "Now, you tell him to call me right away. I mean it. Or we're all going to end up dead!"

I felt a shiver run down my back.

"But—" That's all I managed to get out before Darth banged down the receiver.

For a moment I just sat there staring at the receiver in my hand. Who in the world had that been? And what in the world had they been talking about?

None of it had made any sense, and yet, the caller had known I was a twin. So it had to have been somebody I knew, didn't it?

Or somebody Nan knew.

I reached over, punched in a number, and listened to the phone ring on the other end. I knew, of course, it wasn't really ringing on the other end.

In radio, according to Nan, it's kind of important that the only sound that goes out over the air is what the deejays say or play. Nobody wants to hear phones ringing in the background. Unless it's public radio, Nan says, and that's only when they're having their annual call-a-thon to raise money.

When I visited the WCKI control room not too long ago, Nan had pointed out the large colored lights mounted above the control board. These lights blink to let the deejay know a call is coming in on a particular line. Now I said, as I listened to the phone ring, "Come on, Nan, answer the blink!"

As if Nan had heard me, she picked up. "That you, Bert?" she said.

I wasn't surprised. Nan and I do this a lot. I'm not sure exactly how we do it, but a lot of the times we can tell somehow when it's the other one phoning.

Twin vibes, Nan calls it.

I may not have been surprised that Nan knew it was me, but I was surprised by the odd note in Nan's voice. Her voice sounded strained. And maybe a little bit scared.

"I just got the strangest phone call."

We'd both said the exact same words in unison.

"You did?" I said.

"You too?" Nan said. "Did yours say, *I've got the money?*"

I found I was gripping the receiver so tight my knuckles were white. "What?"

"Money," Nan said, "Mine said, *I've got the money.*" So I say, 'Bully for you,' and I wait. Lord knows we get loonies calling here all the time. The contest hot line number is in the phone book, for chrissake." Nan's tone was almost casual, but I knew, just listening to her, she was really rattled. Even if I couldn't hear the slight tremor in her voice, she was talking a mile a minute. The more upset Nan is, the faster she talks. If she ever sounds like that guy who can rattle off all the classics in about a minute, I'll know she's hysterical.

"At this point I'm figuring," Nan went on, "hey, maybe this is one of our past contest winners. Or that maybe this loony thinks he's called the Kentucky Lottery or something. So I—oh, just a sec. Be right back."

This last is pretty much par for the course when I talk to Nan at work. Our conversation is broken up into two-and-a-half minute spurts sandwiched between the sets when she's announcing songs. I could barely hear the click of the microphone, and then Nan's radio voice boomed over the phone, saying something about John Michael Montgomery.

Nan's radio voice sounds a lot like herself, I guess, except that it has more power behind it—and it always has a kind of sexy overtone. Come hither with a hammer, is what Nan calls it.

The mike clicked again, and Nan came back on the line. "So after I say, 'Bully for you,' there's this long silence," she said, picking up where she left off. "Like maybe the caller's doing some heavy thinking. 'What money would that be?' I ask then."

Nan was on a roll now, performing both voices, hers and

the loony's. "The loony whispers, 'What's the matter?' " Nan was now sounding a lot like Darth Vader herself. " 'Is someone there with you so you can't talk?' "

"And I said," Nan hurried on, now doing her regular voice, 'Well, of course, I can talk. I wouldn't have picked up the phone if I couldn't talk.' I felt like I was explaining things to a baby, for chrissake. Still, after all these years in this business, you learn that the next loony on the phone could be the station owner's wife. It never pays to piss anybody off. After about another minute of silence, I say, 'So, what's all this about money?' That's when the loon hangs up on me. Just a sec—"

Nan's voice boomed once again over the phone. She made the weather report sound faintly suggestive, announced the next set of songs, and then she was back.

"As soon as the loon disconnected," she said, "I immediately hit Dial Return. You know, to call back the last call received. Can you believe, when the phone is picked up, it's a recording that says, 'The number you have reached is out of service to incoming calls.' It was a damn pay phone!" Nan took a deep breath. "So what did your guy say?"

I sort of hated to tell her. What my caller had said did seem significantly worse. "Well," I said, "I'm not sure it was a guy. The voice was so hoarse, it could've been a woman."

Nan jumped in. "OK, OK," she said, "so mine could've been a woman, too, I guess. The way he was whispering, it could've been a St. Bernard, for all I know." There was a noise on the line at this point that I thought at first was static. Then I realized Nan had cleared her throat. "So," she said, "what did yours say?" Her tone was impatient.

So I told her, word for word, the entire conversation, as best as I could remember it. When I got to the part about all of us ending up dead, I could hear Nan do a quick intake of breath.

"Dead?" Nan asked. "Is that really what he said? Dead?"

It was a word I really couldn't misunderstand. "Dead," I repeated.

"Shit," Nan burst out, "you've had a death threat!"

My heart actually started to pound all over again. I realized then that I'd been hoping that Nan would pooh-pooh the whole thing. That maybe she'd tell me that there was really no reason to be scared, that I was just overreacting.

Nan *is* pretty much no-nonsense about just about everything. I mean, you wouldn't believe what she has to say about poor Oral Roberts. Clearly, however, she was not taking this lightly. I think I knew what she was going to say next even before she said it. This time it had nothing to do with twin vibes, either. "Bert, we've got to report this to the police."

Oh God.

"How's about I pick you up at three fifteen after I get off the air?"

I tried just once to change her mind. "Nan, do we have to?"

"We have to," Nan said.

That guy who came up with the saying, the third time's the charm, had obviously never met Detective Goetzmann. As Nan and I approached his desk, Goetzmann leaned back in his chair, putting his hands behind his head. "Well, well, well, whaddya know? The Terror Twins are back."

I didn't know about Nan, but with that kind of encouragement, I was ready to leave.

Nan, however, obviously felt otherwise. In fact, if she'd been a cat, I think she'd have arched her back and spat at Goetzmann. "Look, Goetzmann," she said, leaning on his desk, "I don't care whether you believe us or not. But you need to know that something else has happened, because obviously, you don't have the brains that God gave a—"

Goetzmann's eyes had narrowed considerably. Before they became slits, I cut Nan off. "What my sister means is that we just thought that we should probably report this," I said, my tone placating. "Because if something *should* happen—

"—to either one of us, it's going to be on your conscience," Nan finished for me. "So you'd better get it in your fat head that something strange is going on, because—"

I interrupted again. "—this morning we've each received a—"

"—weirdo phone call," Nan finished again. She was talking very fast. "The call to me at the radio station was this unbelievably creepy whisper, saying he has the money. But then he hangs up on me—"

"—and I got a call at my office, too," I interrupted. "Another whispery voice says for me to tell *him*, like I'd know who that is, that he'd better get in touch or—

"—we'd all end up dead. *Dead*—do you hear what we're saying to you? Bert's actually been threatened," said Nan. "Now what we'd like to know—"

"—is what we should do about it," I finished.

"—is what *you* are going to do about it," Nan corrected.

Looking at the growing scowl on Goetzmann's face, I figured we already had an answer to that question. I realized too late that Nan and I had reverted to doing what we'd done ever since the first grade, when Mrs. Malley, our teacher, accused us of copying off each other on an addition test because we'd both made the same mistakes.

We finish each other's sentences when we're rattled.

It hadn't gone over very well with Mrs. Malley either.

To Goetzmann, it probably looked like we'd rehearsed our fabricated story so well, we had it memorized.

"Don't tell me," said Goetzmann, running his hand over his Marine haircut, "let me guess. You two think these phone calls—whispering voices, did you say?—have something to do with the murder of that John Doe yesterday in the Galleria. The dead guy that neither of you knew. And, natch, it also has something to do with the so-called break-in at one of your apartments. Am I right or am I right?"

"We have no idea what the phone calls have to do with," Nan said, her voice now frosting over. "You're supposed to be a trained professional—you tell us."

Goetzmann took a deep breath. "You know what I hate?" he said. "I—"

I couldn't believe it, but Nan actually interrupted him. "Look, we're not making this up. Check with the phone company. Whoever called me called from a pay phone. There's got to be records."

Goetzmann raised his eyebrows. "So what you're saying is that you two could not have possibly phoned each other? Just to make the records look as if someone else were doing the calling?"

That did it. Nan whirled on her heel and stomped away before I even knew what was happening.

I was left to stand there for a moment, while Goetzmann did a pretty good imitation of Mt. Vesuvius just before the Pompeii incident. I gave him a weak smile, and took off after Nan.

A little later, when I was sitting beside Nan in the front seat of her Neon, I said, "Never again. I will never, never, NEVER report anything to the police again," I said.

For an answer, Nan shrugged.

"To think," I went on, "I took off work just so I could once again have the pleasure of being embarrassed to death by Goetzmann. Gosh. What fun."

Nan shrugged again. "We had to report the phone calls," she said.

"Oh, yeah? Why?" I asked. "What exactly did we accomplish? Except that maybe Goetzmann won't be calling on us to buy tickets to the Policeman's Ball this year."

Nan turned onto Muhammad Ali Boulevard and pulled up behind a UPS truck parked in the middle of the street, obviously making a delivery. And also obviously blocking the one-way street. It was the perfect ending to a wonderful afternoon. "Shit," Nan said. She put on the brakes, glared at the UPS truck, and then turned to me. "Look, Bert, you might as well stop being such a crybaby. You agreed we needed to report the calls."

I turned to glare at her. Crybaby? She had herself a little tantrum and stomped off, and *I'm* the crybaby?

"Let me out of here," I said, opening the car door. "I can get to the office quicker by walking." I did not add that if I stayed in the car with her another minute, I might deliver a few death threats of my own.

I jerked open the car door, crossed in front of the car, and started to walk off.

Nan's voice stopped me. "Bert?"

"What?" I snapped, turning to face her.

Nan had her window down, and was looking straight at me. "Be extra careful, O.K.?"

I just looked at her. The worry in her eyes was unmistakable.

God. What in the world were we fighting about? I threw Nan a shaky grin. 'Sure thing," I said. "You too."

Of course, once Nan and I had this little exchange, I found myself looking over my shoulder every few steps or so, as I walked quite briskly back to Farley, Nevin, and Woods. I probably looked every bit as relaxed as one of the cast of *Alien*, after that monster got loose on the ship. Of course, if I hadn't been looking around so often, I probably wouldn't have spotted the woman following me in the first place.

If she really was following me.

Once I noticed her, I started stopping every few minutes or so, pretending to look in the windows of the stores I was passing. I wasn't really paying attention to what I was looking at. I was just trying to see if the woman behind me would stop, too.

She did, every time.

Even when I stopped in the middle of the sidewalk and just gazed upward, as if maybe I'd spotted some rare birds flying over, the woman stopped, too. I couldn't help but notice that she was at that moment peering into a drugstore window, intently studying a display of athlete's foot cream.

While she studied the display, I studied her. She was wearing—believe it or not—a tan raincoat with the collar turned up, like some kind of female Sam Spade. Only Sam probably wouldn't have been caught dead in the pair of over-sized orange sunglasses this woman had on. Especially if Sam had his hair dyed the same bright red. The color reminded me of the wig that Ronald McDonald always wears. Which, now that I thought of it, made me wonder. Was this a wig?

Sam Spade probably would never have tailed somebody in the four-inch high heels this woman was wearing, either. Her heels were in a distinctive shade of green that Nan calls *baby poop*, and she was carrying a matching baby poop green purse.

It was only when I finally turned into the door of my office building that Miss Spade walked on by, her high heels clicking on the sidewalk like typewriter keys.

I breathed a sigh of relief. Maybe I was just being paranoid.

But, as they say, even paranoiacs have enemies.

I spent the rest of the afternoon jumping whenever anyone came up behind me, and on the way home, I couldn't help constantly glancing in my rearview mirror as I drove to my apartment.

As best as I could tell, no one followed me. In fact, by the time I pulled into my driveway, I was pretty much convinced that I'd watched one too many episodes of *Murder She Wrote*.

That is, up until I saw the front door to my apartment. It was standing slightly ajar.

Hadn't I locked up carefully when I'd left this morning? Come on, sure I had. As I slowly walked up my sidewalk, my heart began pounding in my ears.

I pushed my front door open. Lord.

From what I could see, my living room had become a twin of Nan's from the night before. Drawers stood open. Closet doors were flung wide. Papers, clothes and books littered the floor like confetti.

I swallowed past the lump in my throat. "Oh dear," I said, so softly I could barely hear my own words. Somewhere off in the distance I could hear a car driving up, and yet, all I was really aware of was the wreckage of my poor apartment. I walked over and picked up a Lenox candleholder that had fallen from my mantel. There was a now a tiny chip out of the bottom. Holding the thing, I felt tears prickling at my eyelids. I blinked them away, and moved further into the room.

God. This was just the same as Nan's break-in. Nothing seemed to have been taken—just scattered about.

I had just returned my candleholder to the mantel when I heard the noise on my stairs.

I couldn't help it. I screamed before I saw who it was coming down the steps.

"Jake!" I said. "For God's sake, what are you doing here?"

Jake gave a start when he saw me, and then he held out both hands in a gesture of innocence. "Hey, this place was like this when I got here. In fact, I was just checking around, making sure that whoever did this wasn't lying in wait for you to come home."

I just stared at him. The terrible thing about having somebody you trusted lie to you is that you don't ever take what they tell you at face value any more. "Was my front door unlocked?"

Jake nodded. "It was standing wide open. I just walked right in."

As if on cue, Nan came running in. "Holy fucking shit," she said, looking around the room.

For once, I thought she'd described the entire situation perfectly.

"You two had better see what's upstairs, too," Jake said. His eyes looked grim.

Nan and I exchanged a long look, and then we followed Jake wordlessly up the stairs. Down the hall. And into my bathroom.

There on my mirror, someone had left me a message.

"NO COPS, OR YOU DIE!" It had been scrawled in a garish red-orange lipstick.

Chapter 6

•

NAN

I stared at the bright orange scrawl on Bert's bathroom mirror. NO COPS OR YOU DIE.

That seemed clear.

It must not have been to Jake, however. He shifted his weight from one cowboy boot to another. "Now what the hell do you think that means?"

I just looked at him. Once again, Mr. Stupid Question had not failed us. "Jake," I said. My tone was infinitely patient. "I think we're not supposed to call the police."

Jake shook his head. He was wearing the feather earring again, and it danced its usual jig. "Why, that's ridiculous. Of course, we're going to have to call them!"

Bert had been still staring at her mirror much like I had before—in wide-eyed horror—but now she turned and frowned at Jake. "Can't you read? It says—"

Jake interrupted her. "I don't care what it says, you've got to call the police. Otherwise, you're just playing right into this guy's hands."

Jake was right. I knew that. I also knew—given the alternative of facing a firing squad or facing the police again—that Bert would probably choose the firing squad. And yet, it seemed to me she really didn't have a choice. "Bert," I said quietly, "you really should call the police."

Bert looked over at me and shook her head. "And have some cop start looking through my purse and makeup to see if I wear that particular shade of orange lipstick? No, thanks, I'll pass."

Jake actually looked flabbergasted. It made you wonder just how many times Bert had disagreed with him during the years they'd been married. "Bert," he said, "don't be silly. Of course you're calling—"

I believe if you're trying to convince somebody to do something, calling them silly is not your best idea. Bert looked as if a couple charges of dynamite had gone off behind her eyes. "Jake," she said evenly, interrupting him, "the mirror says no cops, and I—"

Jake cut her off. "Since when did you start paying attention to mirrors?" His tone was derisive. In fact, he made it sound as if maybe Bert was asking the thing every day, *Who was the fairest of them all?*

Bert glared at him. "Since the word *die* was mentioned, that's pretty much when I started paying attention. I don't know about you two—" Here she looked first at me, and then over at Jake. "—but that particular word is a grabber to me. I'm funny that way."

Bert now had that stubborn set to her mouth that, over the years, I've realized always means you might as well as shut up, you're wasting your breath, the subject is closed.

Jake, for all the years he'd lived with Bert, apparently had not learned the significance of the way she was now holding her mouth. Or else, he did know exactly what it meant, and he thought he could still bully her into doing what he wanted.

I shrugged and turned toward the door. Rots of ruck, Jake.

Jake was now running his hand through his shaggy brown hair. "Bert," he said, "don't be hysterical. Either you're going to call the police, or I am. We need to show them this." He nodded his head toward the bathroom mirror.

First, she's silly and then she's hysterical. This man needed lessons on how to win friends and influence people. I took a quick glance over at Bert. She was now breathing through her nose, like a bull getting ready to charge. I'd seen this look before, too. I backed away from her.

It was kind of a good thing I did, too, because right away it cleared a path to the sink. Otherwise, I think Bert might've just run right over me as she rushed toward it. "Oh?" she said. Grabbing a washcloth off the towel rack next to the sink, she began scrubbing at the bathroom mirror.

Jake yelled, "Hey!" and made a grab for the washcloth, but it was too late. The message was now nothing more than long orange smears. Bert stepped back, looking satisfied, and dropped the washcloth into the sink. "There, now you don't have to worry about showing the police anything." She gave her dark head another toss, and walked regally out of the bathroom.

I stood there, watching her go. And she said *I* had tantrums?

Bert was already halfway down the stairs when Jake took off after her. "Are you *nuts?*" he said.

Let me see—silly, hysterical and nuts. The man was on a roll.

"Bert, you're calling the damn cops," Jake hurried on. "It doesn't matter about the damn mirror. I'll just tell them what it said." Jake caught up with Bert at the bottom of the stairs, their backs to the front door. I, of course, was just a few steps behind, and believe me, at this point, I'd decided that I personally had already said all I intended to on the subject of cop-calling. Besides, Jake was saying enough for several people. He was also jabbing his finger in Bert's face. "Look, Bert, I am telling you—"

"You don't have the right to tell me anything," Bert said.

"You tell 'im, little lady," a deep voice drawled.

That one brought us all up short. All three of us turned toward the sound.

A stranger was now standing in Bert's open doorway. Wearing faded jeans, jogging shoes, a white t-shirt, and a wrinkled navy blue linen blazer, the guy bore an uncanny resemblance to Harrison Ford. When Harrison was sporting a neatly-trimmed beard, that is.

I moved to the bottom of the stairs, and I shamelessly stared. The guy might not have looked so much like Harrison Ford if he had not been not wearing his hair cut exactly like Harrison had worn it in *The Fugitive*. He could've been in his early forties or even late fifties, it was hard to tell.

What was easy to tell was he was cute with a capital Q, and he knew it. He was leaning nonchalantly against the door frame, and you could tell he was trying not to smile.

Jake obviously didn't appreciate the look of suppressed amusement on the newcomer's face, any more than he'd appreciated the stranger's input into the charming conversation he'd been having with Bert. "Who the hell are you?" Jake asked.

Harrison ignored him. Instead, he looked past Jake at the current condition of Bert's living room, shook his head and whistled. "Man," he said, "you guys really know how to fight. You could give lessons."

Jake bristled at that one. "This place looked like this when we got here." He took a step toward Harrison. "I asked you a question. Who the *hell* are you?"

Harrison didn't budge. "I got me a card. Wait a second. I never can find one of those damn things when I want one. It's in here somewhere." He stood there, patting down the pockets on his shirt, then going through the pockets, inside and out, of his blazer, and finally coming up with a business card out of the back pocket of his jeans.

The card was almost as wrinkled as Harrison's blazer. He handed the card to Jake, and then looked over at Bert, then over at me, and then back over at Bert again. I half expected the next thing out of his mouth to be the usual, *Are you two twins?* But he surprised me.

"I'm Trent Marksberry," he said. He looked straight at me again, then again at Bert, and then indicated the wrinkled card in Jake's hand with a nod of his head. *"Private investigations. That's* what it says." There was something in his tone that could've been suggesting that, if Trent had not read it for him, Jake might not have been able to figure out what the card said. It wasn't so obvious, though, that Jake could call him on it.

Instead, Jake satisfied himself with just handing the card over to me, holding it by just two fingers, as if it were something unclean. I stared at the thing. It listed an address in downtown Louisville with a Louisville phone number.

Turning back to Trent, Jake said, "You're a private *dick?*" He emphasized the last word.

Trent looked even more amused. He gave Bert a quick wink before he answered. "That's what some call me," he drawled.

Bert stepped forward, extending her hand. She introduced herself, then me, and when she got to Jake, she added, "Jake's my *ex*-husband." I'd say she emphasized *ex* every bit as much as Jake had emphasized *dick*.

The stranger grinned, a charming crooked smile; and unless I missed my guess, it seemed he held onto Bert's hand quite a bit longer than necessary.

I believe Jake thought so, too, because all of a sudden, Jake got very busy reaching for his own business card. Extracting the thing from a gold case he pulled out of his shirt pocket, Jake stuck the card in Trent's face.

This little maneuver accomplished what Jake intended it to. Trent released Bert's hand and took the card.

While Trent read the thing, Jake shifted again from one cowboy boot to the other. "So what is it you want, Marksberry?"

Trent didn't even glance Jake's way. Instead, his eyes still on Jake's business card, he drawled, "I'm looking into the death of the man that a Miss Bert Tatum—that's you—" At this point, Trent glanced over at Bert. "—happened to talk to around lunch time yesterday." His eyes traveled back to the card. "I got your name from that policeman you went to see downtown."

Trent handed the card back to Jake. "Insurance, huh?"

"I own the company," Jake put in.

Trent looked unimpressed. "Oh yeah?" Trent said. "You got a policy on this place?"

"What?" Jake blinked a couple of times.

"Because," Trent went on, "if you don't, I'll just bet this little lady right here is convinced by now that she'll be needing one."

Jake's face turned beet red. "What the hell are you trying to say?"

Yet another stupid question.

I glanced over at Bert. This was getting good.

" 'Course, you're an ex, too," Trent went on in his deep, slow drawl. "And in my line of business, I've seen some ex-spouses who are not even in the insurance biz do some strange things."

"What do you mean by that?" Jake demanded.

I gave Bert another glance. She was actually looking a little amused.

Trent smiled again. "Oh, you know. Spying on their exes, following them all around. That kind of thing—" His voice trailed off, but his eyes wandered around the room.

"Are you saying—" Jake began, but Trent ignored the interruption.

"Sometimes they're harassing their exes at work. Vandalizing their cars. Sometimes even doing things to their homes."

The blood vessel in Jake's right temple was now jumping. "You— You— You—" Jake seemed to be so angry, he couldn't even talk. I stared at him.

Was he overreacting? If what Marksberry was saying wasn't true, why did Jake care what some stranger suggested? I took a deep breath. Maybe old Jake here was a little too outraged. Like maybe he was trying a little too hard to convince people he couldn't be guilty.

Lord. Could it actually have been *Jake* who'd trashed Bert's apartment? And before that, mine?

Bert was now staring at Jake, too; and, from the look on her face, she was wondering the same things I was.

Jake finally found his voice. Turning to Bert, he asked, "Are you going to just stand there, and let this stranger talk to *me* like this?"

Bert's answer was clearly not what Jake wanted. She didn't say a word.

She just looked at him.

Jake actually sputtered. Then he turned to face me.

I would've liked to have told him that I didn't believe for a moment that he could have done any of this. Standing there, however, looking at him, I suddenly saw Jake again, as he'd been last night, squaring his shoulders, and then heading up my stairs to rout my prowler.

Weaponless.

Not even carrying an umbrella. What's more, Jake had even seemed eager to go. Now I wondered. Could that have been because Jake was what I'd always suspected—a total fool?

Or was it because he already knew that he had nothing to fear? That he himself was the intruder?

Would Jake actually trash two apartments just so he could come in and save us? To get his foot back in the door, so to speak, with Bert?

Or—and the thought of Jake's kiss flashed through my mind—even, with me?

With all this to consider, I just stood there and looked at him.

With this kind of family support, Jake looked like he was approaching a stroke. "All right!" he snapped. "If that's the way you two want it!" He marched out the front door without even looking back.

Apparently, that exit was not enough, however. In another second or so, Jake was back in the doorway. He reached for the knob, and slammed the door so hard, the door frame shuddered.

For my part, I just stood there. It's behavior like this

that's earned Jake the nickname of Jake the Flake among Bert's and my relatives.

Trent Marksberry was visibly moved by Jake's exit. "A mite touchy, isn't he?" he said over his shoulder, and laughed. He moved past Bert, and headed straight for the pile of books lying in front of the bookcase. Without even asking, he started putting the books back on the shelves.

It took Bert and me a second to follow his lead. I guess we were stunned that you could get a man to clean your apartment without even asking. Or, for that matter, pleading. We just stood there for a moment, staring at Trent as if he were some rare animal we'd captured.

"Like I was saying," Trent said, "I'm investigating this guy's death." He continued shelving books, and looked over at Bert. "You know, the guy you talked to. The Louisville P.D. has identified the dead man as a Mister Russell Moorman." As he said the name, Trent looked again over at Bert, and then over at me. "That name mean anything to either one of you?"

"Not me," I said, shaking my head, as I picked up the cushions, brushed them off, and put them back on the sofa.

Bert was picking up magazines, and stacking them on the coffee table. "Me neither. I've never heard of him."

I glanced her way. Bert's voice had undergone a subtle change. Or maybe not so subtle. It was now deep and sexy. Lord. Kathleen Turner had nothing on Bert.

I was kind of glad to hear her sounding like this, though. I'd told Bert when she first got her divorce that she ought to start enjoying herself, for God's sake, loosen up, flirt a little. She'd been tied up with Jake ever since her senior year in high school. Moreover, I did happen to recall something that Bert has confided to me over the years. Or maybe I should say *not* confided, since there hasn't been anything to confide.

Bert has never—in her entire life, mind you—slept with anybody but Jake. *And* she'd actually been a virgin on their wedding night.

This last, of course, truly amazes me. I mean, Bert could possibly be the last woman in America who could say such a thing.

The way I saw it, Jake had done Bert the colossal favor of setting her free. It was now her big chance to make up for some lost time. I'd told her so, too. Of course, I'd probably overdone it a bit. I'd actually compared her to the Birdman of Alcatraz, and then I'd mentioned the movie, *The Great Escape*. By the time I was finished, Bert had been looking at me as if I were out of my mind. I'd thought she'd dismissed everything I'd said. Now, it seemed, she'd listened to me after all.

Trent shrugged, and turned back to the bookshelves. "Well, it seems that this Russell Moorman left a hundred thousand dollar life insurance policy. Casualty Life, the company that issued the policy, is the one that hired me." According to Trent, the policy had been issued to Moorman only about a month before, and now Casualty Life, no surprise, wanted to know exactly how he'd died. "Because," Trent said, "that policy won't pay diddly squat if there's a suicide during the first year."

I'd been in the middle of replacing the cushions in both wing chairs, but I stopped and looked over at Trent. "Suicide?" I said. "But his throat was cut."

Trent didn't even hesitate. "Can you think of a better cover for a suicide?"

I had to admit he had a point.

Across the room Bert wrinkled her nose. Apparently, throat-cutting was not a topic for mixed company. "We thought the man had been murdered, Mr. Marksberry," she said. Kathleen was back.

"Call me Trent," he said, smiling at Bert, his dark eyes holding hers for a fraction too long.

Bert returned his smile. "Trent, then."

I was beginning to feel like the Invisible Woman. Back when Bert and I were in high school, we'd had a pact. As twins, you'd expect that the same guy might be attracted to both of us. And, what's more, that we'd each be attracted to the same guy.

We'd had a couple arguments about one guy or another until we came up with The Pact. It was simple. Once a guy declared himself, indicating that he liked one of us or the other, the twin who hadn't been chosen backed off. Of course, before any given guy made up his mind, it was no holds barred. We could both flirt outrageously, we could bat our eyelashes enough that it caused breezes indoors, and we could station ourselves next to the guy's locker, waiting shamelessly for him to show up. Let the guy ask one of us out, though, and the contest was over.

Now it looked as if this particular contest was over before it had even begun. I think my feelings were hurt. I mean, Bert and I are identical. Except, of course, here *I* was, wearing a scoop-necked black body suit, jeans as tight as I can get them and still have blood circulation, and a jeans jacket—an outfit, not to be bragging or anything, that has earned me wolf whistles at the radio station. Bert, on the other hand, had on her usual tailored suit—designer label, of course—with a silk blouse buttoned to her chin and a skirt almost to her ankles.

What can I say? Either Trent must go for the demure type, or I needed fashion counseling in a big way.

Trent's eyes were still locked on Bert, as he continued.

"As I understand it, this Moorman fella had been knocked unconscious. *Before* he got his throat cut. Like maybe he'd planned it that way so that he wouldn't have much pain."

I blinked at that one. "Or maybe the killer had planned it that way, so he wouldn't have much argument," I suggested.

Trent shrugged, frowning a little. "Wouldn't be the first time some poor slob hires somebody to bump himself off. So there'd be a hefty payoff for a loved one." He paused here, and reached for another pile of books. When he spoke again, he'd lowered his voice, as if what he was about to say was strictly confidential. "Actually, we've got reason to believe that's *exactly* what happened."

"Reason?" Bert asked. "Like what, Trent?"

I don't think Bert even cared what the reason could be, she just wanted a good excuse to do Kathleen Turner again. Not to mention, to sit there and stare for a long, uninterrupted moment into Trent's eyes as he answered her.

I suppressed a smile. It was kind of nice for Bert to start acting alive for a change. Lord knows, several times in the last year, I'd been afraid she was going to enter a convent.

Trent gave Bert a gentle smile. "I'm really not at liberty to divulge the reason we think this was a suicide," he said. He winked and added, "Client confidentiality, you know."

Bert's eyes were riveted on his.

I hated to break up this touching moment, but I did want to know—"Who's the beneficiary of the policy?" I asked.

Trent and Bert turned to me as if maybe they'd forgotten I was in the room. "Can't tell you that either," Trent said. "It's not that I'm hiding anything—I just have some restrictions placed on me by my client. It's a pain in the neck, but that's the way it is."

Actually, it sounded to me like he was hiding something.

Across the room Bert, however, was nodding. "Of course, Trent, we understand," she said, her voice huskier than ever.

I got the feeling that if Trent here said we've all got to jump off Louisville's Second Street bridge, Bert would say, "Of course, Trent, we understand."

God. Don't you love hormones?

"Anyway," Trent said, "what I really need to know is what Moorman might've said yesterday." He turned those big brown Harrison eyes, full on Bert again. "What he said to you. Especially if there was any hint about what he might've been planning."

Under Trent's spell, Bert started doing her impression of the Wicked Witch of the West. She was, oh yes, melting. She even forgot to make her voice sexy as she answered him. Unfortunately, by the time she'd told Trent everything about meeting Moorman, complete with Moorman's fashion comments, Trent was wearing the same glazed look Bert and I had both seen most recently on Detective Goetzmann's face.

In desperation, it seemed, Trent then turned to me. And got significantly less information than Bert had just given him. "First time I saw the guy, he was dead on TV."

"That's it?" Trent asked, clearly disappointed.

In fact, Trent looked so disappointed that Bert immediately jumped in, with all the weird stuff that had been going on, ever since she'd met the dead guy yesterday. The break-in at my apartment, the whispered phone calls, and finally, obviously running dry, Bert added, "And, oh yes, there was this redhead who followed me today."

I turned to stare at her. This was news. "Redhead?"

Bert shrugged. "Well, I *think* she was following me. I think she was a redhead, too, but then again, she could've been wearing a wig." She described the woman then, right down to the woman's big orange sunglasses and her baby poop shoes.

I just stared at Bert for a minute. "I thought I was being followed today, too. Only it wasn't a woman." It was true, but until Bert had mentioned the woman who'd followed her, I'd thought I was just being paranoid. I'd returned to WCKI in the afternoon, after Bert had gotten out of the car, and I'd parked in one of the city lots a few blocks away from the station. It was when I was walking back that I first noticed the guy. "This guy was short, bald, overweight, probably in his forties, and he had horn-rimmed glasses," I went on. "He was kind of nondescript. You know, like George on Seinfeld."

Trent was definitely not looking disappointed, anymore. "You're both *sure* that these people were following you?"

"No, I'm not," Bert and I said in unison.

Trent just looked from one of us to the other, and shook his head. He insisted, however, that we give him descriptions of the woman and George all over again. In detail.

He also insisted that we show him the message on Bert's mirror. Bert waved that one away. "Um," she said, "I already cleaned it up."

I turned back to Trent. "Bert is a very neat person."

Staring at us with humorless eyes, Trent suddenly got positively grim. "Look, you two, if either of you ever see this man or woman again, call me immediately. And be careful about who you talk to."

As if we needed that advice.

"And," Trent went on, "if you see either of those people, for God's sake, don't try to talk to either of them. It could be dangerous. Just call me and let me deal with them—that's what I've been trained for."

Bert looked pleased. "Certainly," she all but cooed.

"And, if I were you, I'd stay away from the police," Trent said. "That message wasn't a joke." Bert was already nodding, and Trent looked over at me. What could I do? I nodded, too. I mean, if this guy wanted to handle the bad guys? Hey, no problem here. It was certainly more than Goetzmann seemed eager to do.

Trent's bookcase was now full, and he got to his feet. "With your permission," Trent said, "I'd like to have a look around."

"Of course," Bert cooed again, and we both began to follow Trent around the apartment.

"You need to keep this place as secure as you can," Trent said. "Lock all your doors and windows."

I just looked at him. He was a professional, and the best he could do was tell us to lock things up?

Having told us about the locks, Trent then went around, actually doing it, locking all Bert's windows and examining her sills. Then he marched directly to the front door and opened it. "You need to never, ever leave this door unlocked," he said. "Except for the windows, it's the only way in." He reached over and turned the door lock.

I glanced over at Bert. Was she buying this? She was, indeed. The expression on her face said one thing. *Wow.*

After the lock tour, Trent headed outside. "And always leave your porch lights on at night. Use the peephole. And, needless to say, don't open the door to anyone that you don't know." He stepped away from the porch, and gestured toward the front door. "And, you know, you really ought to get a deadbolt for this—"

A loud crack rang out, and something whizzed by my ear like an angry mosquito.

Trent gave a sharp cry and dropped to the ground.

Chapter 7

●

BERT

Trent yelled and dived for the ground, pulling me down as he went. Believe me, I didn't mind. In fact, I had every intention of lying there, behind the tall shrubbery in front of my apartment until, oh, say, the seasons changed. They could rake me up with the last of the autumn leaves, for all I cared.

Flat on my stomach, I looked around for Nan, my heart sounding like thunder in my ears. Thank God, Nan was lying right next to me—I guess Trent had shoved her down, too. Or else, she'd reacted to that god-awful noise by diving for cover the second the shot rang out.

The shot?

Ohmigod.

I'd never heard a gunshot before—unless TV counts—but I didn't have a doubt in the world as to what that loud bang had been. I all but hugged the ground.

Beside me, Nan and Trent were already getting up on their elbows, trying to peek through the shrubbery in front of us.

"Is—is somebody shooting at us?" I stammered. I know, I know. It was one of Jake's patented stupid questions. But I couldn't help myself. I was so rattled I blurted out the first thing that came to mind.

It must've been such a stupid question that neither Trent nor Nan thought it deserved answering. I guess they both figured that, if the way all three of us were hiding behind ornamental shrubbery didn't say it all, there was no use explaining it to me.

I did rather hate to be the only one left still hugging the ground. I mean, you could get the idea I was a major coward. Nan was now up on her knees on my right, peering through the shrubbery. On my left, Trent was up, doing the same.

I took a deep breath, propped myself up on my elbows, and carefully parted the branches of the yew bush—or whatever it was—directly in front of me, scanning houses and other shrubs across the way.

I gave Trent a quick glance. No wonder he didn't hesitate to start getting up. He had a gun in his right hand. If he saw something, he could at least do something about it. What could I do? Throw a rock?

I mean, you give me a gun, and I'd be getting up and looking around, too. Maybe. Of course, I have heard you ought to have a pretty steady hand for that kind of thing; and, right now, both my hands were shaking.

There was really no explanation for the way Nan had immediately gotten up. Other than, of course, her constant craving for adventure. Which, when you come right to it, is probably some kind of neurosis.

I spread the branches of the shrub a little farther apart, and studied the houses opposite. Here in the Highlands neighborhood, most of the houses are these lovely two- and three-story antique homes, interspersed here and there with your basic brick apartment house or duplex, like Nan's. Old and new alike are often built so close together that neighbors can shake hands out their windows without ever leaving home.

Unfortunately, it just occurred to me that the buildings being so close together also gives a gunman plenty of places to hide. Like alleyways, and behind garbage cans, and next to even larger shrubs than the ones in front of us.

"You see anything?" Nan whispered, turning toward me.

The second she spoke, the shrubbery rustled in front of the Victorian house on the corner. While I ducked my head, Trent took off running. Nan jumped up to follow him, like the neurotic she is. I immediately grabbed her arm, yanking her back down next to me.

"Are you crazy?" I asked. "Let *him* go!"

Nan was trying to wrench her wrist out of my grasp. "Damn it, Bert. Let go of me!"

"Nan, *he's* got the gun! I mean, what are you going to do, even if you actually found the gunman? Ask him to apologize?"

Even Nan couldn't argue with that one. She stopped struggling, settled back down behind the shrubbery next to me, and took a deep breath. "You O.K.?" she finally asked.

"Peachy," I said. "You?"

"Oh, yeah," Nan said. "Nothing like a good shooting."

I gave her a thin smile. "Who could be shooting at us? Do you think it could be someone we know?"

Nan turned slowly to stare at me. "Do you think it's somebody we don't?"

I nodded. "Well, I sure hope so," I said. "I mean, it could be this is just one of those drive-by things that you're always hearing about on TV."

You could tell right away that Nan was really open to this idea. "A drive-by shooting by someone on foot," she said. "Hmmm."

That *hmmm* sounded sarcastic to me.

"OK," I said, "if you're so sure it's someone we know, who do you think it is?"

"I'll tell you who has my vote." Trent's voice sounded behind us, and we both jumped. I hadn't even heard him come up, but there Trent stood, looking down at us, on the other side of the shrubbery. "Jake, that's who."

"Jake?" Nan and I repeated the name in unison.

Trent nodded, as he reached down to help me and Nan to our feet.

"That's right," Trent said. "Jake was pretty mad when he left here, and I've seen exes not nearly as angry do a whole lot worse."

My mouth actually went dry. If Trent had not suggested Jake as a possibility, I don't think it would ever have occurred to me. But now, I couldn't help but wonder. Jake did own a gun. He'd bought it right after a series of robberies down the street from his insurance company.

I turned toward Nan. "Lord. Do you think Jake could've been shooting at us just to throw a scare into me? Because I wouldn't call the police, like he wanted?"

"Oh, sure," she said. "Jake is shooting real bullets at you so you'll call the cops. And, no doubt, they'll haul *him* off. Right."

Put that way, it did seem a bit farfetched. And yet, maybe Jake had been trying to scare Trent off. Jake certainly had seemed to have taken an instant dislike to the guy.

"Whoever the shooter was," Trent said, "he's long gone by now." He took a final look around, and then slipped his gun back into the holster beneath his blazer.

That's when I noticed the dark wet stain on the upper right sleeve of his navy blazer. "Oh my God, you've been hurt!"

Trent just looked at me, as if he didn't quite understand.

Then he lifted his forearm to look. The red-black stain seemed to be spreading. He touched it and his hand came away red.

"Oh dear," I said. I could feel nausea building in the back of my throat.

Trent pulled off his blazer, and then we could all see the ugly red smear on his right sleeve. He pushed up the sleeve. I couldn't help it. I looked away. "It's just a scratch, really."

I was more than willing to take Trent's word for it, but Nan wasn't. "You need to go to the emergency room."

Trent immediately shook his head. "Naw, all it needs is a bandage." He looked straight at me.

I took the cue. "Follow me," I said, trying to sound like I bandaged gunshots all the time. What I really hoped was, I wasn't going to barf all over the hydrangea—or whatever that shrub was—before I got him inside to the bathroom.

Nan followed us upstairs.

Seated on the side of the bathtub, Trent unbuttoned and stripped off his shirt. If there hadn't been any blood, I might've enjoyed the show—his shoulders were muscular, his arms tanned, his chest nicely hairy. I even had visions of Harrison Ford stripping off his shirt in that movie, *Working Girl*.

Unfortunately, however, the sight of blood made me want to puke.

I gritted my teeth and started cleaning the wound—it really was just a scratch—when Nan managed to tear her eyes away from Trent's manly chest. "So," she said. "Did you get a look at the shooter?"

"Not even a glimpse," Trent said. "Just the sound of running footsteps."

"You really ought to go to an emergency room," Nan repeated.

I gave her a quick glance. I was slathering first aid cream

all over Trent's scratch at that very moment. I'd already done the hard part, for God's sake. Wiping off the blood. And *now* she wanted to go to the doctor?

Trent was shaking his head. "It's a scratch. And docs have to report gunshots. No thanks. It's too much trouble." He winked at me. "Besides, considering the dealings with the cops that you all have had, I'd just as soon skip it, if it's all the same to you."

I taped a gauze bandage over the dressing. He didn't need to convince me. I could easily imagine Goetzmann accusing Nan or me of taking potshots at each other. Just to strengthen Nan's ongoing grab for cheap publicity.

"I mean, nobody really got hurt," Trent was going on. "And in my line of work, you make a few enemies. This shot tonight might not have had anything to do with you two."

"How do you figure?" Nan asked. "I mean, this is our home, and the gunshot did seem to be headed in our direction."

"But it was aimed right at *me*," Trent said. "I was the one who got hit. And it was only one shot—not two. It could very well be that it's connected to one of my other cases. I do a lot of domestic work, you know. Surveillance. Gets kind of hairy."

That made sense to me.

"Most important, I'm fine, thanks to you," Trent said. His eyes were intense as he looked over at me. "You could've been a nurse. You've got real gentle hands."

Over Trent's head, I could see Nan rolling her eyes.

I don't know if Trent picked up on Nan's reaction or what, but right after that, he decided to leave. Before he did, however, he reached out and took my hand. "I'll be in touch," he said softly. Looking into his eyes, I felt a stirring in the pit of my stomach that I hadn't felt in a long, long time.

As soon as Trent went out the door, Nan and I finished putting my apartment back together. It didn't take as long as I thought. Of course, after all the cleaning practice we'd had in the last twenty-four hours, we were getting pretty good at it.

Nan ended up sleeping on my sofa, rather than going over to her place. We both told each other that it was just too much trouble for her to walk all the way home, but the truth was, it was just too scary to be alone.

You don't have somebody shoot in your direction, whether they mean to or not, without it making a real impression.

Without either one of us putting it into words, there was one thing we both agreed on. If Nan and I were going to be murdered in our sleep, we might as well do it the same way we were born. *Together*.

Even though it was Saturday, I was up the next morning at seven. I tiptoed past Nan, asleep on my sofa, and I went in search of my *Courier-Journal*. I found it under the shrub we'd hidden behind yesterday. An omen, no doubt.

I have to admit I did do some quick footwork in retrieving the paper, all the while expecting to hear bullets flying overhead. After I'd rushed back inside, slamming the door closed behind me, I leaned against it, breathing hard.

Slamming the door woke up Nan. Who immediately dived for the floor.

I stood there, staring at her.

Nan got to her feet, sheepishly. "We have really got to do something about all this," she said.

I nodded. We couldn't spend the rest of our lives diving under couches and hiding behind bushes. Or, for that matter, looking over our shoulders. We needed to find out who was behind all this, and we needed to find it out before yesterday's gunman learned how to shoot better.

I fixed us both Cokes while she scanned the newspaper. Both of us are non-coffee drinkers, but our morning caffeine fix has to come from somewhere.

The story we were looking for turned out to be on the second page of the *Courier's* Kentucky Region section. "Galleria murder victim identified," read the headline. The third sentence told us what we wanted to know. "The victim, Russell Moorman, of 4451 Taylorsville Road, suffered head trauma, as well as a laceration to the neck, according to Louisville police."

Somehow, the word laceration made you think of skinned knees and scraped elbows, rather than a slashed throat. I sincerely hoped the poor guy really had been unconscious when it happened.

"So," Nan said, looking up from the paper, "how's about a nice drive out Taylorsville Road? I'll put on my tape."

I knew what she meant. Because no one in their right mind likes to work on Saturdays, all the deejays where Nan works take turns every other weekend filling six-hour shifts. Today was Nan's Saturday to be on the air at WCKI.

"We'll stop on the way, and I'll ask the newsguy to put my tape on," Nan said, getting up from the table.

The tape Nan was talking about was her emergency tape. It's a prerecorded one that sounds just like her live show. Except—if you listen closely—you'll notice that she mentions nothing about the time of day, the weather or anything specific. It's kind of a one-size-fits-all radio show.

All the deejays at WCKI have emergency tapes—at management's insistence, if you can believe that. According to Nan, they're so short-staffed that when on-air personalities do remotes, or get sick, or take vacation, the station uses part-timers to run their emergency tapes. That way, SICKIE doesn't have to pay full-price for another full-time announcer.

Nan hurried next door to put on, what else, a fresh pair of jeans and a sweatshirt. Minutes later, we were on the road.

Nan insisted on driving her Neon, instead of our taking my Festiva. I wasn't surprised. Nan often refers to my perky little car as The Turquoise Roller Skate.

4451 Taylorsville Road turned out to be one of those long ranch-style homes, complete with picture window, brick veneer front, and not a ranch in sight. Just a patch of yellowish-brown grass with a blue plastic three-wheeler and a red metal wagon sitting next to the sidewalk. The white paint on the home was beginning to peel, littering the yellowing shrubs in front like dandruff.

As Nan and I walked up, a woman opened the front door, her head down as she fumbled with her key ring and then locked her door. She did this, all the while managing to hang onto the hand of a kid maybe three years old who'd started running even before she'd put him down. As we watched, the kid was jerked backwards when the length of his mother's arm ran out. Then he saw us. And shrieked.

The woman started and then turned to face us. Petite, about twenty-five, with long blond hair held back by a headband, black to match her dress, hose and shoes.

Nan jumped to the obvious conclusion. "Mrs. Russell Moorman?"

"Yes? I'm Alice Moorman," the young mother said. Her eyes darted from me to Nan and back again. "You're—you're twins?"

Nan nodded. "I wonder if we could talk with you—"

"Oh my. I wonder how your mother ever managed?" Alice said.

For a second there, I could tell Nan didn't quite understand what she meant, but I got it right away. Especially when I realized Junior was now lunging for the red wagon, yanking at his mother's arm like he wanted to pull it from the socket. All the while making loud grunting noises. With one tyke like him, Alice must've thought two would be impossible without a tranquilizer gun.

Over Junior's grunting noises, I said, "Isn't he a darling?" Actually, the kid was kind of cute, dressed like a perfect little gentleman in a navy blue suit with a bright red bowtie. The little gentleman, however, was clearly not all that perfect. He was now going for the shrubs, his grunts getting louder by the minute. "How old is the little cutie?" I asked.

"Thirteen months," Alice said. "He's big for his age."

I stared at the kid, then met Nan's eyes. Big for his age? Was Alice kidding? Paul Bunyan wouldn't have been this big. The blue ox, *maybe*.

"His father was large when he was a baby, too," Alice said, her blue eyes tearing up.

"Russell is the reason we're here," Nan said, flashing the press pass she'd gotten from the newsguy at the station. The way she flashed the thing couldn't have been any more casual, but I knew Nan was making sure that Alice didn't get a good look. Mainly, of course, because the photo on the pass showed a man with a walrus mustache. Nan quickly put the pass in her pocket. "I'm doing a follow-up on the shooting," she said, her voice brisk, "for the radio station, and—"

Alice swallowed, her eyes getting even bigger. "Oh," she said. "I—I was just on my way to the funeral home."

"We were so sorry to hear about your husband," I put in.

Nan turned to stare at me. I could tell what was on her mind. So, suddenly we were family friends, paying the bereaved a social call? her expression seemed to say.

I folded my arms across my chest. There was no reason we couldn't be polite.

"Thank you, Miss, um—" Alice's voice trailed off, as her eyes traveled to Junior. The child was now scooping up a fistful of dirt. "No, don't eat that!" Alice said, yanking at his arm. "Drop it! Drop IT! DROP IT!"

Junior promptly ground the clump of dirt into the front of his suit coat and smiled up at his mother. Alice sighed, and, for the first time, I noticed the fatigue in her eyes. "Oh. Now I'll have to change him again," she said. Her voice actually shook a little.

I felt a rush of sympathy. "Here, let me help," I said, scooping the little hellion up. Junior immediately tried to kick and bite me, letting out another eardrum-bursting shriek. Ellie and Brian weren't this big at this age, but at times they'd certainly been this rambunctious. I easily dodged the kid's feet, holding the boy so tightly around the waist and legs that he didn't have room enough to move.

I could see that Nan was amazed. No doubt, her answer would've been to lock the kid in his room until he was twenty.

As I hurried inside, I thought for a moment that the Moorman house had been ransacked, too, just like Nan's and my apartments. Then I realized that all the stuff littering the carpet and floors were kid's toys. And kid's clothes. And kid's bottles and kid's teething rings. Wall to wall.

Alice followed me back inside, picking her way down the hall. She returned with a new outfit for Junior. A little brown suit this time that would probably stay clean for about two minutes after she got it on him.

At least it was brown, though. Maybe the dirt would blend in.

While Nan and I pinned Junior on the couch, holding his chubby little legs down, Alice began to undress him. Surprisingly, Junior got quiet all of a sudden, gurgling happily and chewing on a pacifier that Alice had scooped off the floor and inserted in his mouth, like a cork. I stared at the kid. He looked as if he was enjoying himself. Lord. He'd probably grow up to be a guy who smoked cigars and was turned on by bondage.

Alice glanced up at Nan, as she worked Junior's arm out of a sleeve. "You know, I wasn't surprised when the police told me about Russell. About his being—being—" She couldn't seem to say the word, *murdered.*

"You weren't surprised?" Nan asked.

Alice nodded her head, her eyes now looking almost haunted. "Oh, I just knew something awful was going to happen. Ever since that man showed up on our doorstep. Russell was never the same after that."

He was certainly not the same *now*, I thought before I could stop myself. I cleared my throat. "What man showed up at your door?" I asked.

Alice was pulling the pants of the suit over Junior's diapered rump. "Oh, Russell wouldn't tell me who the man was. Or what was going on. He just said that he and this man were working on some big business deal. And that we were all going to be rich. That's what Russell said. We'd all be on easy street from then on."

Nan and I exchanged looks. I knew she was thinking the same thing as I was. That maybe all this money Russell had in mind was the insurance money Alice would get when Russell set up his own murder. One hundred thousand dollars could certainly help buy an address on easy street.

Yet, what he'd told his wife seemed to imply that Russell was expecting to profit, too. Not something people do very often, by collecting their own life insurance.

"Did your husband say what the business deal was?" Nan asked.

Alice had wiggled Junior's arm into a shirt sleeve, and was now working on the other one. She seemed to be avoiding our eyes. "No. No, he didn't."

I wondered if she really didn't know, but before I could ask, she said quickly, "Oh, I know what you're thinking. That it was something illegal. Like drugs. Or worse. But I asked Russell about that. And he swore to me that the deal was on the up and up."

Oh sure. A drug dealer would certainly be completely honest with his wife. Sure he would. Not to mention, I could testify myself that husbands never, never, never lie to their wives.

"Russell promised me," Alice repeated, "that it wasn't anything against the law." The tears started this time in earnest, running silently down Alice's cheeks. Junior eyed his mother, his small eyes looking worried as he worked on his pacifier.

"I guess I knew Russell was lying all along," Alice finally said. "Because he got real mad every time I asked him anything about what he was doing." She shrugged, tucking a stray blond curl back under her headband. "I didn't let that stop me, though. I kept right on asking him things. I even asked him why on earth he'd go into business with some stranger he'd only just met."

"What did he say?" Nan asked.

"Russell finally admitted it wasn't just some stranger. That this guy was *family*. But that's all Russell would tell me—he says that I don't need to know anything more about it." Alice swiped at her eyes with the back of her hand. "I started having my doubts right then. Because, well, I've met Russell's whole family—he's an only child, you know—and I've never heard of anybody, not even a distant cousin, by the name of Ledford."

Alice had spoken of Russell in the present tense, as if he were still alive. I think she realized it at about the same time as I did, because the tears started all over again.

"Ledford?" Nan put in. "The guy's name was—"

Alice finished for her. "—Glenn Ledford. That's who Russell says he's been meeting."

Present tense again. Alice started on a fresh bout of weeping.

Not that I blamed her. Not in the least. The rug had been yanked right out from under her, and now she'd be raising her little gargantuan alone. I looked at her, and for the first time in a long while, I felt as if I'd been lucky. At least, when Jake and I had split up, the kids were nearly grown.

Alice wiped hastily at her tears, blinking hard. "I don't care what anybody says, though. Russell was a good, decent, wonderful man. He never did a wrong thing in his life."

I wondered if she'd sound so positive if she knew her husband had asked me out just minutes before he was killed.

"Russell really is the sweetest, kindest—"

Uh oh. Nan must've expected Alice to start crying again because she jumped in fast. "Alice, what did this man—this Glenn Ledford—look like?"

Alice blinked. "Oh, bald. Kind of thickset, I guess. And

pudgy—not like Russell at all. Much shorter. And heavier. With glasses."

I exchanged another look with Nan. "Sort of like George on Seinfeld?" I asked.

Alice nodded. "Well, yeah," she said.

My stomach tightened. Could this Ledford guy have been the man Nan thought had been following her? But why? Why would he be doing such a thing?

"Did Russell tell you where Ledford lived?" Nan asked.

Alice nodded again. "I've got the slip of paper on the refrigerator door. It's the address where they always arranged to meet." She handed a freshly dressed Junior to Nan. Who held the child with her arms extended straight out from her body like he was some kind of stuffed animal.

The minute Alice left the room, Nan passed me Junior. Who, Lord love him, immediately spit out his pacifier, shrieked to high heaven, and writhed to get down. I was tightening my grip when Alice strolled back in. She didn't even seem to notice the shrieks. "Here," she said, handing Nan a slip of paper. "It's not a house, though. It's a motel in Jeffersonville. The Blueberry Hill Motel. Yeah, that's where they met, all right."

"Thanks so much," I said, handing Alice her son. I was pretty sure I was just thanking her for the information, but I admit I was pretty grateful to get the kid off my hands, too.

Jeffersonville, Indiana is just across the Ohio River from Louisville, Kentucky. With Nan crowding the speed limit all the way, it took us a little over twenty-five minutes to get there.

I saw the sign as we came off the ramp. "There it is," I told Nan. "The Blueberry Hill Motel. Doesn't that sound nice?"

It wasn't.

Chapter 8

●

NAN

What a dump.

Bette Davis could not have meant it more. And Bert could not have been farther from the truth. The Blueberry Hill Motel was not nice.

Once upon a time, it had obviously been one of those red brick, fifties strip motels that catered to families seeing the U.S.A in their Chevrolet or Studebaker or whatever. Way before Holiday Inn and Howard Johnson became household names.

The Blueberry Hill Motel had, no doubt, been the usual Mom-and-Pop operation. Meaning, Mom goes in to check for mouse shit and bed bugs before agreeing to let Pop register the family. At least, that's what Bert's and my Mom and Pop always did when the entire family took off on a road trip.

Some of these motel relics around Louisville have simply closed, and today they stand stark and vacant with FOR SALE signs rotting out in front. Some, like the Blueberry Hill Motel, have been reborn for purposes more in keeping with today's demands. The hand-painted sign out in front of the Blueberry Hill boasted of its $15.95 DOUBLE!!! With three, count them, one, two, three exclamation points.

I pulled my Neon into one of the many empty parking spaces, and took a long look around. Noting the truly charming ambiance of the peeling white shutters on the windows, the numerous screen doors hanging lopsided on broken hinges, and the rusted-out gutters dangling away from the building in spots. Yep, this was a home away from home, all right.

Beside me, Bert cleared her throat. "Oh, dear," she said.

The manager's office was easy to spot. The door was right next to an ancient Coke machine that still said its Cokes were ten cents a bottle. I stared at the cheerful drawings on the yellow sign bolted to the front of the machine. The drawings all showed men and women dressed in hats and suits clearly from the fifties, all drinking up. Hell, this machine alone was probably worth more than the entire joint.

"God almighty. Is this the No-Tell Motel or what?" I said as I got out of the car. "You could probably get an hourly rate here easy. Hell, they probably rent by the minute."

Bert's lips were pressed into a tight line as she looked around. "You don't suppose this is the kind of place Jake went with his girlfriend?"

"Not if he wanted to impress her, he didn't." The minute I said the words, I wished I could have them back. Bert blinked and looked away.

"Of course," I hurried on, "if she was a real tramp, she probably went to places like this all the time."

I wasn't sure Bert even heard me. She'd already started walking toward the small door marked *Manager's Office*. I hurried to catch up, and pushed open the door for her.

Inside, the first thing you saw was a small black and white TV with a huge rabbit ear antenna sitting on a table in back of the grimy front counter. The reason you noticed it so quickly was that the TV was blaring. A quick glance told me that a Road Runner cartoon was in full progress.

Sitting behind the counter, in a frayed green velour arm-chair facing the TV, was a wrinkled gnome of a man. He had a shock of white hair sticking out around his ears like cotton candy, but the top of his head had no hair whatsoever. It gleamed under the naked light bulb suspended directly above him. He was wearing a yellowed white dress shirt buttoned all the way to his chin, baggy brown polyester slacks, and for a minute or so he didn't even look around.

Bert stepped forward. "Sir? Excuse me?"

The gnome heaved a huge sigh, and without even glancing our way, he got to his feet. What do you know, the guy walked like Walter Brennan on that old TV show, *The Real McCoys*.

Leaning heavily on the counter, Walter looked at us with all the welcoming warmth he'd, no doubt, muster for a summons server.

I started talking. Fast. When I paused for breath, Walter said, "Ledford's sisters, you say?" He'd been looking both of us over the entire time I was talking, his watery eyes lingering on our chests several times. "Twins, ain't ya?"

How he could tell that just by staring at our chests was beyond me, but Bert and I nodded, anyway. "We certainly are," Bert said. She actually smiled at the old geezer.

Walter did not return Bert's smile. "Ya'll don't look much like that Ledford fella."

"We don't have the same dad," I said.

Both Bert and Walter gave me a look at that one. Then Walter's eyes started doing the double take most people do when they first see me and Bert, looking first at one of us, and then at the other, and back again. "Twins," Walter said again. His tone was scornful. He cleared his throat noisily, and spat.

Obviously, not a fan of multiple births.

I rather hoped the old guy had a spittoon at his feet, but I wouldn't count on it.

Beside me, Bert grimaced.

Walter didn't notice, however. His rheumy eyes had wandered back to the television with the rabbit ears antenna. I could see now, in the middle of the easy chair, a deep indentation the exact size of Walter's butt. Apparently, he'd been trying to take root. On the screen, another cartoon was beginning.

Bert started to lean on the counter, and then thought better of it. "Sir?" she said again. "Excuse me?"

Wile E. Coyote had made two futile attempts at the Road Runner by the time Walter finally turned back to us. "Look," he said, "Ledford ain't home now. And he ain't been home for a spell." He eyed us then like maybe he expected us to spin on our heels and head on out of there.

Bert and I didn't budge.

"If we could just get inside his room," Bert said, "our brother Glenn asked us to pick up some of his things for him. The poor thing has, um, sprained his ankle, so he's going to be staying with us for a while. So we can take care of him. And, um, our brother will be needing a change of clothes, like clean shirts and jeans and things, so we thought that we—"

"—we need his room key," I finished for her. Up to then I'd been staring at Bert in slack-jawed amazement. The woman really ought to be writing fiction. But if we were going to get into Ledford's room *today*, I thought I'd better cut this one short. And wait for the movie.

Walter scowled at us, turning back to the Road Runner.

Two more bungled attempts by Wile E., and I was getting impatient. At this rate, Walter wouldn't live long enough to let us in Ledford's room.

"Hey. You!" I said. "Give us the key!"

I hadn't thought I was yelling, but Walter jumped the second I spoke. "All right, all right," he said, dragging his eyes away from the TV screen and turning to glare at us. "Any more of you folks coming?"

Bert and I stared at him blankly.

"No, just us," Bert said. She smiled at Walter again.

Walter, no surprise, did not smile back at her this time either. In fact, he grumbled the entire time he was fumbling around in the registration desk in front of him, trying—I fervently hoped—to locate the correct room key. "Don't understand all these kin coming around," Walter said. "Other tenants don't get much company. Usually bring their company with them, matter of fact. And all this a-getting up and a-getting down—a-letting folks in—a-letting folks out—that's all I been doing since this here Ledford fella got here."

Life's a bitch, I felt like saying to him. But what I did get from listening to Walter's tale of woe was that, apparently, Russell had visited Ledford here often. And, also, that security was an unknown quantity at this lovely establishment.

How nice for Bert and me.

Walter had finally located the key, and now he slammed the thing down on the counter in front of me. "Unit 6 is out back," he growled. "In the rear wing."

I blinked. This place had wings?

The old buzzard had already turned back to the TV when Bert said, "Thanks so much. We're really sorry to inconvenience you."

Yeah, right.

Walter was now replanting himself in the armchair, mumbling to himself. "Don't pay me near enough. Not even close, not with me a-getting up and a-getting down ever' five minutes. Should quit, 'at's what I should do. Should be a damn Wal-Mart greeter."

What could I say? He certainly had the personality for it.

I picked up the room key. Dangling from its chain was a wooden tag with the number 6 in chipped white paint. I headed for the door.

Bert, would you believe, actually dawdled. "We'll just let ourselves in, sir. And, again, we certainly appreciate your—"

She might've gone on and on except that I turned around, grabbed her arm, and pulled her outside with me.

"Really, Nan," Bert said when we were both walking toward Unit 6, "you are so rude."

I didn't even answer her. The woman was worried about being rude to a man who spit on floors.

Uh huh. *Right.*

As it turned out, Bert and I should've paid a little less attention to the floor spitting and a little more attention to what the old geezer had said. Then maybe we wouldn't have been so surprised when we opened the door to Ledford's room.

The first thing I saw was the bed in the center of the room. Apparently, all the drawers of the two scarred maple dressers on either side of the room had been yanked out and emptied right on top of the bed's moth-eaten spread. The mattress was already sagging in the middle, and all the stuff piled on top of it was clearly not doing it any good.

While Bert and I gaped at the bed, some kind of movement at the far end of the room attracted our attention. I was, of course, instantly afraid that it was something of the small, furry, rodent variety. There was a metal closet door standing wide open at the far end of the room.

Heart pounding, I moved closer, Bert at my elbow.

Now we could see inside the closet. There, a dark-haired woman was standing, unmoving, with one hand deep in the pocket of a suit coat hanging right next to her. She stood like a statue in there, her green eyes filling her face.

I'm not sure who the woman was expecting, but a split-second after she spotted Bert and me, her face visibly relaxed. "Oh," she said, her eyes traveling from my face to Bert's and back again. "It's you. Mutt and Jeff."

Her tone was only slightly less scornful than Walter's earlier. Apparently, what we had here was another multiple birth devotee.

"Don't you guys ever knock?" she went on. "I mean, for crying out loud, you two nearly scared me to death." As she said this, she waved at her face as if maybe she were on the verge of fainting, and she was trying to revive herself beforehand.

Bert jumped in. "Oh, ma'am, we really are awfully sorry. We had no idea that there was somebody—"

The woman was clearly not interested in what else Bert had to say. She interrupted. "What's the matter? He lam out on you, too?"

Evidently, the woman was under the impression that Bert and I were playmates of Glenn Ledford. I just stared at her. In *these* sorry surroundings? I took a fast glance at the frayed rug, the scarred maple furniture in the room, the distinctive hole in the wallboard right next to the bed. It looked as if somebody had put his foot through it.

Oh, yeah, Bert and I had definitely been insulted.

Bert must've realized this about the same time as I did, because when she spoke next, her tone was almost haughty. "May we ask who you are?"

I had to hand it to her. She almost sounded as if we were the ones who had the right to be there. And certainly not this dark-haired woman standing in the closet with her hand in Ledford's pants.

The woman smirked. Mimicking Bert, she said, "May *I* ask where Glenn is?" She did not wait for an answer, but immediately turned back to the closet. She was now rummaging through all the pockets of a pair of blue jeans.

I hated to tell her, but the minute she turned around, she got a lot more attractive. The denim jumpsuit she wore looked like it might be some label or another, and it hugged her every curve. In fact, the woman's rear looked as if she was wearing one of those magic girdles that shove your ass about two inches higher. She appeared to be in her early thirties, five-two, slender, with chin-length, brunette hair that had to have been tinted to get that uniformly dark color.

Or else, it was a wig. I peered at the thing a little closer. A few strawberry-blond curls had escaped at the back. Now that was something you didn't see much—a blond trying to be a brunette.

Even from the front, the woman might've been pretty— if she hadn't applied her makeup with a trowel.

It would also have helped if she hadn't had all those deep worry lines around her eyes and mouth. The woman, in fact, was wearing the same look as a dog who'd been kicked so many times she'd stopped wondering *if* and was now concentrating on *when* she should duck.

"Well, *this* is Glenn's apartment." Bert said. "Isn't he here?"

The dark-haired woman shrugged, and continued what she was doing. "I don't have time for games. Where the hell is he?"

Bert and I exchanged a look. "You don't know?" I asked.

The woman shrugged again. "Why should I?" she asked.

Bert and I looked at each other again. Were we missing something here? Maybe we should start all over. "OK," I said. "Let's go back to the beginning. Who are you?"

The woman didn't answer right away. She did, however, turn around this time. In fact, she just stood there, her right hand still in the jeans back pocket, an odd look on her face. As if she were trying to make up her mind about something. "OK," she finally said, evidently reaching a decision. "I'm Maxine Ledford, all right? Glenn's wife. Mrs. Glenn Ledford." As she spoke, there was an odd trill to her voice. "I'm, uh, I'm collecting his things."

Collecting? I could've been leaping to conclusions here, but it sure looked to me as if it were more like Maxine here was *searching* Ledford's things.

She didn't stop just because Bert and I were standing there right in front of her, either. Having introduced herself, she immediately turned back around and stuck her hand in the pockets of a pair of trousers hanging next to the jeans.

"Looks like you guys are little late," Maxine said. This time she didn't turn around. She'd moved on to the next garment hanging in the closet—a plaid blazer—and was now going through the inside pockets.

Bert immediately jumped in. "I guess we should've been by a little sooner. I mean—"

I turned to stare at Bert. What the hell was she talking about?

"—we probably should've come by to pay our respects as

soon as we heard about the death in the family," Bert went on. She was actually looking a little guilty about this oversight. "We really were so sorry to hear about the tragedy. It must've been a terrible shock."

Oh, for the love of Pete. Was Bert playing social caller to the bereaved again? I'd thought she'd gotten this out of her system at Alice Moorman's place.

"What?" Maxine said, again without looking around. "Oh, you mean Russell? Oh, yeah. Quite a shock, I can tell you that. I've been really torn up about it." That touching sentiment lost a little something when she delivered the entire speech in a monotone, as she continued to go through the pockets of the blazer.

Maxine did pause right after that, giving us a quick glance over her shoulder. "Look, I gotta few things to do, if y'all don't mind, what with my—uh—my husband moving out and all, so if you two'll just—"

"Your husband moved out?" I asked. My heart sank. And she didn't even know where he was?

"I'm so sorry," Bert was now saying.

This time Maxine and I both turned to stare at her. "Sorry?" Maxine asked.

"About him leaving you," Bert said.

"Oh." Maxine turned back to the closet. "Yeah. Bummer."

I stared at Maxine. Evidently, the break-up of her marriage was eating her up inside. "So. You getting a divorce or what?"

"Nan!" Bert said. Her voice was shocked.

"Come on, Bert," I said, "we're way past bad etiquette here. The woman's searching the guy's clothes, for God's sake."

Maxine, for her part, didn't look the least bit offended. She stared at me, shifting her weight from one foot to the other, that odd look on her face again. As if she were trying to figure out something. "OK, yeah," she finally said. "Glenn and I are getting divorced. And I'm trying to find his—uh—bank book, you know, stuff like that. Before he, uh, comes back to get his things." That odd trill in her voice was back.

"When did you last see Glenn?" Bert asked.

Maxine was now upending the shoes in the floor of the closet, shaking them and peering inside. She looked up at us with annoyance.

"What? Look, I don't have time to answer your idiot questions. All I know is Glenn ain't here. That's all I need to know."

"Did you know that Glenn was in some business deal with Russell?" I asked.

Mrs. Ledford gave me a searching look, her eyes narrowing. "A business deal? No," she said. "I don't know anything about that." She said that last sentence so fast, the words all ran together.

Now why, oh why, didn't I believe her?

"You sure?" I asked again. "Because Russell's wife knew about it. She's the one who told us about the deal."

"And about this place," Bert put in.

Maxine looked confused. "Russell's wife? You went to see Russell's wife?"

"Yeah," I said. "Alice said Glenn and Russell had gone in together on some deal that was going to put them both on easy street."

"Easy street! Hah!" Maxine was now looking inside a pair of slippers. "Is that where Russell is now? *Easy* street?" Her voice was bitter, and it still had that odd trill.

Suddenly, it came to me. I knew exactly what that trill was. It was *fear*. This woman was absolutely scared to death.

"Maxine, what's happening?" I asked. "What are you afraid of?"

The woman turned around to face me, her green eyes flashing. "You're asking *me* that? Good old Russell gets his throat cut, and you want to know what I'm afraid of? Don't you have a lick of sense?"

I stared at her, not knowing what to say.

"What are you talking about?" Bert asked.

"Good old Russell thought he had it all figured out," Maxine said. "Oh my, yes. The only thing he didn't know was who he was dealing with. But I'd told him. I had already told him." Maxine punctuated this last by jabbing her finger in my direction. "But no-o-o-o-o. Russell knew it all. Sure he did. He was just too damn smart to live. And if we all get as smart as him, we'll end up just like him. Jeezuz!"

Maxine now moved from the closet to the tiny, dank cave that the Blueberry Hill Motel laughingly called a bathroom. There she started pulling out the pockets of the bathrobe left on the floor. "Look, you two," she said over her shoulder. "You better be careful, OK? You ought to go home and forget all about easy streets. Unless, of course, you're smart like Russell. Then it won't matter. You'll be dead anyway."

I stared at her. Was she threatening us? "Look, Maxine—"

"What's that?" she interrupted, her voice rising shrilly. Her head swiveled toward the front window. Bert and I looked, too.

Like most motels, the front windows of Unit 6 were covered bottom to top with draw drapes, along with under curtains of some sheer fabric. Here at Blueberry Hill, of course, they've added a gray layer of dirt. Even through the gray sheers, however, I couldn't see a thing to be scared of.

"What was what?" Bert asked. Her eyes were glued to the front window, too. Like maybe it was one of those 3-D magic eye murals that you can see something in, if you just stare at it so long that your eyes cross.

Now I could barely make out the sound of a motor. It sounded as if maybe somebody had just pulled into the parking lot. Was that what Maxine had heard? If it was, this woman could give dogs hearing lessons.

As the noise got louder, Maxine stiffened. "I gotta get outa here," she said. She ran across the room, grabbing her purse and car keys off the dresser as she passed it. Bert and I were right behind her.

"You've got to tell us," Bert said. "Who is it you're afraid of?"

I made a grab for Maxine's arm, intending to slow her down, but she shook me off. She snatched up a tan raincoat that had been thrown over the one chair in the room.

I stared at the coat. Something nagged at me, in the back of my mind. What was it?

In the distance, a car door slammed.

Maxine jumped at the sound, and turned toward the door. "God, you two don't have any idea what's going on, do you? That's it, isn't it? You two are idiots. Well, you better stop poking your damn noses in where they don't belong. Get it? Or don't you even remember what happened to the Sandersens?"

"Sandersens?" Bert echoed, turning to look at me.

"Sandersens?" I repeated, turning to look at Bert. "Did she say Sandersens?"

It was the name of that couple we'd baby-sat for years ago. The ones who were murdered. But what could something that had happened so long ago have to do with what was happening today? That case had been solved almost twenty-five years ago.

"Maybe we heard wrong," Bert said. "Maybe it was Samson. Or Simpson."

I turned to ask Maxine to repeat herself.

The door was closing with a soft click.

Maxine was gone.

"Shit," I said, hurrying to the window.

A car had already started up just outside as I pulled aside the front curtains. I was just in time to see a late model white Dodge Shadow head out of the parking lot. I could barely make out Maxine's dark head behind the wheel. I immediately looked at the license plate while I still had the chance. The damn thing had been covered with mud. All I could make out was an emblem that said, Econo Rent-a-Car.

It sure looked as if Maxine wasn't stupid.

And if she wasn't stupid—and she had just run out of here—then, correct me if I'm wrong, but shouldn't Bert and I be getting the hell out of here, too?

Even as the thought struck me, the doorknob to the motel room began to turn.

Standing beside me in that cruddy, little motel room, Bert gasped. I knew what she was going to say even before she said it.

"Oh, dear," Bert said.

Chapter 9

●

BERT

The doorknob to the motel room slowly turned.

Nan and I stared at it, as if mesmerized.

Wouldn't you know, there's one thing all these older motels have in common. That is, other than mildew, of course. None of the owners ever seem to get around to installing those newer doorknobs that automatically lock when the door closes. Which, believe me, would have come in very handy right about now.

The door slowly inched open, and I found myself actually suppressing a tiny scream.

A head peeked into the room.

It was Trent.

I was so relieved, I actually felt dizzy. Trent looked straight at me, then over at Nan, but his expression—oddly enough—remained wary. I couldn't help but notice that his right hand was hidden in the front pocket of his corduroy jacket. I didn't have to guess what he held there. "Anyone else in here?" Trent whispered, his eyes sweeping the room.

Nan and I shook our heads in unison.

"Are you sure there's nobody else? Did you check?"

I blinked. Actually, when you came right down to it, all we could say with certainty was that there was nobody now in the closet. Nan and I had just taken Mrs. Ledford's word that her husband wasn't here.

I gave Nan a look that said, And *you* were the one who thought you could be Nancy Drew?

Nan ignored me, and turned to Trent. "We really haven't been here very long, so—"

Trent didn't wait to hear the rest of it. He moved past us into the room.

Watching him, I thought, *Now, this is a real detective at work.* Trent's eyes seemed to miss nothing as they swept around the room, his every muscle tense and ready to respond to danger. It was kind of thrilling actually, watching Trent check the closet, under the bed, and behind the shower curtain in the bathroom.

Naturally, Nan spoiled the entire effect. When Trent disappeared into the bathroom, she leaned toward me and said, her voice teasing, "He's not glad to see you, Bert. That really *is* a gun in his pocket."

I did not dignify that comment with a reply.

Trent emerged from the bathroom, putting his gun back in the holster underneath his jacket. I purposely did not even look in Nan's direction.

I wasn't so sure about Trent not being glad to see me, either. He immediately crossed the room to stand at my elbow. "Nobody here. Y'all OK?" he said. His dark eyes met mine.

My heart started pounding for an entirely different reason than before. "Oh," I said, and yes, my voice did have this stupid lilt to it all of a sudden, "we're just fine. But how are you? How's your arm?"

Trent gave me a quick smile. "It's fine. I had a great nurse."

I smiled back at him.

He glanced over at Nan and then looked back at me. "Mind telling me what you two are doing here?" Trent drawled. "I thought we all agreed that you were going to stay close to home."

I immediately felt a little guilty. He looked so concerned. "Well," I said, "the police weren't helping us a bit. So it was obviously up to us to find out what was going on. So we decided to have a talk with Russell Moorman's widow—"

At this point, Nan started being rude again. She interrupted me. "Mind telling us what *you're* doing here?" she demanded, pinning Trent with a look. "You weren't following us, were you?"

I turned to frown at her. If Trent *was* following us, why would we mind? With bullets whizzing by our heads, and both our apartments getting trashed, it would be kind of comforting to know that somebody was keeping an eye on us. Particularly if that somebody was carrying a gun.

Trent just shrugged. He hooked his thumbs through the belt loops of his faded Levis, and winked at me. "Nope," he said, turning back to Nan, :"I can't say I was following you two. Although it doesn't sound like a bad idea." He glanced over at me again, his eyes warm. "As a matter of fact," Trent went on, "I got a phone call on my office answering machine. Anonymous, of course. Some yahoo whispering."

Nan and I exchanged another look. This sounded familiar.

"This yahoo tells me I'd find an associate of Russell Moorman's at this address. So I figured it might be the guy Russell hired to kill him."

Nan shook her head. "Doesn't look likely," she said. "The guy staying here is named Glenn Ledford. From what Bert and I have been able to find out, Glenn and Russell may have been related. Glenn met Russell here several times, working on some business deal or another."

Trent's eyes widened at that one. "Then who was that woman? I thought I saw some woman leave in a white Dodge Shadow as I walked over here."

I immediately nodded my head. "That was *Mrs.* Ledford," I said. I hurried on, telling Trent what all Nan and I had learned from Alice Moorman and Mrs. Ledford. Of course, there wasn't a whole lot to tell. We didn't know anything about the business deal the two women had mentioned. In fact, by the time I was winding things up, Trent was actually looking a little bored. Up until I told him the last part. "We think," I said, "as Mrs. Ledford was going out the door, she said something about us remembering the Sandersens."

Nan jumped in. "But we're not sure that's what she said."

Trent's eyebrows went up. "Sandersens?"

I nodded. "Nan's right. We could be mistaken."

"What makes you think it was even Sandersen, then? You ladies know anybody by that name?"

Nan immediately shook her head. "Not any more. In fact, nobody knows the Sandersens any more. They're dead."

I gave her a sideways glance. Nan has such a delicate way of putting things. She was now going on, telling Trent all about the double murder, but after a while Trent didn't seem to be listening. In the middle of what Nan was saying, he walked over, cleared himself a spot on the bed, and sat down.

While Nan finished her story, she followed Trent's example. She went over and sat down in the grimy wooden chair in front of the equally grimy wooden desk.

I just stood here, staring at both of them. I had no intention of sitting on anything in that room. In fact, I had no intention of touching anything. Not without a bottle of Lysol and rubber gloves.

Trent was now shaking his head. "I don't know, the whole thing seems pretty farfetched to me." He looked over at me then, and immediately got to his feet. "Oh, I'm sorry, do you want to sit down over here?"

I just looked at him. The only time Jake, in nineteen years of marriage, had ever offered me a seat was when I was in labor. As I recalled, I hadn't sat long.

Since it didn't happen all that often, I kind of hated to turn Trent down. I did it, though. "I don't mind standing," I said.

I *did* mind sitting. I also minded staying. Particularly since I could see, moving slowly on the wall in back of the bed, a gigantic cockroach. Oh God. Apparently, this was truly a roach motel.

I'm not sure what my expression showed, but Trent immediately got to his feet. "Why don't we get out of here?"

I had moved toward the door before he'd even finished the question.

Trent's car turned out to be a burgundy Jeep Cherokee. It was parked next to Nan's Neon, and as we walked over, Trent said, "Look, I really wasn't kidding when I warned you ladies to stay close to home. Obviously, there really is something strange going on, and I can't protect you if I don't know where you are."

I noticed his eyes wandered to mine and held. Like a teenager, I felt a little flutter in the pit of my stomach. God. You'd think at this age, I'd stop being rattled when a handsome man looked at me. Of course, it had been quite awhile since this particular thing had happened. That is, if you didn't count Russell. And I do think, in order for the man to count, he really should still be alive after twenty-four hours.

Besides, it could very well be that you never get too old to be thrilled. And, goodness, Trent did have those big, beautiful Harrison Ford eyes.

"I really would hate," Trent went on, "to have anything happen to either one of you."

Nan shrugged. "Yeah, well, we'd hate it, too. That's why we're not going to sit by and wait for it to happen."

Have I mentioned that Nan is rude?

Trent, being the gentleman that he was, ignored Nan's little comments. "So," he said, his eyes on mine again, "how about a little dinner? Your place? Pizza, breadsticks maybe? And a little wine?"

I stared at him, the flutter in my stomach turning to lead. Was the man actually asking me to fix him a meal? Who did this guy think he was? After nineteen years with Jake, I had pretty much switched off the hot plate.

Trent added softly, "I'm told I give great take-out."

Hold the phone. Wait a minute. It actually looked as if my home cooking was not what he'd had in mind.

As this thought crossed my mind, however, the lead in my stomach got a little heavier. God. You'd think I'd have been pleased. After all, this situation suddenly had all the earmarks of Trent trying to cut me loose from the herd. At least, that's what Nan and I used to call it.

For people not born a twin, being cut loose is not something they even seem to notice. But then, they're not part of a matched set. Being separated from whatever group they're in is no big deal.

When you're a twin, however, some guy trying to get you away from your sister is a major maneuver. What's more, doing that maneuver right under your twin's nose is tantamount to a finesse play. Instead of my being impressed, though, Trent's behavior gave me a little feeling of unease. Mainly because a blatant maneuver like this can be a sign of a guy who has never learned to share. I know this sounds strange, but believe me, Nan and I know. I glanced over at her, and she raised one eyebrow. Oh, yeah, Nan was thinking the same thing, all right.

Nan and I had found out early in high school that the way your potential date cuts you loose from your twin can be a prelude to how the whole dating experience was going to go. We'd found that out the hard way.

One of the first guys I'd dated in high school had asked me out right in front of Nan. Even turned his back to her when he did it. Good ole Peter Ray Hume. At the time, I'd been flattered that this first-stringer on our high school football team had actually asked *me* out.

But that was before he starting calling me at all hours of the day and night, much to our Mom's undying displeasure. It turned out that Pete was just making sure I wasn't talking to anyone else. After awhile, that anyone else included Nan. Needless to say, double-dating was out of the question. Possessive Pete tried to fill my every minute, and breaking up with him had been a nightmare.

Could Trent here be a Possessive Pete, too? Or was I just looking for reasons not to pursue a relationship with him? After what had happened with Jake, I guess you'd expect that I'd be a little gun-shy.

On the other hand, Trent here was gorgeous. With a beard, no less. What on earth was the matter with me?

I looked over at Nan again, hoping she'd get me out of this. She responded right on cue, but it wasn't at all what I expected. Apparently, Nan didn't have anywhere near the reservations about Trent that I did. "You two go on," she said coolly. "Bert, I'll see you back at the apartment later."

I could've strangled her.

"No, no," Trent said quickly. "I meant the three of us. You two head back to Bert's apartment. I'll pick up the wine and pizza, and I'll meet you both there. How about it?"

I caught Nan's eye again. She gave me an almost imperceptible nod of approval. Trent had just passed the Twin-cutting Test with flying colors. Now, if I could just figure out exactly how I felt about him.

The pizza party we had that night seemed remarkably normal when you considered everything else that had been happening. Trent arrived with more food than the three of us could possibly eat—four sausage-mushroom-double-cheeses, a triple order of breadsticks, and a bottle of red wine. Within seconds of his arrival, my entire apartment smelled of tomatoes, sausage, and oregano.

I decided not to go for the Betty Crocker Homemaker Award and served everything buffet-style right off the coffee table. Nan settled on the love seat, and I made myself comfortable on the larger sofa while Trent piled a plate high with pizza slices. He then plopped down on my left.

"Can't sit next to Southpaw Nan, or we'll be bumping elbows," Trent said, grinning at me. I think Nan and I both knew that he was only making excuses to sit next to me. I hoped Trent didn't notice that my hands shook a little as I reached for a slice of pizza. Lord. The last guy that made me feel this way was Jake. And we all know how that turned out.

I sat there, eating my pizza, and I couldn't get rid of the notion that dating was something you did in your teens, not in your late thirties. I felt like a full-grown woman playing dress-up in kid's clothes.

While we all ate, the three of us made small talk. I found out that Trent had been married and divorced while he was still in college, that he'd once worked as a bartender, and that he didn't have any children. I also found out that his favorite movie of all time was *Raiders of the Lost Ark*, and that he couldn't stand Rush Limbaugh.

Almost against my will, I found myself relaxing. More than anything else, I guess I was just grateful to have a conversation that didn't have the M word in it. Murder, of course.

Three slices of pizza and a glass of wine later, Nan suddenly got to her feet, licking tomato sauce off her fingers. "Gonna check my mail and phone calls," she announced and headed for the door.

She might as well have said, "I'm making up an excuse now to leave you two alone."

My mouth went dry. Now what on earth was I going to do?

Luckily, I didn't have to come up with anything. Especially since Trent started giving me one of those long appraising looks, as soon as the door closed behind Nan.

Those dark eyes of his seemed to glow. "I like this outfit you're wearing," he said, his eyes traveling down the front of my body.

In my haste this morning to visit Moorman's wife, I'd snatched up the first thing I came to in my closet. A very simple white silk shirt and khaki twill slacks. While we were out, I'd been wearing a denim blazer, but I'd taken it off when I got home.

The good news was—unlike Nan a lot of the time—I *was* wearing a bra. The bad news was that the silk fabric of my shirt was so thin that, if you looked, you could see the lace of my bra underneath.

Trent did seem to be looking. "And I like how you let your hair go—kind of wild. And sexy." Trent reached out and took a dark curl between his fingers.

Heat surged through me. I would've liked to believe it was the fire of passion, but I pretty much figured it for outright panic.

Trent tugged gently on the curl, pulling me slowly to him. Then, when I was close enough, he leaned over and kissed me.

Trent Marksberry definitely knew how to kiss. He started out all slow and sweet and ended up all hot and deep. With his hands in my hair.

His arms came around me and pulled me closer, his hand sliding slowly up to caress my breast through the thin silk. I moved even closer, my arms going up around his neck.

And, of course, that's when Nan threw open my front door and came rushing in. Talk about rotten timing.

"I heard a noise," she said.

I stared at her. She was *going* to hear a noise—my voice yelling at her to get out of here.

Then, through the open door, I heard something rustling in the bushes outside.

"What's that?" Nan and I asked in unison.

The faint rustle came again. Trent got to his feet.

Then came the snap of a twig. And then another one.

There was no doubt about it. Someone was moving around outside my apartment.

Trent made motions with his right hand like he was moving the mouth of a hand puppet—signaling us to keep on talking. He went over to the coat rack, got his gun out of his jacket, and then slipped out the front door.

I guess I shouldn't have been surprised at who the prowler turned out to be. But I was.

Trent led him back inside, actually prodding him in the back with the gun.

It was Jake.

Jake glared at me, as he shuffled in with his hands in the air, like some kind of desperado. "Bert, would you tell this asshole to put that damn gun away?"

Trent poked him again. "What asshole would that be, friend?"

Out of the corner of my eye, I noticed Nan trying to keep a smirk off her face.

I nodded at Trent, anyway, mutely signaling him to release Jake.

Trent shrugged, putting the gun back in his pocket with an air of reluctance. He had seemed to be thoroughly enjoying himself.

Jake, on the other hand, was another story.

"What the hell do you think you're doing, pulling a gun on me?" He whirled around to face Trent.

Trent shrugged again. "Protecting the ladies? Being careful? Catching a prowler? Take your pick."

"More to the point," I asked, "what are you doing here, Jake?" I was a little surprised to find that I was avoiding Jake's eyes. It was almost as if I had somehow gotten caught in the act of being unfaithful to him. Me, being unfaithful to Jake. Now *that* was a joke.

Jake had the colossal nerve to hold up his hand, like a traffic cop. "Just a damn second. I've got a few questions of my own, you know," Jake said, glowering at me.

The man could glower better than anyone I've ever known.

Again, out of the corner of my eye, I saw Nan moving across the room toward the sofa. Sitting down, crossing her legs, she reached for another slice of pizza and settled back to watch the show.

What could I say? This could possibly be better than *Raiders of the Lost Ark*.

Jake was now indicating Trent with a quick nod of his head. I couldn't help noticing that he wore another feather earring in his ear, this one a dark green. "For starters," Jake said, "what's *he* doing here?"

"Having dinner," Trent said.

"Excuse me, Jake," I said, "but—as I believe I've mentioned before—you don't have the right to ask me questions about anything."

Jake's chin came up. "All right, Miss High and Mighty." He'd assumed the whining tone of a puppy that had been kicked for no reason. "All I was trying to do was make sure nothing happened to you."

Lord, how I hate it when he whines.

"Like what exactly did you have in mind?" Trent asked, not even trying to hide a smile. "What do you think is going to happen to her?"

What, indeed? It suddenly occurred to me that Jake might've actually been out there all along, peeking in my windows. Exactly how much had Jake seen of what had just happened between Trent and me?

Jake was blabbering now. "Well, like . . . like . . . *harm*, for instance. I mean, something weird is going on around here, and you, mister, are up to your neck in it." He took a step forward and thumped Trent on the chest as he spoke.

Trent thumped Jake right back. "I'm here at the lady's invitation," he said. "So what's your excuse?"

The two men were now standing nose to nose, glaring at each other.

At seventeen, I would've thought this entire scene was exciting and flattering. At thirty-nine, I thought it was ridiculous.

Jake now looked away from Trent and turned to me. "Look here, Bert, I really think I ought to sleep over tonight—on the sofa, of course—because of everything that's been happening."

"Like what, for instance?" Trent asked again. His grin was back.

Jake's face turned beet-red. "Like *murder*, for instance," Jake said.

I believe he was referring to current events, and not to any action he planned to take in the future. Although the way he was glaring at Trent, I couldn't be sure.

Trent didn't grin this time. Instead, he took a step away from Jake and turned toward me. "You know, Bert, I think Jake is right. Someone really should stay over until all this stuff gets cleared up. Only I would recommend a professional, such as myself. Rather than an *insurance salesman*." Trent said this last with obvious contempt.

Jake's face colored into stroke proportions.

I stood there, looking from Jake to Trent and back again. Wouldn't you know it? It had taken me until this late in life to manage to have two dates for the same evening. It wasn't half as much fun as I'd imagined back in high school. As a matter of fact, I didn't appreciate in the least being put on the spot. Did these two expect me to choose between them? That was going to be tough, since I still hadn't figured out how I felt about either one.

And I certainly didn't appreciate feeling as if there was some kind of contest going on, and the only part in it that I played was the prize.

Nan caught my eye, and raised her eyebrows. I got her message.

"Neither of you need to stay here tonight," I said. "Nan and I will keep each other company. We'll be just fine."

It took another ten minutes to counter all their arguments, but finally Jake and Trent both left. Together. Pretty much shoulder to shoulder. As if neither one of them wanted to allow the other one even another second alone with me.

I sighed as I closed the door behind them.

That night, I dreamt Nan and I were teenagers again. One of the houses in the neighborhood had caught fire. The air was filled with the smell of acrid smoke and under it, an odd sweetness, like old cooked meat. I awoke gasping for breath, dry-mouthed and covered in sweat.

I tiptoed to my kitchen for a drink of water, anything to get my heartbeat back to normal. On the sofa, Nan tossed and turned. Every once in awhile, she would frown, and I wondered if her dreams were as bad as mine.

Once, when I was around four, I remembered waking in the middle of the night like this and looking over at Nan, asleep in the twin bed—what else?—next to mine. I'd been amazed that I could be awake and that she would still be asleep.

And then I'd realized something that all singles know from the very beginning. It had dawned on me right then that Nan and I really were two different people. That Nan would have a life different from mine. That she would do things I wouldn't do. That we would both live and then die, all entirely separate from the other.

In the quiet of the night, I had cried over what had seemed to be such a lonely future.

Even now, I wasn't sure I could stand it if something terrible happened to Nan. Particularly if that something terrible were my fault. I only hoped I hadn't loosed something disastrous on her—on *us* both. And all because of my casual chat with a stranger on a sidewalk.

Lord.

It took me a long time to finally get back to sleep.

Unfortunately, the news the next morning didn't make me feel any better.

Chapter 10

●

NAN

I must've been even more exhausted than I thought. I was still asleep on the couch shortly after eleven on Sunday morning when Bert came rushing into the living room. With my eyes closed, I heard her bang down the steps, probably two at a time, and then run toward me. She seemed to be making some extremely strange noises.

I opened one eye.

Standing right in front of me, Bert was literally wringing her hands. From the horrified look on her face and the unintelligible sounds coming out of her mouth, I knew that something awful had happened, even before she told me. I sat up and stared at her until she finally got it out.

"Alice Moorman's been murdered! I just heard it on the morning news on my clock radio."

My mouth went dry. "Oh my God."

"That poor woman was strangled. *Strangled*. Can you imagine? One of her neighbors found her. Last night."

I blinked, trying to take it all in. Russell Moorman's wife had been killed, too? Just like Moorman himself? But why? And by whom?

"What about the kid?" I asked, recalling the oversized little fellow who—I might as well be honest here—had irritated the shit out of me yesterday. Now I felt a quick rush of guilt. The poor thing was an orphan, for God's sake. "Is the kid all right?"

Bert shrugged. "I guess so. According to the radio, they found him locked in his bedroom right after they found poor Alice. Oh God, isn't it awful?" Bert was now pacing the living room. "In fact, from what I gathered, it was the baby's crying that made the neighbor go check."

I remembered that ear-splitting shriek. That kid could get work as a civil defense siren. Oh, yeah, hearing that, you'd go check, all right.

Bert was shifting from foot to foot. Either she had to go to the bathroom, or she was so upset, she couldn't stand still. "Lord, Nan. What on earth is going on?"

I got up, heading for Bert's kitchen and a Coke. Hearing this little newsflash was not a great way to wake up. I couldn't complain, though. Alice Moorman was not waking up at all. I felt a little shiver run through me.

"Do you think Alice was killed by the same person as her husband?" Bert asked.

I was putting ice in two tumblers, but I stopped to turn and look at Bert. "Do you think she wasn't?" I didn't want to start an argument or anything, but did Bert actually think that Alice and her husband just happened to have the worst luck a couple could have? That each of them would be murdered within three days of each other? Even as the thought crossed my mind, I wondered. Alice and Russell *had* been murdered in different ways. If there was just one killer, did it necessarily follow that he'd kill his victims in the same way?

I was now pouring Coke into the first tumbler. "It had to

be the same guy. Anything else would be too weird," I told Bert.

"But why? Why would somebody kill both of them? Do you think Alice knew something she shouldn't?"

I handed Bert her Coke, and started to pour mine. I wasn't about to say it, but it sounded to me as if maybe Bert had read too many mystery novels. I mean, for all we knew, somebody had killed the Moormans because of a love triangle, or an affair gone wrong, or maybe because the baby really wasn't theirs. Hell, it could be anything.

On the other hand, maybe I'd watched too many soap operas.

The thing was, Bert and I just didn't know.

"That's got to be it," Bert was now saying. "Poor Alice was killed because she knew something."

I knew something. I knew Bert was jumping to conclusions. Lord, she was jumping period. She hadn't even taken a sip out of her Coke yet. She was waving it around, pacing back and forth. "But what could Alice have known?" she asked.

I just looked at her. She didn't seem to need my input on this. I took a long sip of Coke and tried to clear my head.

"But if she knew something, why didn't she tell us? Why?" Bert started her hand-wringing again. "Oh, Nan, what are we going to do?"

"First, you're going to calm down," I said.

Bert stiffened abruptly and gave me an irritated look. However, she did calm down. In fact, for the first time, she seemed to realize she had a Coke in her hand. She blinked a couple times, and then took a long, long sip. "Oh, Nan, if only Alice had told us whatever it was!"

I just looked at her. "Bert, listen to yourself. Suppose—and it may not be true, so don't get excited—but suppose what you're saying is true. And Alice Moorman knew something that somebody murdered her to keep her from telling. Why on earth would we want to know it, too?"

Bert blinked and this time took an even larger sip.

I took a sip, too, as what I'd just said hit me. Oh God. "I think we'd both better hope that nobody knows we talked to Alice yesterday."

The significance of this was not lost on Bert. Her eyes did that hubcap thing again. "Oh dear," she said.

I nodded. "We haven't exactly been secretive about our little visit, either," I said. "We've already told Trent. We've told Mrs. Ledford. And now all we have to worry about is anybody and everybody they could've told. Not to mention anybody Alice might've shared the news with before she died."

The way I saw it, the only person we didn't have worry about was the kid.

Bert finished off her Coke, and then took a deep breath. "I don't know about you, but I'm not sitting around here waiting for some nut to drop by and do to me what he did to the Moormans." She lifted her chin, squared her shoulders and walked straight over to the kitchen cabinets next to the stove. She opened the door, pulled out a small bottle, shook out a red pill and handed it to me.

"Here's breakfast," Bert said. "Swallow it, then let's go get dressed and get out of here."

I stared first at the multivitamin in my hand. My, this looked tasty. Then I stared at Bert. "Do you have any idea where we're going?"

Bert was now actually looking a little angry. She poured herself some more Coke and swallowed her little, red breakfast before she answered. "The way I see it, we only have one lead to follow. Alice is dead, and we don't know how to find Glenn Ledford or his wife. So . . . that just leaves—"

I knew what she was going to say. "The Sandersens."

Bert shrugged. "It's better than doing nothing." She finished off the last of her Coke. "Do you remember anything about the Sandersen murders?"

I was swallowing my breakfast right then, so I took a minute. "Sure I remember. The lover blew them both away with a shotgun. Because the wife dumped him. That's about it."

Bert just looked at me for a moment. "Thank you, Nancy Drew, for that in-depth analysis. So, what were the Sandersens' first names? When were they killed? What was the lover's name?"

My answers might not have been terribly helpful, but they were quick. "I don't know. I don't know. And I don't know."

"What we need are facts," Bert said. "And I know just where to go to get them. Matter of fact, anybody who's ever helped kids with their term papers knows that."

"WFPL's mama?" I asked, naming the radio station run by the Louisville Free Public Library.

Bert nodded. "Hurry up. We've got some investigating to do."

And she calls *me* Nancy Drew?

I followed Bert's instructions and hurried next door to change into a fresh pair of jeans, a red body suit, a short navy blue wool coat, and Reeboks. Bert, of course, had to wear something with a designer label. She'd put on Liz Claiborne jeans, a red crewneck sweater, and a tailored tweed sport coat.

She was also wearing something that I hate—heels with jeans. They weren't terribly high heels, but they were heels, all right. To my way of thinking, heels and jeans are mutually exclusive. Wearing them together is a lot like wearing rain boots and an evening gown. I didn't say anything, though. I just directed Bert toward the passenger side of my Neon, and we headed downtown.

It took us about twenty minutes to get downtown to the main branch of the Louisville Free Public Library on York Avenue. Usually all the parking spots on York and adjacent streets are taken, but this early on a Sunday, in the middle of the Bible belt, most people are in church. Bert and I, heathen that we are, found a parking spot right in front of the library's side entrance.

This is the entrance I always use. This branch of the library built itself a spacious, beautiful addition a few years ago. It's all sleek modern lines and lots of glass, and I never go in that way. Instead, I always go up the steep stone steps to the side entrance, pass the statue of Abraham Lincoln with the pigeon droppings in his hair, and enter what is now the oldest part of the library. It's a little longer to walk around to the front lobby, but this side of the building looks exactly like I've always thought a library should look. Solemn, and stately, and a little smug.

Bert's heels made little explosions on the gray tile floor as we hurried past the uniformed guard, past the check out desk, and headed toward the elevators and the reference area on the second floor.

The woman who looked up at us from the reference desk was a definite transplant from up north. In these surroundings, her New York accent stood out like a baby's cry in an old folks' home. "May I help you?" The woman's accent was clearly at odds with the old-fashioned wire-rimmed eye-glasses on the elastic cord around her neck, the prim ruffled collar at her chin, and the salt-and-pepper hair pulled back from her face into a tidy bun. She looked like she'd posed for the Old Maid on the children's cards. Only I don't think the Old Maid would ever have worn blue eyeshadow all the way up to her eyebrows.

"Obits from nearly twenty-five years ago?" the woman repeated after Bert. She must've had at least five sticks of gum in her mouth. It made her look a little as if she had the mumps. "You're kidding me, right? Without full names and precise death dates? Puhleeze, you should be so lucky," she said, smacking her gum.

So much for the prim librarian image.

"How about newspaper articles about the deaths?" I asked.

The woman put her glasses on, peered at me, then took them off before she spoke. "There'd be newspaper stories? What kind of deaths were they? An accident?"

"No," Bert said. "A shooting. They were murdered."

"Murder, huh? *Interesting*," she said. "Still—no can do. Not without the exact death date. Could've been any day that summer. That's about five hundred miles of microfilm to look through. Like I said, no can do."

I glared at her. Who was this woman anyway? The Librarian from Hell? "Why don't you get us a few miles and let us start looking?"

Next to me, Bert shifted her feet and cleared her throat. She was, obviously, trying to tell me that I was once again exhibiting my usual attitude problem, as Bert calls it. Attitude, hell. I was being nice. If I wasn't, I would've pulled those eyeglasses on their elastic cord away from that librarian's neck.

And then let them snap back into her nose at about eighty miles an hour.

"We would really appreciate anything you can do for us," Bert put in then, patting the woman's spider-like hand.

The woman jerked her hand away from Bert. Apparently, librarians from New York don't like to be touched. She was eyeing us both uneasily when she shoved a giant book in our direction and a pad of forms. "You want miles, we'll give ya miles," she said. "But first, you gotta sign the register and fill out the proper form. It's The Rule. Then we can only try."

I assumed the "we" she used was the royal "we." I signed the register, and Bert filled out the request form with the name of the deceased and the approximate date. We'd decided that the murders had probably occurred between May and August our sophomore year in high school.

The Librarian from Hell put on her glasses again and eyed the form. Then she eyed us. "You two twins?"

We both nodded in unison. Hell's response was to shrug and to turn back to the form. Her face immediately brightened. "Oh, *Sandersen*. Why didn't you say so? No prob. I can pull the stuff easy." She leaned forward, looked around the room, and lowered her voice. Bert and I looked around, too. There was nobody there.

"Listen," Hell said, "those two must've left a huge estate or something. Like maybe it's just getting settled?" Her voice was getting louder by the minute. "The family must be really slugging it out. I've seen it happen. I bet the lawyers have sucked it dry by now. Probably nothing left. After twenty years. I've seen it happen." She broke off and gave Bert's suit a pointed stare. "Oh. You're not a lawyer, are ya?"

Great. Now Hell had gotten talkative. I might have to do that thing with her glasses to get her moving.

Bert was looking flattered. "A lawyer? No, no, no," she said, smoothing her hair away from her face. "What makes you ask?"

"Oh, honey—" Bert was a honey now? "—there's already been two or three people in here over the last few months or so, asking about this Sandersen thing," Hell said. "They said they were lawyers. The last one—about a month back—was a woman, though, wearing a hot pink jumpsuit and cheap orange sunglasses. That sound like a lawyer to you?"

Bert's head went up. "She wasn't wearing a tan raincoat, too, was she?"

Hell immediately nodded. "Yeah, she was, come to think of it. One of those trenchcoat getups, probably trying to cover up that trashy jumpsuit. We're talking trashy, believe you me." She broke off again and once again stared pointedly at Bert. "Oh. She isn't a friend of yours, is she?"

I was tempted to say, *No, that's Mom.* Bert spoke first, though. "No, we don't know her." Bert seemed to realize in the middle of what she was saying that this didn't exactly explain how she'd known about the raincoat. "But we know people who do."

Hell blinked at that one.

Bert was now nudging my ankle with her pointed shoe. Before I required first aid, I gave her a slight nod to tell her, *Hey, I got it, already.* I knew, for God's sake, that Hell's description sounded just like the woman Bert thought might've been following her.

In fact, now that I thought about it, this description also sounded like Mrs. Ledford. That was what had been nagging at me yesterday when I'd seen her raincoat. Lord. Could these two women be one and the same?

I looked over at the large book now in Hell's hands. "Did

the woman in the jumpsuit sign that register, too?" I asked.

Hell tapped the book with a bony finger. "My dear, *everyone* who wants microfilm has to sign the register. It's The Rule."

She made it sound as if Moses had brought this particular Rule down from the mount.

Bert and I turned the large book back around to face us and started skimming through the back pages.

"You're not trying to find her, are ya? Oh my dear, you'll have to look through miles of pages. Miles, we're talking. Even so I don't see how you can possibly figure out which signature was hers," said the librarian, smacking her gum again. "I couldn't. I wouldn't even try."

I believed that.

As it turned out, we did find the signature. Only two pages back, someone had signed the page with a name we recognized. In black ink with lots of swirls.

Tonya Harding.

Call me skeptical, but I figured it was a pretty safe bet that Tonya hadn't skated into the Louisville library any time recently.

Seeing Tonya Harding's name on that page should've struck me as funny. I mean, it seemed like such a ridiculous thing to do. It was even more ridiculous that somebody had signed Tonya's name and gotten away with it.

But, instead, the name gave me a little chill. Because it meant that someone was really out there playing games.

And the proof was right here in black and white.

I couldn't believe that the Librarian from Hell hadn't even noticed.

"Tonya Harding?" I asked, pointing to the signature.

"Oh. Do you think *that* was the one?" Hell considered it

for a moment and then gave her gum a little extra chomp. "Now that you mention it, I guess that might've been her. I remember thinking at the time, wouldn't it be just too tacky to have the same name as somebody famous? Like Lizzie Borden or Oliver North?"

Those were two names I'd never expect anyone to use in the same sentence.

"Of course, I never said anything to that Tonya person about her name. I didn't want to embarrass her."

Maybe using a famous name had not been so stupid, after all.

"Did you see any identification?" I asked.

Hell shook her pepper gray head. "Of course not," she said. "It's not The Rule."

That certainly explained it.

Bert and I studied the entry. Tonya's signature was dated about a month earlier. That meant that whatever had been going on with the Sandersens had been in the works for at least a month. Way before Bert ran into an about-to-be-dead guy on a street corner.

"I wonder if we could have some of the newspaper issues from around the time of the deaths?" Bert asked Hell. "Before and after? In addition to the obituaries?"

Hell put her eyeglasses on and sighed. "Is that all?" She didn't sound so friendly any more. However, in only a few minutes, she did bring out several small microfilm canisters and showed us how to thread the things on the machines, as well as how to twist the little cranks to advance our way through.

"OK, that's it," Hell announced and returned to her desk.

I sat down next to Bert, threading microfilm on my machine. Bert must've gotten the entire library gene, because she was already skimming through the first pages on her machine, locating the first news item about the murders like a pro.

The Sandersens' first names turned out to be Ted and Jane. Certainly bland enough. No wonder we couldn't remember them.

In fact, we couldn't remember much. The newspaper accounts of the double murder that had been splashed across the front page of the *Courier-Journal* back then were only vaguely familiar. It was the one large photograph of the victim's bodies covered in sheets that I thought I recognized.

Today the *Courier-Journal* is usually pretty reserved when it comes to gruesome details. Apparently, twenty-five years ago, they'd had a field day. The *Courier's* front page not only included the one large photograph of the victims' bodies, but what looked like the couple's wedding portrait. A nice touch, I thought.

There was also, at the bottom of the page, an inset photograph of a house engulfed in flames. It took Bert and me a moment to realize that this picture also belonged to the story.

June 26, LEITCHFIELD, Ky. *The charred bodies of Ted and Jane Sandersen were discovered by firefighters in the burned-out ruins of their vacation home early this morning.*

Beside me, Bert stiffened. "Lord. I dreamed of a fire last night. And yet, none of this sounds familiar to me. Could I have been remembering all this on some level, and not even know it?"

When Bert starts talking metaphysical, I just ignore her. I moved closer to Bert so that I could read, too.

Located at Rough River, Kentucky, the couple's secluded cabin had been the site of a getaway weekend, according to close friends.

"I guess that was why we were babysitting for them in the first place," I said.

Bert waved at me to be quiet, as she continued to read.

Arson was first suspected when firefighters discovered evidence of an incendiary substance that was apparently used to spread the blaze. Searches of the surrounding area by police produced empty cans of kerosene, found in the woods near the cabin. Investigation into the case continues.

"So Loverboy set fire to the cabin, hoping to destroy evidence," I said.

I turned to my machine then and advanced the microfilm. Newspaper accounts following the days of the murders had carried even more grisly details. They also mentioned more than once that the Sandersens' arson-related deaths had been upgraded to premeditated murder.

When the headline, LOUISVILLE MAN SOUGHT, appeared on my screen, Bert and I leaned forward to read the article.

June 28, Louisville. *A warrant for the arrest of a Louisville man was issued today. On Monday the charred bodies of Ted and Jane Sandersen were found in their burned-out vacation home.*

"The term *charred bodies* gets kind of overused, don't you think?" I asked Bert.

This time she ignored me, and continued to read.

Evidence of shotgun blasts to the heads of the victims prior to the fire has launched a four-state manhunt, according to Louisville police. Sources inside the coroner's office confirm that the shotgun blasts were made at close-range. Les Tennyson, sought in the warrant, has been named as a close friend of Jane Sandersen by sources inside the family.'

"I guess the term *close friend* meant the same thing then as it does now," Bert said.

I shrugged and read on.

Tennyson had been seen in the vicinity of the cabin by neighbors, just prior to the double murder.

Just below the news item was a photograph of Les Tennyson.

Bert and I leaned forward and squinted. It didn't help. The photograph looked as if you were viewing it through water. As best as I could tell, it showed a man in his late twenties, with light hair parted on one side and neatly combed across, dark eyes, and an easy-going grin. Not exactly the expression you'd expect to see on the face of a murderer.

Bert frowned. "Ever notice that newspaper pictures of people accused of murder are always blurry?" asked Bert.

I just looked at her. Sometimes she reminds me of Andy Rooney.

"I think they're always out of focus because the photographer is shaking in his shoes," I said. "He's standing too close to a killer." I squinted at the screen again, finally shaking my head. "Hell, I don't remember this guy at all. Do you? Ever see a blurry guy hanging around the Sandersens' house?"

Bert just looked at me for a moment. "I don't even re-member the Sandersens all that well, to tell you the truth." She tapped her index finger against the photograph on her own screen.

Ted and Jane Sandersen in more pleasant times stared out at us. Ted, a tall, thin, sandy-haired guy with round cheeks and a toothy grin, stood ramrod straight, looking directly at the camera. He was wearing tailored slacks, a dark polo shirt, and a captain's cap. Ted's arm was around the waist of a pretty brunette in a sleeveless print dress. The brunette only came up to her husband's shoulder. Both were smiling, and the pho-tograph looked as if it might've been taken on a marina.

"Oh, dear," Bert said. "They look so young."

I was still studying the screen. "And so unfamiliar." I don't know why I'd expected otherwise. We only babysat for them a few times.

Bert turned to look at me. "All I really remember," she said, "was that Mr. Sandersen acted very interested in our being twins. Do you remember that?"

I shook my head again.

Bert turned back to the screen, and now looked sad. "One day he asked us all about being mirror twins—you know, what was different about the two of us. He was such a nice guy. Actually, I don't think he was even interested—he was just trying to make us feel comfortable." She sighed. "I can't believe I don't remember him any better than I do."

I shrugged. "Well, at fifteen, we were probably a lot more interested in what he thought of us, rather than what we thought of him."

When you're still in high school, everything is filtered through this little quiz program. Do I look all right? Did I act all right? Do they like me? What do they think of me?

Only, of course, with Bert and me, all the *I*'s and *me*'s got turned into *we*'s and *us*'s. Back then, the adults around us had just seemed to fade into the background.

Bert cranked ahead to the end of her microfilm, and the obituary section appeared on her screen. They used the same photo of the Sandersens on the marina, but it had been cropped tight into little more than head shots.

We scanned the information that chronicled the short but unhappy lives of Ted and Jane. It boiled down to little more than they had been survived by only three people. The little boys we'd babysat for that summer, Carl and Edward, had been three and four respectively at the time of their parents' deaths. The only other survivor was a younger sister of Ted—a woman by the name of Wilma Sandersen Cartland.

I took a pen and notebook from my purse, jotting down the name. There was a chance this sister was still in town. After all, Bert and I were still here after twenty-five years. Why not Wilma?

While I was making notes, Bert disappeared into the research stacks and returned, lugging the Louisville residential phone book. We flipped it open. No Wilma Cartland.

There was, however, a W. Cartland at 39173 Winchester Road.

We headed for the nearest pay phone. W. Cartland—that is, Wilma Sandersen Cartland—answered the phone on the first ring.

And, what do you know, she *was* willing to be interviewed by WCKI news.

Chapter 11

•

BERT

Meeting Wilma Cartland was a big disappointment.

I didn't know about Nan, but the whole time she and I were traveling out of downtown Louisville—first on I-65 and then on the Watterson Expressway—I was expecting that W. Cartland—alias Wilma Sandersen Cartland—would turn out to be someone we'd already met. Like, oh, for example, the woman in the orange sunglasses and the tan raincoat who'd followed me back to my office.

Or, at the very least, I was hoping that Mrs. Cartland would've had a little throat surgery in the past. So that she'd have to whisper when she talked. That would at least have started to tie a few things together.

Thank God I didn't mention any of this to Nan, though. She would probably still be teasing me.

The woman who opened the door of 39173 Winchester Road in the suburb of St. Matthews was tall, skinny and, let's face it, kind of old. I took one look and realized she was about twenty years older and twenty pounds lighter than the woman who'd followed me. "You the people from the radio?" Wilma asked, her voice about as grating as fingernails scraping on a blackboard. Even though she was speaking to us through a screen door, she yelled as if her front door was still shut.

So much for the whispering theory.

Nan had been staring pointedly at the two small metal signs stuck in the yard, on either side of the sidewalk. The one on the left read, KEEP OFF THE GRASS. The other one said, ARE YOU RIGHT WITH YOUR LORD? When Wilma spoke, though, Nan stepped forward. "Yes, ma'am, we're from WCKI News." She hurried through the introductions.

From over Nan's shoulder, I was studying Wilma. The woman wore what I believe people used to call a house dress—one of those shapeless cotton things with long sleeves, a Peter Pan collar, in a tiny pink print. Her chin-length, gray-streaked brown hair was curled under pageboy style, and held to the sides by—of all things—two Mickey Mouse barrettes. Mickey grinned at us from just above each of Wilma's ears. It was the way any little girl might have worn her hair. But Wilma was hardly a little girl. Deep lines etched the sides of her mouth and between her eyes, and her lips were pressed together in an expression that my Kentucky relatives have always described as "looking as if she'd just bit into a persimmon." In Wilma's case, it looked as if the persimmon might've bitten back.

"We appreciate your seeing us, Mrs. Cartland," Nan was now saying. Since it had worked so well before with Alice Moorman—something in my throat caught at the thought of her—Nan flashed her walrus mustache press pass and then quickly put it in her pocket.

Behind Nan, I smiled and tried to look journalistic.

Wilma had made no move yet to open the door. "We'll only take a little of your time, Mrs. Cartland," Nan said.

"It's *Miss* Cartland," Wilma corrected, her tone and compressed lips implying that being a *Mrs.* would be remarkably distasteful. Nan might not agree, but, considering my own recent experiences, I thought Wilma might have a point.

"Actually, I'm a widow," Wilma went on. She still made no move toward the door, but just stood there, looking Nan up and down. Nan's coat was unbuttoned, and Wilma's eyes seemed to linger longer than necessary on Nan's red bodysuit and jeans. Judging from the way Wilma's eyes narrowed, I could tell she didn't like what she saw.

"I've been a widow for a great many years now." Wilma's tone made it sound as if widowhood had been just one more annoyance in a lifetime of annoyances. "I use *Miss* these days rather than *Mrs*. It saves long explanations about where my husband is or isn't."

Like, in the grave, for instance? What a sweet way to put that, I thought.

Wilma's eyes had now moved to me. She glanced briefly at my tweed sport coat and my designer jeans, apparently found nothing to disapprove of, and turned back to Nan.

"Naturally, *I* don't listen to the radio very much." Wilma said this with some pride, as if anyone who would stoop to listen to such a thing was strictly low class.

I was kind of glad to hear it. That meant the woman would not recognize Nan's name, and realize that Nan had never done the news on WCKI. I also knew Nan didn't care whether Wilma listened or not.

This happens to radio personalities all the time—even to the ones with the best ratings in the market. For some reason, there are those who seem to enjoy going out of their way to tell somebody on the radio that they never listen to them. Nan tells me it's because these people want to cut you down to size.

I think it's because these people are rude.

Beside me, Nan was shrugging. I knew what she was going to say. Lord knows, I'd heard her it say it often enough. "I don't blame you for not listening," she told Wilma with a smile. "Some of that stuff you just don't want to hear."

Apparently, that wasn't the reaction old Wilma had hoped for. She turned abruptly, gesturing over her shoulder for us to follow her inside. As she walked briskly through the foyer, she didn't look back once to see if we were following.

We ended up in her living room—a room completely filled with knickknacks. Every horizontal surface seemed to contain figurines or vases or some kind of porcelain something. There were no pictures of family, no framed art on the walls, but there were enough little ceramic doodads to fill a large van. Shepherdesses, elves, and clowns smiled giddily at us from end tables. On the coffee table, an entire village had sprung up, complete with interior lights and an ice-skating pond.

I stared at the thing. This woman had too much time on her hands.

Wilma quickly perched on a Queen Anne armchair, crossing her skinny legs daintily at the ankles and folding her hands in her lap. Then she just sat there, staring at us.

Nan and I glanced at each other, wondering where we should sit. We both started for opposite corners of the sofa, when Wilma snapped, "No, not there! In the middle." Nan threw me a *this-woman-is-nuts* look and settled herself in the center of the couch.

There wasn't room in the center of the couch for both of us. Unless I sat on Nan's lap. I headed, instead, for the only other chair in the room, an armless occasional chair with a cane seat. About as comfortable as a rock, the cane chair was standing next to a small table with castered legs and a mirrored top covered with—you guessed it—figurines. I stared at the closest figurine to my elbow and thought I recognized a Hummel—the one where a little girl is kissing her doll. It was one I've always particularly liked. "Oh," I said, "how sweet," and reached for it.

"Don't touch that!" Wilma yelped. "You'll break it!"

I jerked my hand away. Now I knew why Wilma here had made Nan sit in the middle of the sofa. The sofa's end tables were covered with figurines, too; and Wilma wanted to make sure that Nan wouldn't accidentally break one.

It was my guess that Wilma and her deceased husband had never had any kids. Or pets either, for that matter.

Nan had been looking over at me with widened eyes, but now she cleared her throat and turned back to Wilma. "Well, it's like I said on the phone," Nan said. "We're working on a radio documentary on famous murders in Louisville."

Wilma's lips pressed together even tighter. "Are you now?" Her tone implied she didn't quite believe it.

"Naturally," Nan went on smoothly, "we thought of your brother and his wife."

Wilma stiffened. "That was a long time ago—I can't imagine why you'd want to rake up all that filth again," she said. "I certainly don't have anything else to add about it at this late date." Her eyes darted back and forth between Nan and me. "You two aren't twins, are you?"

Why wasn't I surprised to hear her phrase that question in such a negative way?

Nan nodded. "Yes, ma'am, we are," she said slowly and evenly. I shifted position in the cane chair. Nan sounded almost excessively polite. It was so unlike her, it made me a little nervous. I mean, I knew Nan had to be swallowing what she'd really like to say to the charming Wilma. In my estimation, it was only a matter of time before Nan couldn't hold it back anymore. "About your brother and sister-in-law's murders, Miss Cartland," Nan went on in that same unnaturally polite voice, "we were wondering what you remember—"

Wilma held up a bony hand. "Oh, please. I'm sure you can get all that trivia from the old newspapers," Wilma said. She gave Nan's outfit a piercing stare. "If you'll take the time to do a thorough job, of course."

Nan's eyes flashed. Uh oh. "Now just a *darn*—"

I cut Nan off.

"I suppose," I said, leaning toward Wilma, "it must've been terrible for you back then. I mean, the murders must've created quite an unexpected problem for you."

Nan turned to look at me, one eyebrow lifted. I know. I know. So maybe *problem* was an odd way to put it, but Wilma here struck me as someone who liked her life nice and neat and orderly. She'd have viewed the murders as quite an intrusion on her daily life.

"Oh, yes, indeed," Wilma said, turning toward the three-tiered wooden table beside her chair. She reached for a ceramic teddy bear. "You've hit on it exactly. That's precisely what it was for me. A terrible problem. Terrible." She stared into the bear's laughing eyes. "I had to take off work, of course—I was the office manager for a car dealership in town. A very important position. And very difficult for me to miss any work. But, of course, I missed several days just getting the estate settled, as well as arranging all those funeral details. Just mountains and mountains of details."

"Not to mention dealing with the police," Nan said.

"And the reporters." Wilma threw a contemptuous look at both of us. "Land sakes, what I had to go through because of them. Between reporters and the police, I was answering questions night and day." She pulled a handkerchief out of a side pocket and began to polish the bear in her lap. "I thought things would never get back to normal. And it wasn't as if *I* had done anything to bring such a problem on myself." She lifted her chin as if she were bragging.

I stared at her. Was she implying that Ted and Jane had done something? To deserve to be murdered that way?

From the sofa, Nan just sat and gaped at the woman.

I pretty much gaped at her, too. Then I said what I knew Wilma wanted to hear. "Oh, you poor thing."

"Well, it's a violent world, you know." She put down the teddy bear and picked up a ceramic rabbit. "No doubt about that. It's violent and evil." She made the comment off-hand, like one might say the weather was stormy.

"Yes, it is," Nan put in. "I guess that, back then, you certainly had more than enough to take care of."

"Well, first off, I had to be the one to identify poor Teddy's body." Wilma lifted her chin again, and began to polish the rabbit in short, angry strokes. "There wasn't anyone else to do it. Just me. My husband was still alive back then, but he was no help. He'd have fallen apart if he'd had to do it. So I was all by my lonesome. But I did it. And what a thing to see. I'll never forget it. Ninety-eight per cent of his body. That's how bad they said Teddy was burned. Well, I don't care what they said. It looked like one hundred percent to me."

An important distinction, no doubt.

"It looked like so much burned hamburger. Really, I could only identify Teddy by his rings and what was left of his

clothing. Everything else was just black. Just black and goo
and gunk. That was all. A black mess. And me having to look
at it."

She carefully replaced the rabbit on the table and then
coolly looked straight at me. As if what she'd just said hadn't
been the grossest thing I personally had ever heard. She was
talking about her *brother*, for goodness sake.

Wilma had delivered her last little speech with all the
emotion of a dead salamander. I swallowed and looked over
at Nan. To be honest, I was beginning to feel a little queasy.
I was beginning to regret that I had jump-started the old girl
into blabbering, after all.

"But, like I said, somebody had to identify him," Wilma
went on, that chin of hers lifting again. "Who else but me? I
mean, who else could? Not those poor kids. And it wasn't like
I hadn't expected it. Oh, heavens, I could see it coming. It
was—what's the word? Inevitable. Oh, my yes, I wasn't surprised."

Nan gaped at her again. "You weren't surprised that they
were burned?"

Wilma shot her an irritated look. "Don't be silly. Of course
I was shocked when I first heard about it. But I'd known before then that something evil was going to happen. It just had
to, you know. Evil begets evil. The Good Book says so."

I glanced over at Nan again.

"Begets?" Nan asked, just a trace of sarcasm in her voice.

Wilma noticed it, though. She lifted her chin again. I'd
begun to realize that chin action of hers was one of those unconscious movements we all make from time to time. Like
chewing on your lip when you're nervous. Only Wilma's chin
evidently became airborne anytime she started praising herself for something. "I can recognize evil, young lady," she

boasted. "And evil begets evil—it's in the blood. I could just see it. The way they carried on. Drinking and partying. Partying and drinking. All hours of the day and night."

"Sounds like a fun couple," Nan said.

Wilma shot her a scornful look. "I'll have you know that both of them were sinners. Teddy and that wife of his. *She* was just plain evil. Playing around on Teddy, *fornicating* with that other man. Well, it was scandalous—that's all I've got to say about it."

I certainly wished that were true, but unfortunately Wilma went right on.

"And it wasn't like Teddy couldn't have married someone else. He was so good-looking, he could've had his pick. He could've had a fine, God-fearing woman. He was raised just like I was, with a good church upbringing."

I just looked at her. No wonder he'd wanted a little fun.

Wilma grabbed up a tiny ceramic mouse this time, and started scrubbing it with her handkerchief. "So I wasn't surprised when evil ended with evil. With blood and death and fire. Just like the Bible says that evil ends. That *sinners* end. It is the judgment of the Lord. It had to happen." Wilma's voice had taken on the sing-song cadence of a fundamentalist preacher.

I was beginning to understand the metal signs Wilma had in her yard. She would definitely equate being right with God with keeping off her grass.

"And now here it is again," Wilma went on in her sing-song tone. "Evil starting up once more. Dark evil. Pure and simple evil. And, once again, I'm not surprised. Not surprised a bit that the evil is happening again. Because evil just naturally begets evil."

Nan was nodding. "Begets," she said, as if she actually understood what in the world this crazy old woman was talking about. "You say it's happening again?"

Wilma looked back and forth from Nan and me. "Why, I figured that was why you were really here. I saw it on the news," she said. "It was just like I said. Evil breeds. And now the oldest son of Teddy and Jane has gotten himself murdered, too. *And* his wife."

Oh my God.

"What do you mean?" Nan asked slowly, but I think we both knew already what Wilma was going to say, even before she said it.

"Why, Russell Moorman. Dead just like his mama and daddy. Russell was Teddy's oldest boy. Now I hear he got himself killed downtown somewhere. Murdered, too. His throat cut."

I blinked and looked at Nan, knowing we both were thinking the same thing. That about-to-be-dead guy who'd tried to pick me up a couple of days ago was actually the same little boy we'd *baby-sat* for, almost twenty-five years ago.

I sat there, letting it sink in. Thinking about the horror of it.

Certainly I was horrified at the idea that the little boy we'd known long ago had ultimately grown up to be murdered—that much was sure. And, also, that his wife had been murdered.

But, I might as well admit it, there was something else that horrified me, too. Lord. I felt *old*.

Naturally, I started grasping at any little straw that Russell Moorman couldn't really have been that same little boy. "But his name was different," I pointed out.

Wilma glared at me. "Well, of course, it was. Both boys were put up for adoption after their parents got killed. Their new families thought it best to change the boys' names, of course. I couldn't blame them. They certainly didn't want people pointing and staring at their new little boys all the time. What with their real parents blown to smithereens in a love nest and all."

Like I said, the woman had such a sweet way of putting things.

Wilma's chin went up again. "*I* helped arrange the whole thing, of course. I got the boys' adopted, helped find just the right parents—but it was only proper. It was something I had to do. The whole thing was arranged through my church. The Apostolic Church of the Holy Scriptures."

I'd heard of that one, actually. Mostly because it had made the news on Nan's station. The Apostolic Church of the Holy Scriptures had gone out of business last summer—for a short time. It had closed briefly, with a sign out front saying CLOSED ON ACCOUNT OF THE RAPTURE.

Apparently, the entire congregation had been expecting to be transported to heaven en masse. Naturally, the church had been nicknamed by the news team covering the story as the "Beam-Me-Up-Scotty Church." I personally would've liked to have been there the next Sunday to hear the pastor explain to his flock why they were all still earthbound. Now that I think of it, the acute disappointment could possibly explain Wilma's general mood.

Wilma seemed to take our silence for condemnation at having her nephews adopted out. She drew herself up. "Of course, *I* couldn't take those little boys in myself," she said. "Not to live with *me*."

I glanced around at all the figurines. She was absolutely right.

"Especially after the way they'd already been reared,"

Wilma went on. "They were so ill-behaved. Just little demons. And it wasn't like I was sure they were really my kin. Their mama being that kind and all. Not to mention, I've been down in my back all my life . . ."

I almost smiled. "Down in my back" is a phrase I hadn't heard since Nan and I were little. Our aunt Ginny Sue, on our father's side, who has since—as they say—passed on, used this quaint little phrase all the time. It can pretty much mean anything from having a ruptured disk to suffering from a muscle pull. As I recall, however, in Aunt Ginny Sue's case, it mainly meant that Uncle Ray had better keep his distance.

Wilma was still going on. "Being down in my back, well, it's just my cross to bear."

I remembered her brisk walk into the living room. She'd certainly not seemed to be in any back pain.

"And," Wilma hurried on, "it wasn't as if there was any money to help take care of the boys. Teddy and that woman may have lived high on the hog, but when they died, it turned out they owed everybody. Selling that big house didn't even pay all their debts."

I opened my mouth to make a sympathetic comment, but Wilma didn't need any encouragement to continue.

"I did make sure, of course, that the boys found good homes," Wilma said, her chin again airborne. "It was the least I could do."

Once more, Wilma was right.

"And Russell's brother?" Nan asked. "What was his new name?"

Nan and I already knew the answer. Family—that's what Alice had called him. And his wife had told us, too, in so many words. Nan and I looked at each other and said the name in unison with Wilma.

"Glenn Ledford."

"Why, how did you know?" Wilma asked us, frowning. "Has somebody been talking? Has somebody been telling tales out of school?"

"Actually, we ran into Glenn's wife recently," Nan answered.

Wilma's frown got deeper. "Oh, no," she said, shaking her head. "I've kept up with the boys all these years." That chin of hers went up again. "I even kept in touch with the families while they were growing up, just to be sure everything was as it should be. Church twice on Sunday and, of course, Sunday school and Wednesday prayer meetings and Christian Youth Group. Even if those boys might not be real family, it was my Christian duty to make sure they were getting a proper raising."

I could just see those adoptive moms and dads hiding under the beds every time they saw old Wilma coming by for a visit.

"And I've followed along with the boys when they got grown, too. So I'd know if Glenn had been joined in holy matrimony," she said, pointing the ceramic mouse she still held in Nan's direction. "Up to just recently, I even knew where he lived. In a rundown motel over in Jeffersonville. Before that, he was in Chattanooga."

"You don't know where he lives now?" Nan asked.

Wilma looked offended. "He'll turn up. He always does. Especially when he wants to borrow a few dollars." She smiled for the first time. "I give him a real good interest rate."

She was all heart.

Nan pressed on. "How about Glenn's adoptive parents? Do you know where they are?"

Wilma looked at Nan as if she'd asked one of Jake's dumb questions. "Well, of course, once the boys were grown, there wasn't any reason for me to keep track of strangers. It wasn't like they were real kin." She shrugged, and started polishing her mouse again. "Besides, I couldn't find them that last time. They'd moved—out of state, their neighbors said—and, can you believe, nobody seemed to know their forwarding address."

I believed it. They either hadn't known, or they weren't about to tell Wilma.

Nan wasn't through. "But, if you don't know where Glenn lives now, and you don't know where his parents live, how do you know he didn't get married?" Nan asked.

Wilma glared at her, and put the mouse down so hard, it rattled for a moment. "I *said*, Russell was the only one of the boys that was married."

I exchanged a look with Nan. A look that said, *If Wilma is right, then who in heaven's name was that woman at the motel?*

Chapter 12

●

NAN

Sometimes it's hard to believe that Bert and I were ever the same thing. And yet, from what I understand, she and I are supposed to have been at one time a single, fertilized egg. A single egg that—for some reason that nobody seems to understand—decides to split one day and make two people, instead of just one. Bert and I were even one thing for a longer length of time than most identical twins. Because, apparently, that's how you get mirror twins in the first place. If the egg dawdles making up its mind—which, considering that it was me and Bert, does not surprise me—you get mirror images.

So, according to all the twin studies, the woman sitting beside me in the front seat of my Neon is supposed to be me. Same genetic makeup, the whole bit. And yet, as I pulled onto Breckinridge Road, off of Winchester, Bert actually turned to me and said, "Oh, that poor Wilma Cartland. Don't you feel sorry for her?"

I almost ran off the road. "Are you kidding?" I felt sorry for anybody who had to spend time with old Wilma, that's who I felt sorry for. Hell, by the time we left, I was beginning to feel sorry for all those figurines.

Bert shook her head. "I mean, that poor, poor woman.

Just think about it. A long time ago, she had to choose be-tween people and things. And she chose *things*."

Like I said, I felt sorry for the figurines.

Bert was now clucking her tongue. "That poor, lonely, sad woman."

OK, I'd heard enough. "Bert," I said, "you are a very nice person. Wilma Cartland, on the other hand, is not. The only good thing that came out of meeting that bitch was that now at least we know that what's been happening really is con-nected somehow to the Sandersen murders."

Bert nodded. "But what are *we* doing in the middle of all this? I mean, we haven't seen those little boys since we were fifteen. Do you suppose it could be a coincidence that one of them showed up on the street one day and started talking to me?"

I waited until I pulled out onto the Watterson before I an-swered her. Mainly because the Watterson is one of the few expressways in America which shoots you into sixty-five mile-an-hour traffic right off the ramp. You need every bit of your concentration to avoid catastrophe. Every time I enjoy the heart-pumping excitement of risking life and limb getting on the Watterson, I long to find whoever designed it and drop him in front of a herd of stampeding cattle just so he could see how it feels.

Accelerating off the ramp, I narrowly avoided certain death beneath the wheels of an oncoming eighteen-wheeler by deftly changing lanes, and—when I could talk again—I looked over at Bert.

"You think all this could be a coincidence?" I asked. "That the guy who talked to you just happens to be one of those kids we baby-sat for. That the woman in the motel just happens to tell us that she's married to the other brother. And that the last thing she says to us just happens to be the boys' birth name?"

Bert had been staring wide-eyed at the eighteen-wheeler that had hurtled past us, but now she turned to look at me. "So, all right, it's not a coincidence. Where do we go from here? I mean, who else is there to talk to? Glenn Ledford's gone, and it'll be all but impossible for us—who aren't even relatives of his—to find his adoptive parents—"

"—and we've got no way to trace whoever that woman was back at the No-tell Motel," I finished for her.

Bert was very quiet for a long time after that. Believe me, it's not like her. According to our mother, Bert was the twin who talked first. And loudest. Of course, she did have a ten-minute head start on the use of the English language. From her chatter ever since, I always figured she'd already made it to complex sentences by the time I began mumbling *Mama*.

Bert, however, would tell you that the opposite was true—that I was the talker. And she'd point, as proof, to the fact that I talk for a living. Me, I think I'm just making up for lost time.

At any rate, I'd just taken the Newburg exit when Bert finally broke her silence. She tucked one leg up under her and swiveled so she was facing me. No easy task wearing a seat belt. Then she said, "So what do you think? Is it possible the Moormans' killer is the same person who killed Ted and Jane Sandersen?"

I actually let my foot off the gas pedal while I considered that one. "You think Les Tennyson killed Russell Moorman and his wife? But why?"

Bert shrugged. "Maybe Tennyson has been on the loose all this time, and he ran across Russell accidentally, and he thought Russell could identify him to the cops."

I shook my head. "Russell was only four years old when his parents were murdered. Glenn was only three. Neither one of them would be much of a witness now. And why would Tennyson kill Russell's wife? She wasn't around when the first murders happened. She never even saw the guy."

"We *think* she never saw him," Bert said. "But maybe she met Tennyson some time when she was with Russell."

"Then why not kill Glenn, too?"

"Maybe he has. We haven't met up with this Glenn Ledford yet. Or maybe Tennyson can't kill him because Glenn already moved out of that motel. Maybe Tennyson can't find him any better than we can."

I pulled into the passing lane, trying to get around a minivan. "That's a lot of maybes," I said.

"OK. If it's not Tennyson, then Russell and Alice's deaths have got to be linked to that business deal Russell had cooking with Glenn."

"Maybe the two of them made a bundle doing something together, and Glenn decided he didn't want to share. Maybe he killed Russell and Alice so he could keep all the profits for himself."

"I don't know," Bert said. She paused for a moment, thinking, and then she went on. "You know what else it could be?"

We said it together. "Blackmail."

"Maybe Russell and Glenn actually located Tennyson somehow," Bert said, "and they were blackmailing him. You know, pay up or else they'd turn him in to the cops."

"That still doesn't explain what it's got to do with us," I said. "We don't even remember Tennyson."

"Maybe he's superparanoid," Bert said. "Especially after getting away with murder for so long. Maybe he's killing anyone he thinks might remember him. That would certainly explain Russell's murder. And the shot at us."

"It doesn't explain who that woman was at the motel," I said.

Bert frowned, rubbing her forehead. "God, this is giving me a headache. I have a feeling there is someone out there we should know about. Or *something*."

"Of course, there is. We don't know anything. We don't even know if Les Tennyson was ever caught for the Sandersens' double murder. If it was ever in the paper, we were probably in college at the time, and we'd have missed it."

Bert sighed. "We could probably do another microfilm search, but we'd have to check every year since the murders."

I glanced over at her. "There's another way." In fact, once it had occurred to me, I couldn't wait to put it into motion.

I was getting low on gas, so I went on past the turn onto Napoleon Boulevard, and stopped at the station on the corner of Trevilian and Bardstown Road. The phone booth there was one of those handy jobs that let you pull right up and dial, without ever getting out of your car.

I rolled down my window, plunked in the quarter Bert handed me, and punched in the news hot line number at the radio station. Dale Curtis, WCKI news director—the only person I know who actually adores his job—was, believe it or not, joyfully at work on a Sunday afternoon. Dale also looks a great deal like a mix between an elderly hippie and Les Nessman of WKRP fame—with the groovy wardrobe to match—so it's not exactly a surprise to anybody that he doesn't seem to have a life.

What he does have, as a newsman, are connections at the Louisville Police Department. Those unnamed sources that reporters refer to all the time. People who can give him information without asking a lot of questions. Dale picked up on the first ring, and I explained what I needed to know.

"Sure thing, doll," Dale said. "Ring you later at your pad with the scoop." Really, he talks like that. This could also explain why he doesn't have a life.

"I'll be there or at my sister's apartment." I gave him both phone numbers.

"Righto, doll," Dale said, and hung up.

I filled my gas tank and then headed for Napoleon Boulevard. We were still about five houses away when I spotted the dark outline of a man seated on Bert's doorstep.

My stomach knotted up, and I immediately slowed down.

"Who's that?" Bert asked, her voice suddenly shrill.

Still too far away to make him out, I started doing a rapid review of who this could possibly be. Trent. Jake. Glenn. Goetzmann. One of the Clod Brothers. And, oh, yes, Mr. Deranged Killer.

The dark figure had evidently recognized my car, and was now standing up, waving. I peered at him. Do deranged killers usually wave?

Surely not. I could feel myself relax. This was probably Trent again, back for a replay of last night's pizza party. Only this time, he'd probably want to go solo with Bert. Strike while the passion was hot, so to speak.

I speeded up a little, giving Bert a quick glance.

I was pretty sure she was thinking what I was thinking, because she had actually started to smile.

I smiled, too. It looked to me as if Bert really could be smitten with this detective guy. More power to her.

I was almost up to my driveway, and Bert and I could easily make out the waving figure now.

It was Jake.

Next to him on the stoop were several large white bags. With small white cartons in them, their wire handles sticking out. Well, well, well. It looked like Jake had decided to follow Trent's lead, and he intended to trump Trent's pizza with Chinese.

As soon as Bert and I got out of the car, Jake walked over to us, his eyes glued to Bert's face. Jake was wearing what must be a uniform for him these days—skintight jeans, boots, plaid shirt, with exactly three buttons left open down the front, cowboy hat, and a denim jacket. At least, he'd gotten rid of the chicken part in his ear. He'd replaced it with a discreet diamond stud.

Jake approached Bert almost sheepishly. If he'd been carrying his cowboy hat, instead of wearing it, I think he would have been twirling it in his hands nervously, like Gary Cooper asking the rancher's daughter for a date. As it was, Jake had one hand behind his back.

"Howsitgoing, Nan?" he tossed at me, but his eyes were still on his ex-wife. I was beginning to feel foolish for ever entertaining the idea for even a split second that Jake could've been hitting on me. Obviously, he was still crazy about Bert.

"Howyadoing, Bert?" Jake asked, moving closer to her. "I've brought dinner? I thought the three of us might spend some time together?"

Lord, everything he said was a question. I didn't know about Bert, but I know I preferred the old cocky Jake to this new wimpy one.

"I guess I might have been a little out of line last night?" Jake said. "I'm sorry? I don't know what got into me?"

Bert tried to look angry at him, but I could tell she was weakening. I, of course, was ready to start opening little cartons. The aromas emanating from the white bags sitting on Bert's doorstep were making my stomach rumble.

Jake took the hand he'd been hiding out from behind his back, and—with a big grin—presented Bert with a bouquet of brightly colored mums.

A wilted bouquet of brightly colored mums.

Good grief, how long had he been waiting on Bert's doorstep?

Bert stared first at the drooping flowers and then back up at Jake. Finally, she broke into a wide grin much like Jake's own. "That would be great, Jake," she said, taking the flowers. "Come on in."

Jake picked up all the white bags, flashed me a triumphant little smile, and followed Bert inside.

Unfortunately, Jake reverted to type as soon as his feet touched the living room carpet inside Bert's apartment. I guess he could keep up the wimpy nice guy facade for only so long. "So where have you two been?" he asked. There was a sharp little something in his tone.

Bert stiffened, and I gave Jake a warning look. "I guess that came out wrong," he said quickly. "Sorry. What I mean is, I was worried about you two. What with the murder of that guy and all you've been through lately. You know, having to deal with the police and that private investigator."

He said *private investigator* just like you might say *venomous snake*.

"Not even mentioning the break-ins," Jake added. "I mean, you've been through a lot."

Oh, yeah, I thought. Bert's dealings with Trent had been

a real hardship. Kissing someone that attractive can really wear you down.

Actually, Jake here didn't know the half of it—we hadn't even told him about being shot at. Or about Alice Moorman being killed. If he knew about all this, Jake probably wouldn't have prowled around in the bushes last night. He'd have slept in them.

"We're just fine, Jake," Bert said, an exaggeration if I'd ever heard one. She headed into the kitchen, put the mums in a crystal vase, filled it with water, and immediately reappeared to place the pitiful bouquet in the middle of her mantel. It was a nice gesture, but if those particular flowers ever perked up, I'd eat them.

In my present condition, it was a distinct possibility, regardless. My stomach continued to rumble. Was it possible we hadn't eaten all day?

Bert returned to the kitchen, and began getting out paper plates and cups. I followed her, getting out plastic forks and knives. When Bert was married, she would never have served meals on anything but china, but in the past year she's become a great believer in throwaway dinnerware.

On the other hand, Jake apparently was a great believer in the saying, 'He also serves who only stands and waits.' While Bert and I were setting the table and opening containers of Chinese food, Jake crossed his arms over his chest and waited. "Considering everything that's been happening, I think it's only natural that I would wonder where you've been," he said.

It was the same question he'd asked earlier, only in a nicer package.

Bert looked over and motioned Jake to take a chair. "Nan and I were out," she told him, smiling sweetly.

Jake looked taken aback, but clearly he was going to avoid a fight at all costs. "It *is* none of my business. You can do what you want, of course. I was just concerned, that's all."

Bert gave him another sweet smile, and sat down opposite him. "That's so nice of you, Jake."

I took the chair at the other end of the table, and opened the two-liter Coke I'd carried in from the kitchen. Pouring it into my paper cup, filled with ice, I took a long sip.

"I mean, I can't help you if I don't know what's going on," Jake went on. I believe he was giving Bert an intense, concerned look, but I wasn't watching him. I was busy opening the nearest carton, and helping myself to as much Moo Goo Gai Pan as I could without looking as if I wasn't willing to share.

Bert gave Jake another smile, as she helped herself to Kung Pao Chicken. "Well, if you weren't sneaking around my shrubbery," she said sweetly, pointing at him with a plastic fork, "and flying off the handle at the least little thing, maybe I would feel more inclined to tell you things."

Jake made an little exasperated sound in the back of his throat. For a moment I thought he'd lost it. But, no, this New-and-Improved Jake had evidently developed self-control overnight. He caught himself just in time and took a long breath. "So why don't you tell me now," he said quietly.

While I finished off my Moo Goo Gai Pan, and started on an egg roll dripping in hot and sour sauce, I couldn't help but notice that Bert was creatively editing the story she told Jake. She told him about poor Alice Moorman, our little trip to the library, our visit with Wilma, and how all that had been happening seemed to be connected to the Sandersen double murder so long ago.

Oddly enough, Bert omitted the part about our being shot

at, and the part about her playing Florence Nightingale to Trent, *sans* shirt. I was sure she did this little editing job just to keep Jake from being overly concerned.

About which particular thing, however, I wasn't exactly sure.

I could understand why Bert might not want to give him a play by play of her stint at nursing. I was a little surprised, however, when she didn't tell him about the gunshot.

Until I thought about it for a moment.

Maybe Bert was leaving it out because she just didn't want Jake to worry about us. Or maybe she just didn't want to see the look on Jake's face. I mean, she might say the word *gunshot*, and he might immediately get a look on his face that said, *Been there. Done that.*

"So," Bert finished, "we have a double murder that happened years ago, two murders that just happened, weirdoes calling us and maybe following us, and our apartments trashed. And we don't know what any of it means."

I nodded. That was basically all I could do, because my mouth was full of fried rice.

"Well, I'll tell you what it means," Jake said. He reached over to take Bert's hand. "It means you ought to let the police handle it. That's what it means. Surely you two don't think you can solve this thing on your own, do you?"

That remark wouldn't have been so bad, had Jake not added a little chuckle at the end. Apparently, just to show how very silly Bert and I were being.

I was in the middle of heaping Kung Pao Chicken on my paper plate, but I glanced over at Bert. Oh yeah, she hadn't taken that well.

Bert was pulling her hand away from Jake's. "Don't start."

"Really, Jake," I put in, "you've already seen just how

helpful the police have been. And it's not as if we're trying to catch a murderer here. We're just trying to figure out how we're involved."

As I was saying all this, I gave him a pointed look. What I was trying to tell him was that, if he had any intention of getting back into Bert's good graces, this was not the way to do it.

Jake must've gotten my message. He took a bite of his Moo Goo Gai Pan, swallowed, and then said, his voice soothing, "Bert, what I meant was, I can't stand for you two to be putting yourself in danger. The truth is, I really care."

I had a mouthful of Kung Pao Chicken, but I smiled to myself. Now if Jake could go straight into begging and pleading, he might actually have a chance. If nothing else, it would certainly do wonders for Bert's ego. And I was all for that.

Jake reached over and took Bert's hand again. It was a good sign that she let him this time. "Bert, I know I haven't been there for you for a long while," he said.

I noticed Jake failed to mention where he *had* been all that while. Which was probably just as well. I reached for more fried rice.

"But I really want to start making everything up to you," Jake said, his voice low and husky. "Let me help. Please."

This was getting good. I looked over at Bert. Her eyes were glued to Jake's. "I don't know, Jake," she said. But she didn't pull her hand away.

What do you know, she'd been saying all these terrible things about him, but I was pretty sure Bert still cared. After all, Jake was the father of her children. And, I guess, nineteen years of marriage was a tough habit to break.

I took a breath. I, of course, wouldn't know.

"Bert," Jake said. His voice sounded so odd, I looked over at him. The man's eyes actually looked a little moist.

Uh oh. It looked like I was making a crowd again. I knew I really ought to leave these two lovebirds alone, but I didn't relish standing out in the kitchen, knowing everything out here was getting cold. I know it sounds selfish, but let's remember, I hadn't had anything to eat all day.

Reaching for the little white containers, I started filling my plate as fast as I could.

Jake was now leaning across the table, his eyes intense, as he held Bert's hand. "I've really missed you." Unbelievably, his eyes darted to me and then back to Bert again. "I never realized before just how gorgeous you are."

I was now practically a blur, trying to get out of there. I grabbed two more eggrolls, a couple of packets of soy sauce, and I started looking for the fortune cookies.

"Bert," Jake was now saying, "I've thought about it, and I know there's no reason why you'd want to marry me again. Not after the way I've acted."

My head jerked up at that one. Oh, for God's sake. Was he proposing? Right in front of me?

Where the hell were those fortune cookies?

Chapter 13

•

BERT

I stared at Jake, my heart pounding. I could not believe what was coming out of the man's mouth. If I didn't know better, I'd say it actually sounded as if Jake were proposing. Right in front of Nan.

Of course, I don't know why this would surprise me. This *was* the man who liked to pop the question in front of an audience.

Speaking of which, Nan was now scooting back her chair. "Well," she said brightly, "I think I'll just go get me a little more Coke. Out in the kitchen."

She was gone before either Jake or I could say a word. I did notice that for a woman who only wanted more Coke, Nan had taken two heaping plates of food with her.

Jake squeezed my hand. "Bert, I want you to know that I understand how you feel."

I turned to look at him. His dark, good looks really hadn't faded over the years. He still reminded me of that tall, cocky boy I'd been so crazy about in high school. That boy had been such fun, always ready to go to new places, to try new things. It had been Jake who'd talked me into riding the old rickety wooden roller coaster at Fontaine Ferry Park. It had been

Jake who'd taken me horseback riding for the first time. Lord. He'd seemed so exciting.

Back when I was in the throes of divorce, I'd read that the quality that makes you marry a guy is often the very same quality that makes you divorce him. Now I think that could be right. Sitting there at my dining room table, I was looking at a cocky, middle-aged man who'd decided a little over a year ago to go new places and try new things. Bimbette's apartment had been a new place. And sleeping with other women had been a new thing.

Jake squeezed my hand again. "I also want you to know that I don't blame you for feeling that way."

I didn't even blink. That was big of him.

Jake hurried on. "But I've been thinking. Maybe we could start all over again. Start *seeing* each other again. Maybe even be close again."

I looked into his dark eyes. This was the man who had shared my bed for nineteen years. Sure, all those years hadn't been exactly bliss, but they did count for something, didn't they? He was the father of my children, the man I'd left my parents' home to make a life with. And Ellie and Brian adored him.

I'm not sure how it happened, but it seemed as if all of a sudden Jake was next to me. He pulled me to my feet, gave me a gentle smile, and kissed me. It was a kiss that held the familiarity of all the years we'd spent together. There was the same smell of soap and shampoo and English Leather, and the same intoxicating taste of his lips. And yet, there was something different, too. A tentativeness, a question that I'd never felt with Jake before.

It was like kissing a familiar stranger.

I moved closer, and Jake encircled me with his arms.

Of course, that was precisely when the telephone on the dining room wall started ringing.

And, shortly after *that*, was when Nan came rushing back into the living room. She seemed to be making a habit out of interrupting men kissing me.

"Oh," Nan said, coming to an abrupt halt when she spotted Jake and me with our arms around each other. "Were you going to answer that?" She pointed to the phone on the wall. "Because, uh, I'm waiting for a phone call." Nan didn't wait for me to answer her, but went over and snatched up the receiver. "Hello?" she asked, turning her back to us, like maybe by doing that, she'd be giving us back our privacy. "Dale? Yeah, it's me."

It was the news guy Nan had phoned from the gas station, asking about the Sandersen murders. As Jake and I stood there, pretty much just staring at her, Nan stopped talking and listened for a moment. "Oh," she said. There was another longer pause. "You're absolutely sure?" Nan's shoulders seemed to droop a little. "OK. All right. Thanks for the info. Bye."

I know I was supposed to be pretty absorbed in Jake and the magic of the moment and all, but I couldn't help myself. I pulled away from him, and asked, "What did Dale say?"

I could already tell from the look on Nan's face when she turned around that it wasn't good news. "Les Tennyson was never apprehended," she said. "The Sandersen murders are still open. Unsolved."

My stomach twisted into a knot.

"Oh my God, maybe it really *is* Les Tennyson out there," I said. Nan looked as alarmed as I felt. "And he's killing anybody he thinks can identify him."

Now it was Jake's turn to look alarmed. He looked first at me and then over at Nan. "Would either one of you be able to identify him if you saw him again?"

"Not me," Nan said. "I don't even know if we ever really did get a good look at the guy. I mean, I don't think Mrs. Sandersen would've exactly been parading her lover in front of her baby-sitters. It seems to me that she would've been keeping him pretty secret."

"I think he might've come by the house once when we were there," I said, "but I'm not even sure about that."

"So, if you can't identify him, then you two are in the clear," Jake said.

"If he knows we can't identify him," Nan said.

That did seem to be the crux of the matter.

Beside me, Jake took a deep breath. "God, Bert," he said, turning back to me, "I don't know what I'd do if anything happened to you."

Apparently, that was Nan's cue to bolt for the kitchen again. All at once, Jake and I were alone again.

"It's taken me a year to realize what I've lost," Jake said. "I think maybe I really *was* going through a midlife crisis, just like you said."

I looked at the earring in his ear, the ponytail, and the Tex Ritter getup. And he said, *maybe?* Wisely, I managed somehow to keep my mouth shut.

"Now I know," Jake said, pulling me closer. "Bert, I keep thinking about you and how exciting you were in bed. How wonderful it was to be close. Now I realize I never have to look anywhere else. I can find all the excitement I ever wanted right here."

"Jake, I don't know." That was the truth. Was I supposed to just forget that he'd dumped me for Bimbette? Was I supposed to just forget that he might only be here now because Bimbette dumped *him?*

Thank God the phone rang again. This time I turned and ran for it. "Hello?"

"Mom?"

I blinked, at the sound of the familiar voice. These days, this particular voice always sounds to me exactly like a nineteen-year-old Nan. But then again, why shouldn't it? I guess she's half-Nan if she's half-me.

"Ellie?"

I noticed when I said the name, Jake's head sort of jerked in my direction.

"Yeah, Mom, it's me," Ellie said. "I, um, just thought I'd call, and—you know—see how you're doing."

I blinked again at that one. I would've liked to have been touched by my daughter's sudden concern for my welfare, but I couldn't help being a little suspicious. Ellie had phoned only twice since the semester started, and both times she'd wanted something. The first time it had been twenty dollars to tide her over until she got paid from her part-time job. The second time she'd wanted to borrow my car for the weekend. I'd sent her the twenty dollars. The car had been another story.

"So, Mom," Ellie was now saying, "how's it going? Is everything all right with you?"

"Sure," I said immediately. "Everything's great." If, of course, you didn't count having my apartment trashed and my life in jeopardy. Across the room Jake shifted his weight from one boot to the other. I decided to cut to the chase. "Ellie," I said, "is everything OK with you? Is there something you need me to—?"

Ellie interrupted me with a laugh. "No, Mom, really, everything's fine." She paused for a moment, and then, her tone deliberately casual, she said, "I, um, I was just wondering if you'd seen Dad lately."

I turned slowly to look over at Jake again. He was now leaning against the wall across the room, hands in his pockets, the picture of nonchalance. And yet, he didn't quite meet my eyes.

It didn't take Hercule Poirot to figure this one out. Obviously, Jake had put Ellie up to calling me about him.

"Why, yes, Ellie," I said evenly, "I have seen your Dad. As a matter of fact, he's standing right here. Did you want to talk to him?"

"Oh." That's all Ellie said for a moment. And then, in a sudden rush of words, she added, "Um, no. No, I don't need to talk to him. I, um, was supposed to call you earlier, but, good grief, Mom, I had a date, you know. Um, tell Dad I'm sorry, OK? I meant to, I really did. And, Mom? Just listen to what Dad has to say, OK? I—I'll call you later."

As I hung up the phone, I didn't know whether I should be angry at Jake or not. After all, if Jake were soliciting testimonials from the kids, then it could possibly mean that he was actually serious about our getting back together.

Either that, or Jake was just playing his strongest card.

"Jake," I began, "I really wish you hadn't called Ellie—"

"Ellie?" Jake said, interrupting me. He actually feigned surprise. "Why, what are you talking about? I didn't call Ellie," Jake said, crossing his arms over his chest.

I ignored him, and went right on. "—because this is just between you and me—"

The phone interrupted me still again.

"So help me, Jake, if this is Brian . . ." I began, reaching for the receiver.

But it wasn't our son.

When I heard the voice on the other end, I could feel the blush start at my toes and rush upwards.

"Hey, Bert," Trent drawled. "It's me. I just wanted to check in with you and make sure everything is O.K."

"Oh. Well." I said. I tried to make my voice sound perfectly normal, but what came out sounded like a squawk.

Hearing me sound like a chicken apparently alerted Jake. He moved to stand right in front of me, so that I couldn't miss his questioning stare.

I looked away. "Everything's just fine," I told Trent brightly. "We're just fine. Nan's just fine. And I'm just . . . uh, you know . . . fine." Lord. I sounded deranged.

Trent gave a soft laugh. "Well, that's good to hear. I take it, you've got all your doors and windows locked?"

"Check," I said. Jake was moving even closer, obviously trying to listen in.

Trent laughed again. "And, I take it, you're staying inside?"

"Check," I said. I know. I know. Nan and I had not exactly stayed home all day, but technically, we were staying inside right now. Besides, right that minute, with Jake's eyes on mine, I couldn't think of a single reason why I should spend time telling Trent all about our trip to the library or to Wilma's.

"Well, I've been running down some leads on my own," Trent said. "I'll fill you in the next time I see you." His voice changed then, lower and more serious. "I *would* like to see you soon."

My cheeks had to resemble tomatoes by now. I was so rattled, I spoke without thinking. "Sure, Trent, that would be nice," I said.

Next to me, Jake stiffened.

"Because, you know," Trent went on, "there's something I can't get out of my mind."

"What's that?"

Trent's answer was raw and husky. "The way you kissed me."

I blinked.

"I'll call you again soon."

The dial tone sounded in my ear.

Ohmigoodness.

I hung up the phone and tried to get my breathing back to normal before I turned back toward Jake.

Jake was wearing a familiar expression. It was his "you've-got-some-'splaining-to-do, Lucy" face. "I'd just like to know one thing," he said, his words clipped, "I'd just like to know what this guy Trent means to you."

I looked at him. I'd like to know that, too. The truth was I didn't know myself. Was the feeling I got around Trent the beginning of something serious? Or did I feel so wonderful around him because his attention was such an ego boost? Particularly after my ego had been trampled so badly by the man now standing directly in front of me?

I shook my head. "I—I don't know, Jake."

"You don't know? What do you mean, you don't know?" Jake reached out and pulled me into his arms. "You do know me, Bert. You've known me for years."

Did I? Did I really know Jake? I certainly would never have thought that he was capable of throwing away a nineteen-year marriage for a twenty-year-old child. My head was spinning.

And yet, how well did I know Trent Marksberry?

Jake's arms tightened around me. "And I know you, too, Bert. I know you so well, I know you're scared about everything's that been happening. And I know you need somebody with you."

Jake's arms felt strong and comforting. I guess maybe he did know me. I *was* scared. I was also lonely. I leaned my head against his shoulder, feeling the familiar warmth of him. He kissed the top of my head.

"You know, after all these years," Jake said, against my hair, "I understand about you and Nan, too. About how special being a twin is. I understand how important she is to you. Because she's important to me, too," Jake said. "I've always cared a great deal for her. I want the three of us to be close."

I snuggled nearer to him. It was true. Jake had always made a special effort to include Nan. He had never been a Possessive Pete. Maybe, now that he'd gotten straying out of his system, he was ready to make a real commitment.

Jake tipped my face to his and kissed me. For a very long time. Then he put his lips to my ear. "Let me stay tonight, Bert," he whispered. "I've got all I'll ever need right here. And we could try something new—"

Of course, that was when Nan made her appearance again. The woman must have some kind of kissing radar.

"Oops," she said, staring at me and Jake with our arms around each other. Again. "Sorry, sorry," Nan said, looking flustered. "But I just couldn't stay in that kitchen any longer. You two just go right ahead with what you're doing, though. I'm going to get my coat and head on home. I know three's a crowd."

Nan started to go right by us, but Jake grabbed her hand, pulling her over toward us. "Oh, no, it isn't," he said. He put his arm around Nan's shoulder and pulled her even closer. "Bert and I were just talking about my spending the night."

Nan looked over at me. "Yeah?" she said. She glanced over at me.

I wasn't sure why Jake was making an announcement, but hey, he did like an audience. Maybe he wanted to make sure everything was OK with Nan.

"So how about it?" Jake said.

His eyes, however, were now on Nan.

"What do you girls think?" Jake said, tightening his arms around both of us. "It'll be a trip, huh?"

I just looked at him, a cold kernel just starting to form in the pit of my stomach. Surely, the man wasn't suggesting what it sounded as if he were suggesting.

Nan pulled away. "Run that by me again?" she said.

Jake actually grinned, looking a lot like the cat who'd caught the you-know-what. "Do I have to spell it out? You know what a ménage à trois means, don't you? So what do you say, why don't we give it a try?"

I blinked.

Jake had finally come up with the ultimate stupid question.

Nan's mouth dropped open. I wasn't sure what mine was doing.

Jake threw his head back and laughed. "It's all right, Nan. I know it's what you want, too. I mean, let's face it, you didn't exactly pull away when I kissed you the other night."

Now my mouth dropped open, too. *He kissed her? Jake kissed Nan?*

Nan immediately turned to me. "Bert, it was a peck. Like a brother."

I didn't doubt it for a minute.

Jake was undaunted. There was a cold wind blowing

through the room, and he didn't even feel it. "Come on, Nan." He reached for Nan's arm again. "It'll be so great. Like a game for grownups."

I think I was in shock. Staring at Jake, my mind started running through all the things he'd just said to me. How exciting I'd been in bed—when we were *close*. How he knew I wouldn't want to marry him again. But that maybe we could be *close* again. How *all* Jake ever needed was right here. I'd thought he was just talking about me, but Nan had been here, too. Of course.

What an idiot I was.

And now Jake wanted the three of us to be *close*.

It wasn't as if this was the first time Nan and I had gotten this kind of invitation. In college, we'd certainly gotten this little proposal more than once. It was never from anybody we knew very well, though. It had always been some guy we'd just met. Some guy eager to act out his Playboy fantasy about making it with twins.

Back then Nan and I had agreed that the biggest turn off in the world would be watching the other one in bed. And I personally couldn't think of anything more inhibiting than having Nan watch me making love.

What's more, I didn't even particularly want to see *myself* doing some of the things I'd done with Jake in the privacy of our bedroom. Let alone have Nan see me do them. I mean, Nan and I shared a lot of things. This, however, would never be one of them.

Call me a Possessive Pete, but I've always thought of lovemaking as just involving me and a man I cared deeply about.

Apparently, Jake, however, was still that cocky kid I'd known in high school, even after all these years. He still wanted to try something new and different. The years hadn't made much difference to him—he still hadn't matured. Lord. If anything, he'd gone in the opposite direction. He'd immatured.

And he'd actually had the gall to get our daughter to call me so that I'd hear him out.

I took a deep breath. I didn't even feel hurt any more. Maybe that would come later. What I did feel, however, was anger.

"Come on, you all," Jake was saying. "You know you've fantasized about you two doing it with just one guy."

Nan met my eyes. Then she moved closer to Jake. "You're right, hon," she said, her voice as husky as I've ever heard it over the radio. "We've talked about it, haven't we, Bert?"

I made myself smile at Jake. "That's right," I said.

Nan now linked her arm through Jake's. He was grinning now. "We've fantasized about going to bed with just one guy, all right." She leaned closer to Jake so that her lips were right next to his ear. "But, Jake? That guy was Richard Gere."

Jake's grin vanished, as Nan moved to stand beside me.

"Get out of here," I said. I didn't even think before I said the rest of it. "Get out, you fucking ASSHOLE!"

Chapter 14

•

NAN

Having done it once, Bert apparently enjoyed it so much that she wanted to repeat the entire obscenity experience.

"YOU FUCKING ASSHOLE!"

I couldn't have said it better myself.

Now, wouldn't you think, if you had two women looking at you as if you were scum, you would just cut your losses and leave?

Not Jake. He actually stood there and looked offended.

"There's no need for that kind of language," he said to Bert. He sounded as if what Bert had just said was far more indecent than the proposition he'd just made to us. "A simple no would have been sufficient. I mean, we're all adults here."

Bert shook her head. "No, Jake. Nan and I are adults. You are an idiot. Now, I believe I told you to get out of here."

Looking at Bert's face, I would've immediately obeyed. Jake, though, didn't budge. "Now, come on, Bert," he said, "I was just making a suggestion, that's all. If you're not into that scene, then so be it. But surely you're not going to hold it against—"

Bert didn't let him finish. She walked over, grabbed Jake's ponytail, and dragged him to the front door. You could tell it flashed through Jake's mind that he could definitely get away from Bert—the man *was* a lot bigger than she was. But apparently he drew the line at fighting with a woman. Particularly in front of a witness.

"Bert, come on now . . ." Jake started to say again, but Bert opened the door and shoved him through it.

I may have been wrong, but it seemed to me that Bert took a great deal of pleasure out of slamming the door right in Jake's simpering face.

As soon as the door was closed, though, it was a different story. "Oh, God," Bert said, and she covered her face with her hands. I went over and put my arms around her.

Bert cried for about one minute tops, and then she pulled away, wiping her eyes. "I can't *believe* I had two children with that man," she said. "I just can't believe it!" She looked like she should be wringing her hands any second now. Instead, she started pacing. Up and down, up and down.

"Look on the bright side," I said, as she went past me. "At least you've got two great kids."

Bert stopped dead in her tracks and looked at me. "I can't believe," she said, "that I married a guy who would come on to my sister and me at the same time!" She was pacing again. Up and down, up and down.

"Look on the bright side," I said. "At least you've been married."

Bert stopped and gave me another look. "I can't believe I was actually considering letting that jerk back into my life!" Oh, yeah, she was back to the pacing. Up and down, up and down.

"Look on the bright side," I said. "You didn't let him back in your life."

I was trying to cheer Bert up, for God's sake, but evidently, she was not listening. Abruptly, she turned to me, hands on her hips. "Look, Nan," she said. She actually sounded angry with *me*. "No wonder you don't think this is all that awful. And you can keep right on happily looking on the bright side. Your life is perfect. I mean, you've never been tied down, you get to date all the time, and you can come and go as you please. You've always had only yourself to spend your money on, and you've gotten to travel to some pretty wonderful places, like Hawaii and Europe. And you've got a great job. You can't get any more perfect than that."

I almost choked. "Perfect? Let me tell you about perfect." I brushed my hair away from my face, and plunged in. "Bert, do you know what dating is like right now? There's tons of men out there pretending they're something they're not—like unmarried, for example. Or telling you they'll love you forever just to get in your panties. Then once they've had the nickel tour, it's *So long, Sally.* And I'm not even mentioning AIDS and all that really scary crap."

Bert blinked. "Gee, thanks, Nan, I'm going to be dating now, and you've certainly cheered me up."

She was beginning to get on my nerves.

"I don't think I need reminding," Bert went on, "that while I've been at home, being faithful to a jerk, you've dated lots of men—"

"Wait a minute—" I said, holding up my hand. I knew what she really meant by *dated*. Bert was making it sound as if I had gone to bed with—if not the entire US Army—at least a small platoon.

Bert ignored me, starting to pace again. "—but it's not just that," she said, cutting me off. "It's everything." Bert swiveled around to face me. "I mean, just look: You own your own home—"

"You mean, me and the bank."

"You've got no responsibilities except to yourself—"

"Which some people might call self-centered and lonely," I said.

"You've got a really and truly fascinating job—"

"Which may or may not last until retirement."

Bert shrugged. "You've got everything."

I really thought I must be hearing her wrong. Were we really this far apart in the way we looked at each other's lives? Whatever had happened to those twin vibes we'd always thought we had?

"Bert, honey, listen to me. There is a real important difference between us. I don't have any children." I tried for a light tone, but wouldn't you know it, my voice cracked a little with emotion. "It could be that I won't ever have them. Now, if I'm calculating this correctly, if I don't have kids, it's going to be very hard for me to have grandchildren. Something that *you* will probably get to do."

Bert stopped and just stood there, looking at me.

While I had her attention, I hurried on. "You may not have noticed, but I have never had anybody love me enough to marry me. You have, and maybe it didn't turn out so well, but you can always say you have had that kind of love."

Bert shrugged. "Like it means so much."

"It does. It means you're capable of that kind of commitment. I don't know for sure if I am. More important, I don't even know if I'm capable of being faithful to somebody. To be absolutely honest, the idea of staying true to one guy for the rest of my life scares me to death. I just may not be able to do it."

Bert blinked. Then she said, "Well, you've got a great job."

I stared back at her. *This* was all she could come up with?

I bare my soul, for God's sake, and I don't hear all about how I'm going to be able to love someone. Or how that someone will truly love me someday. No, apparently, Bert bought everything I'd just said, no questions asked. Evidently, everything I'd just told her was true, but, don't worry about it, I've still got this great *job?*

If I didn't watch it, cheering Bert up was going to depress the hell out of me.

"OK, Bert," I said. I went over and started clearing the dining room table, picking up empty white cartons and soiled paper plates. "I admit I do like my job. But let's be realistic here. Radio is male-dominated, and a youth market. Meaning that the older I get, the more likely it is that some young guy is going to come along and knock me out on the street." Bert followed my example, and started clearing her dining room table, too. "At the very least," I added, "one day I'm going to have to start calling myself Granny Nan on the air."

I took a deep breath, and looked Bert straight in the eye. "Think about it, Bert. You're the one who has it all."

Bert has got to be the stubbornest woman in the world. I don't know where she gets it. "Nan, you listen to me," she said. She was in the middle of collecting paper cups and napkins, but she stopped and pointed a cup at me. "I was married for nineteen very, very long years. I had two children with one particular guy—to whom, as it turns out, I was foolishly faithful. I followed all the rules—I didn't let myself go after marriage, I kept the house *and* the kids spotless, and I never, *ever* told Jake I had a headache."

I stared at her. And she called *that* a marriage? Good Lord. Then, tonight might've been the first time Bert had ever turned Jake down? No wonder he'd looked so stunned.

Bert was hurrying on. "And what do you know, it turns

out there was still no guarantee that I wouldn't wake up one day to find out that my husband was leaving me. Or that he was a first-class jerk. A thing which, I do believe, we both just found out."

What could I say? She had a point. I turned back to the table, and started gathering things up to put in the trash.

"As far as a job goes," Bert went on, "I've spent my entire adult life being the Happy Homemaker. I'm not trained to do anything else. The only thing I do well is cook and do laundry." She glanced over at me. "I'm sure you'll tell me that there's a great career in there somewhere."

I nodded, trying to look supportive.

Bert frowned. She was stacking garbage, too. "Finally," she said, "while it's true I've got two wonderful children, where exactly are Ellie and Brian right this very minute? When she's not doing telephone solicitations for her father, Ellie is not here. And Brian is certainly not here. They are both off living their own lives, and that's how it should be."

Uh oh. Bert's eyes were filling with tears again. "And what am I going to be if I'm not a wife and a mother?"

I blinked. When you came right down to it, that was the same question I'd been asking myself.

"The bottom line is that I'm still alone." Bert went on. Her voice broke.

I reached over, picked up a clean paper napkin off the table, and handed it to her. "No, Bert," I said, "you're not."

Bert took the napkin, swiped at her tears, and finally smiled a little. "You're not, either," she said.

I grinned at her. "So maybe you and I are luckier than most?"

Bert's smile widened a little, and she nodded, still swiping at her tears.

OK. OK. I figured it was time to stop all this sappy talk. And get to something really important. "Bert?" I said. "How about some cocoa?"

Bert's smile got even wider. Cocoa has always been our treat. Whenever we got upset about something, we reached for the Hershey's. It was the surefire all-round cure for whatever ailed us. Cocoa had been the cure for F's on report cards, the cat tearing up your pantyhose, and not being asked to the junior prom. "Sure," Bert said. "I'll fix us some."

We made a couple trips into the kitchen, throwing stuff away. "While you're making the cocoa," I said, "I think I'll go over to my place to check my answering machine, and get any messages." I slipped on my jacket. "I'll be right back."

I went out Bert's front door, and hurried across the lawn to my own. The night air was cool, and oddly calming, and I found myself taking deep breaths on the way.

In no time at all, I was going up my steps, unlocking my door, and flipping on the lights. I keep my answering machine on a small mahogany table next to my couch, and the minute I walked into my living room, I could see that the message light was blinking. I hurried across the room. And then, I heard it.

A soft click.

Was that my front door?

I started to turn toward the sound.

Then someone rushed up behind me.

Chapter 15

●

BERT

It was just like Nan to leave me sitting over here, watching her cocoa get cold. She was, no doubt, over at her apartment right now, blithely returning phone calls and totally forgetting about the time.

I took a sip of my own cocoa. It was hard to believe, but after talking to Nan, I was feeling a little better. Apparently, there's nothing like realizing that neither Nan's life nor my life was a bed of roses. What do you know? Sharing a little misery can really cheer you up.

I didn't even want to think about Jake. Could it be that he had always been a jerk, and I just hadn't noticed? Or had he really changed so much? All the talk shows say that men go through a midlife change, but this was a total metamorphosis. Only instead of becoming a butterfly, Jake had gone in reverse. He'd become a slug.

I determinedly pushed all thoughts of Jake out of my mind, and took another sip of cocoa. As I did, I glanced over at Nan's full cup. If she didn't get back soon, I was going to have to reheat this in the microwave.

I got to my feet. If Nan was going to talk forever, I'd just take her cup over to her.

I'm not sure why, but as soon as I left my apartment, carrying both cups, I started feeling uneasy. I know it sounds crazy, but there seemed to be something odd about the way Nan's front windows looked. They weren't dark or anything—in fact, her living room lights and her porch lights were all on. Her doorstep was bright and inviting in the cool autumn night. All around me, there were the familiar autumn smells—of leaves and wood fires—and I could hear the steady hum of traffic on Bardstown Road in the distance. Everything seemed normal, and yet, I found myself glancing around nervously as I closed my door, heard the lock snap into place, and turned toward Nan's.

Of course, the reason I was feeling so rattled was pretty easy to figure out. I do believe if you've ever had a bullet whiz by your head, it does change your perspective a little. The world suddenly becomes a very dangerous place. And right now I was all by myself. In the dark.

I quickened my steps, my eyes on Nan's front windows. They still looked strange to me. Sort of hollow and empty. How odd.

I started moving even faster. I would've broken into an outright run, but I would've spilled the cocoa. I wasn't about to show up on Nan's porch with chocolate stains all down my front. If I did, they would no doubt be able to hear Nan's laughter across the river in Indiana.

No, I wasn't going to let Nan know how suddenly afraid I was. Or how loud my heart was pounding by the time I reached her doorstep.

With a cup in each hand, I didn't even try to knock on Nan's door. Instead, I pushed her doorbell with my elbow.

I could hear the chimes inside.

But Nan didn't appear.

I swallowed, fighting that uneasy feeling again. Could she

be talking so loud on the phone, she didn't hear the doorbell?

I pushed the bell again.

Once again the chimes sounded, but Nan didn't appear.

It looked as if I were going to have to knock, after all. I set both cups down on the porch at my feet, and I rapped sharply on the door.

Still, no answer.

OK, the explanation was simple. Nan was probably in the bathroom, with the door shut and maybe the water running, and she just didn't hear me. Sure, that was it. Of course, if I really believed it, that didn't exactly explain why at that moment my heart was pounding so loud, it sounded like rushing waves in my ears.

I reached for the doorknob. It was unlocked. This was just like Nan. A killer is running around loose, and she leaves her front door unlocked.

I opened the door, and I stuck my head in.

"Nan?"

Once again, there was silence.

I moved inside, and took a quick look around. The living room was empty.

"NAN?" I called again.

I hurried down the hall to the half bath. The door was standing open. There was no one inside.

I suppose I sort of lost it then. I took off running, checking the entire downstairs, the kitchen, dining room, utility room, all the while yelling Nan's name.

Where could she be? I took the stairs two at a time, hurrying first into Nan's bedroom, then her bathroom, and finally down the stairs again, back into the living room. Where should I look next? I started to move toward the hall and the closet there, when my eyes fell on the answering machine.

My heart seemed to stand still. The little red message light was blinking on and off. I stared at it. Nan had the same answering machine as I did. If she'd already gotten her messages, the light would not be blinking.

So, what in God's name happened so fast, that Nan hadn't even had time to retrieve her phone messages?

And, oh dear God in heaven, where *was* she?

I tried to calm down. OK, OK, I told myself, don't jump to conclusions. Maybe all that's happened is that Nan ran out for something. Like, maybe, oh, I don't know, marshmallows for the cocoa—that could be it.

She could even be back over at my apartment even now, wondering where I was. And yet, hadn't I just seen her Neon in the driveway?

I moved quickly across the room, pulled back the semi-sheers and peered out. Nan's car was parked right next to mine in the double driveway we shared.

I took a deep breath. OK. OK. Her car being here really didn't mean anything. Maybe Nan had walked. There was a Quik Mart down the street. Maybe she'd walked there. Even as I tried to talk myself into it, I knew it didn't make a whole lot of sense. Nan? Walking several blocks in the middle of the night when she had a perfectly good car? Nan was the twin who'd always said that the only thing she ever wanted to exercise was her imagination.

Oh God.

On the other hand, maybe my imagination was getting the best of me. Maybe everything that had happened to us lately had pushed me over the edge. Maybe Nan really was—please God—waiting for me next door at my house.

She could be pulling a prank. If she was, I might kill her myself. I hurried out her front door, almost tripping over the cups of cocoa I'd left on Nan's doorstep. I kept right on running, though. I'd get them later.

"Hey, Nan? You here?" I yelled, as I unlocked my front door.

Silence. I walked through my entire apartment, quickly checking all the rooms just like I'd done at Nan's.

The apartment was empty.

I ended up back in my living room, turning in circles, trying not to cry.

Nan wasn't here. She wasn't anywhere.

Standing in the heavy stillness of my apartment, I felt a fear so overwhelming I thought I might faint. And I stopped lying to myself. Nan wouldn't have gone on any errand without telling me. She wouldn't be pulling a practical joke because she knew I was already spooked enough by everything that had been happening since I'd met Russell Moorman. She wouldn't have scared me this way.

I stood there, hugging my arms to my chest, my mind racing. What *should* I do now? What *could* I do?

Maybe I should call the police. But would they believe me? Or would Detective Goetzmann and the others just think Nan and I had cooked up another segment from Fantasy Land for the free publicity?

What if the cops refused to help me find Nan? What would I do then? Other than, of course, go absolutely screaming insane. My stomach knotted with fear. Where, oh God, where could Nan be?

I really didn't have a choice. I had to call the police. And I would make them believe me, so help me God. I reached for the phone.

The sudden shrill ring of the telephone made me jump.

I grabbed up the receiver. "Nan, honey? Is that you?"

"In a manner of speaking," a calm male voice said.

My mouth went so dry, I could hardly speak. "Who is this?"

The caller gave a little chuckle. "A friend of your sister's." His tone was mocking. "Yep, I'd say she and I are real close." He chuckled again.

Oh my god. Oh my god. Oh my GOD.

"Where *is* she?" I asked, fighting panic. "Is she all right? PLEASE. Please tell me where she is." My voice sounded strange even to my own ears.

"Now, don't you get all in an uproar. Your sis is right here. No reason to get all in a dither." The caller actually sounded as if I were being unreasonable. "You just do as I say and no one will get hurt."

I thought of Russell Moorman and his wife Alice. Had whoever this was, said the same thing to them? Had they believed him, and now they were dead?

I swallowed past the lump in my throat, and tried my best to keep my voice from shaking. "Please, whoever you are, please let Nan go. She doesn't know anything about anything. Neither do I. This is a mistake. You've got to understand, we don't know anything."

There was a short silence. "This ain't no mistake. It's you that don't understand," the caller said. There was another little chuckle. "If you ever want to see your sister again, you better do just like I say."

"What do you mean?"

"I mean, I want you to do me a little favor," the caller said. His voice had changed. It was now a steady monotone. "I want you to meet a man. On the Belvedere, in front of the fountains, at ten o'clock tonight."

The Belvedere is a sort of huge patio, located in downtown

Louisville, overlooking the Ohio River. Outfitted in the summer with umbrellas, tables and benches, and in the winter with a huge ice-skating rink, the Belvedere is usually teeming with people during the day. At ten o'clock on a Sunday night, though, the place would be practically deserted.

Just the sort of place I wanted to walk around alone.

"And then what?" I asked. I couldn't keep my voice from shaking.

The caller went on in the same steady monotone, "The man you will meet will give you a package. You will take the package back to your apartment, but you will not open it."

I gripped the phone a little tighter. Wait a minute. It sounded as if the caller were now reading from notes. Why on earth would he read to me? My guess was that either he had the brains of a chicken, or he wanted to make sure he didn't forget anything.

Either way, I felt a little better. It didn't look as if I was dealing with somebody who did this kind of thing all the time. Maybe he'd make a mistake.

"You will hold onto the package, and then you will wait for another phone call," the caller continued.

I wondered if he was following each word with an index finger. I took a deep breath. "Some man's going to give me a package? But how will I know this man?"

There was that little chuckle again, as if he enjoyed the sound of fear in my voice. "Don't you worry. You don't need to know him. He'll know you. And don't you even think of calling the cops. Because I'll know. And if I smell cops, anywhere around, I guaran-damn-tee you won't never see your sister again." And then—can you believe it?—he actually chuckled again.

I think it was all those chuckles that finally did it. This

creep was having a great time, laughing at me. He was laughing at Nan, too—laughing at both of us.

The way I looked at it, he was having way too much fun. Especially for a dimwit who actually had to read his threats from crib notes. What kind of kidnapper was he, anyway? It might just be that the creep was as inexperienced at this kidnapping thing as I was. So he was just playing a part. Maybe those little chuckles of his were just his way of showing what a high old time he was having, threatening women and playing Dirty Harry. This was making his day.

In the split second that followed that chuckle, all the crap that had happened to me and Nan since I'd made the mistake of talking to a stranger flashed through my mind.

Enough, already.

To use one of Nan's favorite expressions, I was *pissed*. That could possibly explain why I blurted, "Look, buster, I'm not going anywhere to get anything unless I talk to Nan."

"What—what?" he stammered. For the first time, the creep seemed to be at a loss. Apparently, what I'd just said hadn't been in his notes.

"You heard me. You put Nan on the phone right this minute, or you can get your own package."

"But—but—"

"No buts," I snapped. "Put Nan on the phone. NOW!"

"But I just tied her up in the chair," he said, his voice now a petulant whine.

I actually shivered. Tied up? Oh my God, what was he doing to her?

"Put Nan on the damn phone this minute!"

The creep sounded a little bewildered. "But the cord on the phone won't reach all the way over where she is. And I ain't gonna untie her. She's a spitfire."

I couldn't help smiling. Didn't I know it?

"Then get your package yourself," I said. I hoped I didn't sound as frightened as I felt.

"Oh, all right," Creep snapped. I heard him slam the phone down, and, in the background, the sound of a chair being scooted across the floor. Then I heard a series of grunts, as Creep apparently lifted the chair Nan was in and moved it bodily closer and closer to the phone.

From the sound, I guessed the chair couldn't scoot any more. Maybe it was now on carpeting?

"Damn!" Creep muttered. And then, "I'm taking off your gag, and you better not scream."

I felt tears spring to my eyes. This awful person had actually tied up Nan and *gagged* her.

"Now, you talk to your sister," I could hear Creep saying to Nan. "You tell her—" He coughed and went on. "—to do as I say." He sounded a little winded from carrying Nan to the phone. "Or—or—" Here he paused for breath. "—else."

This guy was going to have work on his threats. Wheezing and coughing just didn't get it.

Then Nan was on the phone. "Bert?"

"Nan!" I didn't want her to know how scared I was, so I tried to sound calm. "You OK? He hasn't hurt you, has he?"

"I'm OK," she said, "but there's *no-tell* in' what he's going to do." Nan was talking so fast, her words almost ran together. "You'd better do like he says, or—"

The phone was snatched out of her hand. "You satisfied now? Be on the Belvedere at ten," Creep snapped. "And get that package." There was a moment of silence, and I thought he was hanging up when he came back on the line. "And remember, no cops." The dial tone sounded in my ear.

I stared at the receiver. What was it that Nan had said?

There's *no-tell*in' what he's going to do. No-tellin'. She'd put extra emphasis on those two words.

I was afraid to hope. But it seemed to me that I had a pretty good idea where Nan was. And if she was indeed there, I even had a pretty good guess who was holding her.

I turned toward the door, and then stopped, looking back at the phone. Should I call the police? But I'd be risking Nan's life. And it might take forever to convince them what I was saying was true.

I'd never see Nan again. That's what Creep had said. And, just because he might need crib notes, didn't necessarily mean he wasn't dangerous.

I looked at my watch. It was seven minutes after eight. Almost two hours before I was supposed to meet some stranger on the Belvedere and pick up a package. If everything turned out right, maybe I'd still have time to call the cops after I made sure Nan was safe.

I grabbed my purse and my car keys, and I ran out the door.

Chapter 16
●
NAN

I really hated this.

Being tied up was not a bit of fun. It was certainly not what some of my ex-boyfriends have tried to tell me it was. But, then again, the experience could possibly lose a little something when you're fully dressed.

I glared at the twerp who'd done this to me. I would've loved to have shouted every obscenity I knew at him, but it was a little tough with a gag in my mouth. Of course, I'd seen this twerp before. He was, without a doubt, the guy I'd thought I'd spotted following me back to the radio station on Friday.

For a kidnapper, he was pretty innocuous-looking. Late twenties or early thirties, and shorter than me. Also balding, horn-rimmed glasses, beady little eyes, with a pretty good-sized paunch. Oh yeah, it was George from *Seinfeld*, all right. George with several more pounds and an endless appetite for junk food. My captor was, at the moment, chowing down on Nutty Buddies.

Lying back on three pillows on the queen-sized bed, his fat legs crossed at the ankles, with a pile of Little Debbie cakes, Fritos and assorted snacks beside him, the guy was actually watching a rerun of *Gilligan's Island*. He was laughing and nodding his fat bald little head, the remote control in his lap.

Seeing him actually laugh out loud at *Gilligan's Island* should have given me hope. Surely, somebody with that kind of intellectual depth could be outsmarted.

There was, however, the gun to contend with. It lay beside him on the bed, always within reach, right smack in the middle of three packages of Ding Dongs. I only hoped the jerk would pick up the gun accidentally, take a bite, and shoot himself in the tonsils.

It was the gun, of course, that had persuaded me to come along with him in the first place. That and what he had said back at my apartment, right after he'd come up behind me and stuck the gun in my back.

I believe if he'd just threatened *me*, I might've actually put up a fight. But what he said was, "Come with me, or we'll go next door and ring the doorbell. I'll shoot your sister the minute she comes to the door."

It was the way he said it, as much as anything else, that raised the hair on the back of my neck. He spoke so matter-of-factly. As if he were talking about going next door and borrowing a cup of sugar.

There was not a doubt in my mind that he'd do what he threatened. He'd do it without batting an eyelash.

When he nudged me with the gun again, I started moving. He directed me out my front door and down the street, toward an ancient, brown Dodge Dart parked at the corner. On the way I kicked myself for being so stupid as to leave my front door unlocked.

And yet, I'd only been running inside to get phone messages, for God's sake. I hadn't been planning to be inside for very long, and then I was heading right back to Bert's. How was I supposed to know that some twerp would be outside, hiding in the shrubbery, waiting for either Bert or me to be alone?

"I thought y'all never would split up," my captor complained, as we walked toward his car. "I was getting real cold, too, waiting on y'all."

What could I say? My heart bled for him.

We were passing Bert's door then, and I couldn't help glancing that way. Maybe if I called out?

The twerp must've noticed my glance, because he poked me with the gun again. "Don't say nothing. I mean it. We can always go and ring your sister's doorbell."

I blinked, and tried to swallow the fear rising in my throat.

When we got to the twerp's car, I realized the thing wasn't brown, after all. It had apparently been done in rust. Not rust, the color. Rust, the stuff that eventually turns metal into brown powder. I could have been wrong, but it looked to me as if there was every chance this car's body was about to disintegrate right before our eyes.

Great. As if I didn't already have enough to worry about.

Behind me, the twerp said, leaning so close that I could feel his breath on my neck, "You and me are going to take a little ride now. If you do your part right, you'll be back here before you know it."

My mouth went dry. Wasn't this the sort of thing all kidnappers told their victims? Just to make their victims easier to control? This guy wasn't going to tell me that there was no way I'd ever get out of this alive, or else I might decide I had nothing to lose. And I might make a grab for his gun.

Or try to kick him in the crotch.

The twerp must've known what I was thinking. "I mean it," he said. "I'm really, really, really not going to hurt you."

Three *really's?* Oh yeah, he was believable. I'd put him right up there with Richard Nixon.

"Get in the car." This time his voice shook a little as he spoke, and I suddenly realized he was almost as scared as I was. This is not the best thing in the world to notice in a guy holding a gun on you. I began to wonder what the chances were that his hands could shake so bad, he'd shoot me by accident.

The passenger door was unlocked, and I slid in, actually thinking for a moment of sliding right out the other side, and taking off running. And yet, if I did such a thing, would he just go to Bert's and make good his threat?

I stayed where I was.

When he got in behind the wheel, it was the first time I got a good look at him. I stared at him, pretty sure already that I knew who this was. Hadn't Alice Moorman described him herself? Like George on *Seinfeld.* Oh yes, this had to be Glenn Ledford. Can you believe, once upon a time I'd actually baby-sat this creep?

Before Glenn started the car, he turned and actually smiled at me. He needed to floss. Bad. "I hope you ain't thinking of trying nothing funny. I reckon you'd feel real bad if you made me shoot your sister." I noticed that he did not say that *he'd* feel real bad.

Glenn drove for the next few minutes without saying anything. He didn't put the gun down, though. He held it in his left hand, pointed directly at me, while he drove with his right.

I tried not to look at the gun, particularly at the end where the bullet comes out. I don't know, I guess I felt if I looked at that small, round opening long enough, something really would come out. Heading very rapidly in my direction.

I turned instead, and looked out the windshield. We were taking the Bardstown Road entrance ramp to Watterson Expressway.

Oh boy. That's what I needed. More excitement.

Glenn hurtled off the ramp, narrowly avoided sideswiping a van, and then pulled into the far lane.

Can you believe, once he'd survived getting on the Watterson, Glen started getting chatty. No doubt, it was just the relief of getting on the expressway in one piece that loosened his tongue. "Tell me," he said, as we headed west, "how long have you lived around here?"

I stared at him. Was this a trick question? Was he trying to get an estimate of how long I'd lived because he knew he was going to cut it short? "All my life," I said.

Glenn actually smiled. Not a pretty picture. "I've lived all over. Tennessee, and Ohio, and Kentucky, and Indiana. I've been around."

Oh yeah, he was quite the globe-trotter. "No kidding," I said. It occurred to me that if Glenn was asking me questions, there was no reason why I shouldn't ask him a few.

"You married?" I asked. I was, of course, thinking of the lady Bert and I had seen at the motel.

Glenn gave me a sideways look. "Naw," he said. "Never been married. Never had enough money to treat a lady right. But soon—" Here he gave me another sideways look. "—real soon, I'm going to have me a lotta money."

"A lot, huh?" I said.

The idiot grinned at me. "Yeah," he said, nodding his fat head, "a perty lady like you could have a real fine time with somebody like me."

Oh God. Too late, I realized he thought I was flirting with him. Not exactly the best thing I could think of doing with a guy holding a gun on me. I certainly didn't want to give him any ideas. Like, oh, say, raping me, for instance.

I glanced over at Glenn again. Oh yeah, I'd rather him shoot me, than rape me.

Old Glenn must not have been as stupid as I thought, because right away he saw the look on my face and seemed to know what I was thinking. He actually looked hurt. "Hey, now, before you go thinking I could do something awful—"

This, from the man who'd calmly threatened to shoot Bert.

"—I'll have you know, I ain't no pervert. I never forced a lady in my life."

I just looked at him, taking in the beady eyes, the fleshy lips, the doughy face. If Glenn were telling the truth, then he had to be a virgin.

"After tonight," Glenn went on, "I'm going to have me so much money, I'll have my pick of women."

Two words occurred to me. Bull and shit. I said neither, however. What I did do was give Glenn a warm smile. "Oh, really? And where are you going to get that kind of money?"

Glenn grinned back at me, apparently having no trouble believing that the word *money* was some kind of aphrodisiac for the female half of the population. He said the next slowly, as if he were titillating me with the idea. "One-half-a-million dollars. Just think about all that money. Now, won't that buy a perty lady like you a whole lot of presents? Jewelry and clothes and trips. Don't you worry none, neither—that money's free and clear. Not even from something illegal. Not really, anyway. I'm just finally getting paid by somebody who owes it to me."

I gave a low whistle. "Half-a-million dollars—that's some kind of debt."

Glenn glanced over at me and frowned, then turned his eyes back to the road. "Half-million is cheap. Real cheap. From the man who killed your parents. That man stole me and my brother's lives."

I stared at him. So it was true. Russell and Glenn had somehow found Les Tennyson and were blackmailing him.

Glenn must've thought I was looking at him so steadily because I was fascinated by what I was hearing. He immediately began embellishing his story. "I remember how it was, you know," he told me. "I remember how, when I was real little, I lived in a great big house, got drove around in a big expensive car, and had the best of everything. My folks had it all. Then, that man up and killed them and left me an orphan with nothing. Nothing but strangers to raise me."

I noticed that Glenn's right hand on the steering wheel had turned white at the knuckles. I also noticed that Glenn's poor-pitiful-me speech had quickly cut his brother Russell out of the equation. I tried to look sympathetic, no easy task when there's a gun involved. "How awful," I cooed.

Glenn nodded his bald head, his eyes on the road. "My brother at first only asked the guy for a quarter million. But that was before the sum-bitch went and killed my brother, too. *And* his wife."

I blinked. Les Tennyson had killed Russell and Alice?

"After that, I called the sum-bitch up at work, and I told him he owes me *another* quarter million. On account of my having four murders I could report to the cops, not just two." Glenn actually chuckled, as if getting the chance to ask for twice as much had been something that greatly amused him. "Yep," he said, "that sum-bitch owes me big time. And I'm gonna collect."

I stared at Glenn, remembering the phone call I'd gotten at the radio station. "I've got the money," a male voice had whispered. It must've been Tennyson. I'd actually spoken to the murderer of four people. The thought sent shivers down my spine. Had Tennyson been trying to lure me to meet him so he could do to me what he'd done to Russell Moorman? It must've puzzled the hell out of him when I'd acted as if I had no idea what he was talking about.

But why on earth had Les Tennyson called *me?*

Glenn was now staring pointedly down the front of my red body suit. My skin crawled. He looked back at the road, as he said, "Now, if you was to be nice to me, *real* nice, why I might just want to spend some of that half-million on you."

My stomach twisted. What do you know, I'd found Mr. Right.

Glenn glanced over at me again, a little faster than I expected, and I guess he caught the look of revulsion on my face. He immediately frowned, turning back to the road, his knuckles getting white again.

I took a deep breath. What was done was done—he'd seen the expression on my face—so what the hell, I decided I might as well make things abundantly clear. "If I were to be nice to you," I said, *"real* nice—why, I'd get *real* sick."

Glenn's eyes flashed. "You've got a smart mouth."

"You've got a dumb face."

I don't know what had gotten into me. Clearly, I had not thought all this through. Because it doesn't exactly take a rocket scientist to come to this conclusion: It's a bad idea to piss off a man with a gun.

Maybe if I'd kept my stupid mouth shut, I wouldn't have found out what a good, strong knot Glenn could tie. As soon as we'd gotten out of his car and into the room, Glenn actually seemed to enjoy himself, winding lengths of rope tighter and tighter around my body, until I could barely breathe.

The ropes he'd used to tie me to the damn desk chair didn't seem to be the kind that gave any, either. Even though I'd pulled at the things as hard as I could when he had me sitting over by the little refrigerator, they hadn't slackened at all. Judging from the way my wrists were stinging, I was pretty sure I'd scraped some of my skin off, trying to get a little breathing room.

Of course, if I'd been able to keep my jacket on, its sleeves might've protected my wrists some. Glenn may have been dumb, but he'd known enough to make me take the jacket off before he tied me up. He flung it angrily on the floor, and there it lay, absolutely useless to me, just in front of the door.

Things like this could make you think that dumb old Glenn might actually know what he was doing.

He seemed to enjoy putting the gag on me, too. "Now let's see how many smart remarks you can make," he said. Made of a washcloth wadded up and stuffed in my mouth, then held in place by a strip torn from the motel's thin bath towel, the whole thing made my mouth feel as if it had been stuffed with dead leaves. Only the taste was far worse. That is, I've never actually tasted dead leaves, but I think I'm pretty safe in saying this. The corners of my mouth ached.

Now, while Glenn snickered at Gilligan and the skipper, I wondered if Bert had understood my message. Surely, she had. Our twin vibes couldn't fail us that badly, could they? Unfortunately, Lester Jeffries, the high school nerd bird with whom Bert had accepted a date on my behalf, immediately came to mind. Oh, yeah, twin vibes *could* fail miserably.

The castaways on Gilligan's Island were fondly waving goodbye when Glenn finally roused himself from the bed. He got up and immediately stuck his gun into the waistband of his trousers. It was a tight fit. But, hey, I'd settle for him blowing his balls off instead of his tonsils. I wasn't picky.

Glenn headed for the door, and without looking at me, said, "Gotta get me something to drink."

No wonder. With all the sugar and salt he'd just taken in, it was a wonder he had any spit left at all.

"I'm going to run over to the Food King for a few six-packs." He turned to look at me then, his tiny eyes twinkling. "You stay here," he said. As he went out the door, he was chuckling at his little joke.

Oh yeah. He was a laugh riot.

I heard him turn the key in the lock, and groaned. Damn. He'd locked me in. I could hear the car starting outside, and then it pulled away.

I looked around. The television set across the room was off now. Maybe if I could get hold of the remote control, I could turn the TV back on. Maybe I could turn it on with the volume so high, it would bring complaining, angry neighbors to make me turn it down.

On the down side, I hadn't seen many neighbors when we'd pulled up. But then again, all I needed was one.

Besides, I had to do something. I craned my neck and located the remote control. It was still in the middle of the bed, still surrounded by snack cakes, candy bars, and now empty wrappers. Let me see. My chances of getting to it, while I was still tied to a desk chair, were pretty much what you'd expect. Remote.

I looked around a little more. OK, I'd seen this kind of situation on TV before. People are always getting tied to chairs, their hands bound behind them, just like mine, and they still move their chairs around and get to safety. All I really needed was a phone. Except the phone in this room was over on the wall, just inside the door. I could reach it only if I could fly.

OK, then maybe I could scoot this damn chair over to the wall. If I could kick the wall, I might attract the complaining, angry neighbors I'd mentioned earlier.

I tried to scoot the chair. Shit. It wouldn't budge. Now I knew why, when Bert wanted to talk to me, Glenn had picked me up, chair and all. It must be some kind of law of physics. When a body is tied to a heavy desk chair, and both are sitting on thick—very ugly, by the way—green carpet, it tends not to move.

Next, I tried to jump the chair forward. It could take some time, but it would still get me over to the wall. And yet, this time I couldn't get the chair to move even a quarter of an inch. Shit. Shit. Had to be another physics law. A body tied to a chair tends to stay in one place. Hell, Arnold Schwarzenegger tied to this chair couldn't have lifted it.

I realized then that I was sitting about halfway between the bed and an interior wall. Maybe I could rock the damn desk chair, and sort of teeter myself in the direction of the wall. In fact, if I could get the whole thing rocking, I could work my way over, and finally bang up against the wall with my shoulder. Alerting, you guessed it, hordes of complaining, angry neighbors.

This, of course, was when I tested out yet another law of physics. This law is right up there with, A body in motion tends to stay in motion. It is: A body in motion tends to fall and hurt itself.

I began lunging, like a complete idiot, from side to side, and, sure enough, the whole damn shebang started to rock. I was not, however, moving forward even an inch. So I rocked harder. And harder.

And then—Shit. Shit! SHIT!—all at once, the back legs of the chair slipped out from under me, and I hit the floor backwards, with a loud bang. You'd have thought that the carpeting would have cushioned my fall, but you couldn't tell it by me. My head ricocheted off the floor like a billiard ball.

I saw stars. Bright, sparkly stars.

Then blackness.

I don't think I was out for very long.

When I opened my eyes again, all I saw were my knees in the air. I can't say this was a big improvement over the stars. On the positive side, at least I was not wearing a dress. Or else, I would be dreading Glenn's return even more than I was already.

My temples throbbed, and a jackhammer had started up at the back of my head. I wanted to open my mouth and scream, but the gag wouldn't let me. Instead, I moaned. I also, I might as well admit, whimpered a little.

Again, on the positive side, the gag had probably kept me from biting off my tongue when I'd hit the floor.

I looked around again. There wasn't a whole lot to see. Other than the really ugly green carpet close up, and of course, my knees. Now that I was down here, I also noticed a faint odor. A lovely combination of urine, vomit, and rug shampoo.

I really needed to get out of there.

Lying there on my back, knees in the air, I came up with another plan. I would roll onto my side, and then wriggle toward the wall that way. Sort of like a snail with a really heavy shell on its back. I began to rock the damn chair again, only from side to side this time.

I'd just realized that I was, once again, going nowhere when I heard the glass break in the front window.

My heart leaped to my mouth. Was that Glenn? Was he already back? And yet, how could it be Glenn? He had a key. Surely, he wouldn't need to break a window to get in. What's more, even if he'd lost his key, wouldn't he go to the office for another one before he'd break a window?

In the position I was in, with my knees in the air, it was hard to see anything. I craned my neck to the side. Had somebody been waiting outside for Glenn to leave? Oh God, Les Tennyson had already killed four people, maybe he wanted to up his total to five. Maybe he'd followed Glenn and me here, and now that Glenn was gone, he was going to do what Glenn had not yet done.

He was going to take care of me. Permanently.

I heard the front door open, and I swallowed once, tasting dead leaves again. This could also be somebody else, of course. I shut my eyes. Please, God, let it be *her*.

"Nan!" Bert said, coming around the end of the bed. "Thank God you're here!"

God, she'd never looked so great.

"You poor thing," she said, rushing over to me. She dropped to her knees. "Are you all right?"

Like I could answer her.

As Bert struggled to pull me to a sitting position, she said, sounding almost giddy, "I knew this is what you meant. I knew it! You said *no-tellin'* so I would think of the No-tell Motel, right? The Blueberry Hill Motel!"

Bert had me right side up now. I shook my head, lifted my eyebrows, grunted, and did just about everything I could think of except wiggle my ears to get Bert to take the gag out of my mouth.

Naturally, Bert immediately began tugging at the ropes binding my *hands*. Oh yeah, our twin vibes were amazing.

"Oh dear. Oh dear," Bert said as she worked at the knots. Loosening them hardly any, I might add.

I grunted again and shook my head at her all over again.

"Oh," she said, finally seeming to focus on the gag. She pulled the towel strip down from my mouth, dug out the wash cloth, and, hallelujah, I could speak.

"Hurry, Bert," I said. My voice sounded hoarse and unnatural. "Hurry, for God's sake! He's going to be right back!"

Bert's face went pale, and she started tugging on the ropes binding my hands with renewed energy. "It's Glenn Ledford, isn't it?" Bert asked, as she worked at the knots.

I nodded. "He never moved out of this motel, after all." My voice was so hoarse, I swallowed once before I spoke again. "Hurry up, Bert!"

"Then his wife lied to us?" Bert asked, still tugging.

"I don't think that was his wife," I said.

"If that wasn't his wife, then who—"

I cut her off. "Bert, for God's sake, can't we talk about this later?" I glanced toward the door. "Please hurry!"

Bert kept tugging, but it didn't look to me as if she were making much progress. It didn't help to have her ask, "Isn't there a knife around here, or—or something?" She stood up and looked vaguely around the room, as if she truly expected to see a switchblade lying out on a counter or maybe in the middle of the bed.

I tried to stay calm, but let's face it, when I'm tied to a chair, I'm not in my best mood. "Bert, he has a gun, O.K.? He doesn't need a knife. And if there *were* a knife anywhere around here, don't you think I'd have already mentioned it by now?"

Bert blinked once, then without a word, dropped to her knees again, yanking furiously on the ropes. After awhile, I could feel them loosen a little, especially right around my wrists.

I could also hear an automobile in the distance. "Oh, God, Bert, he's coming back!"

Bert sat up like a hunting dog, pointing towards the front window. "But I almost had the ropes off," she said, sounding distracted. She moved quickly to the window, and pulling the drapes back just a little, peered outside.

Whatever she saw made her immediately stiffen. She spun around, and hurried over to me. "Nan," Bert said, "I'm sorry." With that she reached for the back of my chair, and quickly shoved me backward again. It wasn't as bad a fall as earlier, because Bert didn't let go until I was almost to the floor.

"What the hell are you doing?" I asked. My knees were airborne again. And my mood had not improved. "Are you nuts?" I yelled.

"Be quiet!" Bert hissed at me. She took off her tweed coat, grabbed my denim jacket up off the floor, and hurriedly put it on. Returning to the front window, she waited there for a moment, looking out. "Get the rest of those ropes off, and then call the police, OK?"

With that, she dashed out the front door.

Right after Bert left, I heard a car door slam outside, and then, shortly after that, the sound of a car starting and then pulling away. Oh, for God's sake. Was Bert leaving me here?

Outside, another car door slammed. "Shit!" I heard someone yell. "How'd you get loose?" The voice sounded like Glenn's.

That's when it hit me. Bert wasn't leaving me. She was *saving* me.

Wearing my jacket, she knew Glenn would think it was me—*escaping*.

Bert was acting as a decoy.

Outside now, I could hear the sound of somebody running, and then more curses. "Damn you! Come back here!"

Can you believe, Glenn actually shouted this. As if he really expected to be obeyed.

Now, the running sounds stopped, and there was the sound of footsteps headed this way.

Oh God. Maybe Bert hadn't fooled him after all.

I lay very quiet. Where I was right now, lying between the bed and the wall, even if Ledford looked in the window, he wouldn't see me. But would he notice the broken glass?

I don't think he even looked. I heard a car door slam one more time, and then a car started up and peeled out of the parking lot.

Chapter 17

•

BERT

"Oh God, oh God, oh God," I heard this voice saying, as I jumped into my little Ford Festiva and started it. It took me a second to realize that the voice was mine. The worst part of it was, the voice didn't sound terribly sure of itself.

I saw Glenn Ledford walking leisurely toward the motel room from his own car, carrying what looked like a heavy grocery sack. He did a double take when he spotted me.

"Shit! How'd you get loose?" he yelled, dropping the sack he was holding, its contents spilling out on the parking lot. One of the cans from a six-pack inside landed at Ledford's feet with a small explosion of fizz.

I yanked on my seat belt and put my car into reverse, just as Ledford began to run toward me. For a split second, he was actually running alongside, but then I pulled away. No surprise, he began to spout a string of swear words. Then he turned around, sprinting for his own car.

Oh my God, it had worked. He really was going to chase after *me*. And totally ignore Nan.

I could hardly believe I'd done this. This was *me* willingly getting into an honest-to-God car chase? Just like Gene Hackman and that other guy in *The French Connection?* Lord, it had made me dizzy even then, just watching it on the screen.

Now *I* was the one being chased? Me, the woman who'd failed her driver's license test three times? Nan, I could believe—she'd passed the darn test the very first time. Of course, Nan was the twin who'd just jumped on a bicycle the first time, too, and rode off. While I took down every fence post and mailbox in our neighborhood before I got the darn thing under control.

In my rearview mirror, as I pulled forward toward the exit, I saw Ledford reach his car. For a chubby little guy, he could run pretty fast. Even this far away, I could hear the car door slam after he climbed behind the wheel. I could also see how dark red his face had become. No doubt about it, this guy looked really, really mad. He threw his brown sedan into reverse and then gunned it, just as I was looking both ways and pulling out of the motel parking lot.

I pulled my own car into the traffic on whatever-street-it-was in Jeffersonville, traveling as quickly as I could. Before I knew it, I was passing cars left and right, honking as I went. Breezing right over the speed limit. Please, God, I prayed on the way, let me be lucky, let some cop catch me on radar and haul my terrified butt off to jail. Where said terrified butt would be safe and not going anywhere over fifty miles an hour.

Darn it, where were the cops when you really wanted to be stopped for speeding?

I peered at street signs as I went, trying to figure out where in the world I was going. Lord, if I were really going to have to do this chase thing, I wished I'd at least done it in Louisville. Because I really didn't know my way around Jeffersonville. I could get lost way too easily.

The only thing I did know about Jeffersonville was that the I-65 South on-ramp would take me into downtown

Louisville, and I did know how to get to that ramp. Or was it I-265 West that took me to Louisville? No, no, that was to New Albany, still here in Indiana. It *was* I-65—I was sure of it. Pretty sure, anyway.

I glanced into my rearview mirror. Oh God. Ledford was gaining on me, maneuvering his rusty heap around the other cars like they were standing still. No, more like they were backing up. I pressed harder on the gas.

The green highway signs for I-65 appeared overhead. I felt a surge of hope. Up ahead, I could see several cars already in the right lane, waiting to get on the interstate. Oh God. If I got in line with the other cars, Ledford would, no doubt, be able to just get out of his rust-bucket, and walk right up to my Festiva.

He'd be yanking me out of my car by my hair, before I even got a chance to get to the on-ramp. He could do it, too—I'd seen him. He may have been pudgy, but his upper arms looked like Oscar Mayer hams.

Unless I had something in the car I could fight him off with. I looked quickly around the inside of the car as I drove. Oh, sure, I could take Ledford easy—with a plastic coffee cup, a parking garage receipt, and a stick of gum.

I passed the line of cars entering I-65, feeling a huge sense of loss as I went by them. I turned left on some other street, the street sign a blur as I sped by. Next I turned onto another unknown street. Lord. What I really needed was to get to some place with crowds of people—I could get out of my car, blend into the crowd and get someone there to call the police. I'd seen it done all the time in the movies.

Surely Ledford wouldn't gun me down in front of witnesses. I leaned forward, trying to peer down the streets I passed, looking for groups of people. But, let's face it, it was

Sunday night in Jeffersonville, Indiana—not exactly your teeming nightspot.

I glanced in my rearview mirror again—Ledford was only two cars back now, weaving to the left as he tried to get around a minivan. A minivan whose occupants apparently had coined the phrase *road hog*. Bless their hearts, they were all over both lanes.

I passed street signs like Spring and Maple and Chestnut, but I couldn't tell if I were actually on those streets or just going by the signs. Like it would mean anything to me, anyway. Ledford whipped his car around the minivan. A Chevette stuffed with teenage boys was now all that was between me and him. I pressed even harder on my gas pedal, but I felt no change in my speed at all. None. Oh dear. This was all I was going to get out of my car. I'd maxxed.

Up ahead, a church spire stuck its lighted pyramid into the sky. I only hoped the parishioners there at Sunday night services were praying something generic that would cover me, too.

Sunday night services. Of course. That was it. What better place to find a crowd of people on a Sunday night than at a church? Behind me, Ledford was moving to his left to pass the teenagers.

I waited till the last minute to swing wide into the church parking lot. Once I made the turn, I could see that it looked indeed exactly like a church parking lot—only minus the cars. Good grief, what time was it anyway? Was church service already over? Obviously, it was. Ledford swung in behind me and gunned his engine. He came up alongside me on the left, and wrenched his steering wheel hard to the right.

Oh God. Our cars made that awful, screeching noise that metal makes when it scrapes against more metal. Great, just great. I was idly wondering if my insurance covered this kind of thing, when my car started doing this crazy shimmying. I veered from left to right, smacking Ledford one more time. Oh, great! Just GREAT!

I grabbed at my steering wheel, steering into the slide, just like I'd read somewhere that you were supposed to do. Naturally, my car's shimmy got worse. I smacked into Ledford again. By now, I was nearing the far end of the parking lot and heading toward two concrete poles that marked the exit.

I braked a tad—that's a scientific measurement—and what do you know, my Festiva stopped shimmying. I sailed between the poles; alongside, Ledford was forced to drop back to avoid hitting a pole head-on.

We were in the streets again, Ledford again a car-length behind me.

I really didn't think I could stand another session like we'd just had in the parking lot. I figured I'd been lucky up to now, but I was afraid it was only a matter of time until my luck ran out. I needed a break.

Like magic, the Golden Arches appeared up ahead on my left, as I came around a turn. It's amazing how much your mind can process in a short time, especially when you are totally and completely panicked. I could see one car pulling up in the drive-thru lane, with other cars heading for the drive-thru after entering from the front. I could also see that this particular Mickey D's drive-thru allowed only a single car at a time at its drive-thru speakers. Mostly because it was banked on one side by the restaurant itself and on the other side by this lovely concrete wall, with an absolutely beautiful turn about halfway down the lane before you got to the windows.

In the drive-thru lane, Ledford might not be able to see what I was doing. Maybe he'd think I just wanted a Coke.

A second later, I'd cut my wheel sharply to the left, racing up the drive-thru, and screeching to a halt in front of the speaker. Whoever was manning this thing probably thought I was incredibly hungry. I watched my rearview mirror. A Toyota station wagon pulled up right behind me, and, thank the Lord, a VW Beetle pulled in behind him. Glenn Johnny-Come-Lately Ledford was next in line.

"Welcome-to-McDonald's-may-I-take-your-order?" a perky voice said, making the entire speech sound like one word.

"Call the police!" I yelled.

"Excuse me?" The voice was still perky, but now it had a hesitant edge.

"Call the police! The man in the brown car in back of me is trying to kill me!"

There was a moment of silence while she digested this news bulletin. I looked for and then spotted the large round mirror mounted at the turn. In the mirror, I got a look at Miss Perky. Blond curls, wide eyes, petite—oh, Lord, she looked like she was only twelve. I sincerely hoped she was mature for her age.

In my side mirror, I could see Ledford sticking his head out of his car window, trying to see what I was doing.

"Call the police! I mean it!" I yelled into the speaker.

Another silence. And then came a distinct giggle. "This is a joke, isn't it?" Miss Perky asked, followed by another giggle. "Is that you Stephanie?"

I suppressed a scream. "No, this isn't Stephanie! And this isn't a joke! Call the cops—NOW!"

"Oka-a-ay," said Miss Perky, obviously deciding to go along with the fun. "Will the cops be for here or to go?" she added. "How about it, *Stephanie?*" Now she laughed out-right.

In the rearview mirror, Ledford had already gotten out of his car and was walking toward me, one hand stuffed in his trouser pocket.

I floored the accelerator and careened down the drive-thru, making the turn and passing Miss Perky. When she saw me coming, her face went from pink to white, her blue eyes showing the whites all around as I raced by.

In my side mirror, as I headed down the street, I could see that Ledford had already made it back to his car, and he was now making a fast exit out of the entrance to the restaurant. Obviously, the man was cheating. He'd backed out of the drive-thru line when he saw me take off, and he'd immediately headed toward the entrance.

In what seemed like no time at all, he was right on my tail. This close, under street lights, I could even see the expression on his face in my rearview mirror. If anything, he looked even angrier. His dark red face now looked more like the color of violets.

Green highway signs appeared overhead again, and, would you believe it, somehow I'd gotten around to the on-ramp to I-65 again. I wasn't sure how I'd done it, but this time, there was no one waiting to get on. I wrenched the wheel to the right and sped up the ramp, hoping and praying that the bridge to Louisville would not have any accidents on it stopping traffic. Or, if there were, the cops were already on the scene. In swat team formation.

I couldn't believe how much I was hoping and praying for

a glimpse of a police uniform—it just goes to show you how quickly things can change. I'd have even welcomed Goetzmann but, hey, any traffic cop would do.

As luck would have it, the bridge was pretty much deserted. Concrete stanchions and street lights whipped past me, as Ledford came roaring up behind me.

Th-wump!

Oh God! My car took a sudden jolt forward, and my neck snapped back sharply against the head rest. For a split-second, I saw stars.

Ledford was actually ramming my car!

I glanced back at my rear window, only to see Ledford rushing forward to hit me again.

Thwu-u-ump!

I jolted forward again. Lord, that really hurt. If I lived through this, I was going to have one dilly of a headache. I certainly wasn't in good enough shape to put up with this for long. I looked back to see Ledford dropping back a little so he could build up speed to hit me again.

Oh, my. This had to stop. One thing about my little Festiva, its small size made it a lot more maneuverable than most. In fact, I'd bet it was considerably more maneuverable that Ledford's Dodge Dart. I moved my Festiva into the inside lane, going south on the bridge. And, then—I couldn't believe I was doing this—I rolled down the window and gave Ledford the finger.

My goodness, the man had a short fuse. Ledford took one look at my little gesture, and went an even darker red.

It seemed to me to be an excellent time to get out of there. We were just passing the Welcome to Kentucky sign when I hit the accelerator and moved ahead of Ledford.

Ledford must've stomped on his own gas pedal with all his

weight. He shot forward, coming straight at me. He was almost on my bumper, when I suddenly braked, simultaneously turning hard to the right. Our cars barely made contact, my little car spinning all the way around, coming to rest facing the other way.

Ledford's Dart, though, clipped me on the left and shot on by, while he was still trying to turn right to follow me. Then, before he could brake, he slammed into a concrete stanchion.

There was a sickening crash. And then, suddenly, everything was quiet.

I sat there for a minute, my head throbbing, more or less, waiting for Ledford to start up and come at me again.

I looked out my back window at his car. There was some kind of weird steam coming out from under his hood, which now looked a whole lot like an accordion. His front windshield was cracked. Inside, nothing moved.

I wondered if Ledford were all right. I mean, surely, he'd had on his seat belt. Nobody goes on car chases without putting on their seat belt, do they?

I undid my own seat belt and got out of my car, walking very slowly up to his steaming car. A sharp odor filled the air, and I wrinkled my nose. Radiator fluid, maybe? I moved closer, braced to dash for my own car, if Ledford should start after me.

On the passenger side, which was now missing its glass, I peeked in. Glenn Ledford was slumped sideways, leaning in my direction, bleeding profusely from a cut on his forehead. I felt a little faint at the sight of all that blood. His right arm was bent at an odd angle and his left arm was resting against the dashboard. I couldn't see his legs—the dashboard now seemed to be lying in his lap. Oh, God, that didn't look good. This was going to need the Jaws of Life or something.

I probably should have been worried about the gun, but it was nowhere to be seen. And, after seeing the condition Ledford was in, I didn't even think about it. I yanked on the door to open it, but it wouldn't budge. At the sound, Ledford opened his eyes and squinted at me, blood still oozing down his face.

A wave of nausea washed over me, and for a moment I had to look away.

I turned back to him when Ledford tried to speak. I leaned forward, expecting something like *Help me* or *Get a doctor.* But his three whispered pearls were, "You . . . fucking . . . bitch."

A thing like this could make a person question the entire Good Samaritan concept.

Ledford struggled to speak again. "You . . . cost me . . . a half-a-million dollars."

I blinked. "I did what?"

Ledford frowned, as if he were irritated at having to answer me. Or maybe he thought I was arguing with him. "You . . . and whoever left their keys . . . in that damn . . . Festiva."

I knew what he meant about the car keys. He actually thought Nan had stolen a car back at the motel, and escaped in it. I really didn't think it was the time to break it to Ledford that it was really my car at the motel all along. And that I was actually Bert—not Nan. Besides what I wanted to hear about was that part about the money. Matter of fact, that's pretty much why I asked what I did. "What was that part about the money?"

The magic word *money* brought him to, all right. Ledford's eyes popped open, staring at me. He studied me for what seemed a long time, as if he were thinking something over. Then, apparently, he made up his mind, because he said,

"It's not . . . too late." As he talked, his voice seemed to get steadily stronger. Maybe he wasn't as badly hurt as I'd thought. Although having an engine in your lap certainly couldn't do you any good. "I'll share it . . . with you," Ledford said.

I stared back at him. If I understood correctly, Ledford here was offering to share five hundred thousand dollars with me. The entire Good Samaritan concept could be looking up.

"All you gotta do is . . . meet Sims at the Belvedere," Ledford went on. "At ten o'clock."

This was how I was supposed to come by that much money? This was the same message he'd given me on the phone. Except for one small, but important addition. "Sims?" I asked. "Who is Sims?"

Ledford frowned again. He seemed a little put out that he was having to spell all this out for me. "Elliott Sims. The guy who killed my folks."

I stared at him. Elliott Sims had killed the Sandersens? At the risk of repeating myself, I asked it again. *"Who* is Elliott Sims?"

Would you believe, behind his horn-rimmed glasses, Ledford actually rolled his eyes. As if I were trying his patience beyond belief. "Les Tennyson," Ledford's voice was getting ragged again. "He changed his name . . . moved to Corydon."

I blinked. Corydon was a small town in Indiana, only about an hour or so from Louisville. Lord. Had Tennyson been living there all this time? Within driving distance?

Ledford closed his eyes for a minute. When he opened them again, he went on. "He started a company making ice dispensers—"

I blinked again. Ice dispensers? Was I hearing right? Was Ledford trying to tell me that a cold-blooded killer had ended up manufacturing ice dispensers? He was kidding, right?

"—and got rich."

Ledford's voice was stronger now. He was obviously finding energy somewhere. Of course, just thinking about a half million dollars probably gave him strength. "Just pick up the blackmail money . . . and bring it to me. I'll give you a fourth."

Oh, sure thing. Glenn Ledford was going to give me one-fourth of the money he was going to get from blackmailing this Sims guy. Right after which, in all probability, I would end up just like Russell and Alice Moorman. I mean, what a wonderful business opportunity. Thanks, but I thought I'd pass.

I looked around. Where were the police? We'd had several cars go by, and one truck whose driver, I'd noticed, had been talking on his CB radio. Surely, somebody had notified the police about this accident by now.

Maybe I was going to have to leave and do it myself. I sort of hated to leave Ledford here all alone, though.

Even in his condition, Ledford must've noticed my eyes darting around. Only, apparently, he thought I was just feigning disinterest to negotiate with him. "All right," he said, his tone disgusted. "I'll . . . give you a third, OK? It's only right. You two . . . earned it . . . you and your sister."

Ledford certainly knew how to get my attention.

"We *what?*"

Ledford groaned, and then struggled to shift into a more comfortable position, pulling on the steering wheel in his lap with his one good arm. He wasn't going anywhere. He fell back with another groan, and then looked over at me. "It was you two . . . who finally made Sims believe us," he said. Ledford's strength must've been fading rapidly, because he was pausing a lot now. "When Russell told Sims we knew about the . . . murders, Sims acted like . . . he didn't know . . . what we were talking about."

I stared at Ledford, feeling a shiver run down my back. So what exactly had the brothers done to convince Sims they were wise to him?

"It was . . . Russell's idea," Ledford went on, actually smiling a little now. "Russell was plenty smart . . . he told Sims something he knew he . . . would remember from . . . back when we were kids. It was . . . something Russell and me remembered real clear . . . these twins who'd baby-sat for . . . us back then."

Ledford glanced over at me. Even in pain, he managed to look sly. "Fact is, Russell made Sims think . . . it was really you two . . . behind this whole thing. He made that moron think that y'all had found out who Sims really was . . . and come up with the whole blackmail idea."

I swear, if the man hadn't been lying there in his own blood, all busted up, I'd have slapped him silly. I could hardly believe it. This idiot and his brother had actually told an honest-to-God *murderer* that it was Nan and me who were blackmailing him?

Ledford hurried on, his voice growing weaker, "It was easy . . . to find you two . . . what with you being on the radio and all . . . and living right next door to your sister."

It was on the tip of my tongue to tell him I was Bert, just to see the stunned expression on his face, when Ledford went on. "Russell told Sims he'd prove . . . it was you two behind everything. Told him to be watching on the corner in Louisville when he talked to one of you about the *arrangements*."

Lord. In my mind's eye I could see me, as clear as anything, standing on the corner with Russell Moorman as he'd

turned to look at someone across the street. So this was what
it had all been about—Russell Moorman had been proving to
a murderer that he really did know us. Oh my God.

Ledford gave a weak chuckle and then coughed. "That
there Russell . . . he had brains."

That there Russell's brains got him killed, I thought.

Ledford coughed again, his face definitely paler than it
had been just a minute before. I guessed that all this talking
was starting to wear him down.

"Look, you need to be quiet now," I said. I looked in both
directions, trying to see further down the bridge. In the distance, finally, I could hear the faint whoop of a siren, coming
closer. Thank God, it seemed the cops were on their way. Or,
at least, an ambulance. From the looks of Ledford, they'd
better hurry.

Apparently, Ledford heard the sirens, too. He roused
himself one more time to try to look at me again, but quickly
fell back, groaning. He licked his lips, his eyes tightly closed.
"Now you go get that money," he said. ". . . Belvedere at ten
. . ." He began to cough, harder this time, and grabbed at his
chest each time with the pain. His lids fluttered. "You meet
. . . Elliott Sims . . . I'll give . . . you . . . half."

What do you know, he'd raised the ante again.

And yet, it really didn't matter how much he raised it.
Dead people, I have noticed, don't generally get to spend
much money.

I shook my head. "I don't think so," I said.

Ledford, however, didn't hear me. He had passed out.

Chapter 18
●
NAN

Another ten minutes and I would've been free. I'd worked the ropes almost completely off my arms and wrists—no easy task when you're lying on your back, attached to a chair. I'd just started on the cords around my ankles when Bert and the cop walked in. They'd evidently gotten another key from Walter Brennan in the manager's office, because the cop didn't kick the door in or anything. Which, I believe, is what cops always do on television. Evidently, in real life, a cop's entrance is not nearly so dramatic, but a lot more practical. The policeman just unlocks the damn door, and walks in.

Have I mentioned that it's a little embarrassing to say hello to a strange man when you're flat on your back, with your knees in the air? I mean, this is precisely why I go to a female gynecologist. I said it, anyway, though. "Hi there."

Bert hurried to my side, and sank immediately to her knees. Evidently, so that she could see me glare at her right after she spoke. "Nan, you're still tied up!"

Believe me, I'd noticed.

"I was *sure* you'd be able to untie yourself," Bert went on. "Really. It never occurred to me that you wouldn't be able to get loose."

Apparently, before she ran out the door earlier, I should

have reminded her that at the last summer camp we went to—the year we were fourteen—I'd skipped every one of the knot-tying classes. Instead, I'd gone off to the pool to flirt with the lifeguard. It had seemed a good choice back then. Now, of course, I realize that lifeguards come and go, but a handicraft can last forever.

"It's OK," I told Bert. I wasn't lying. I was maybe exaggerating a little, but the bottom line was that, in order to rescue me, Bert had put her very own self in jeopardy, getting Glenn to chase after her. So it certainly seemed tacky at this point to complain about her not taking the time to untie me. Not to mention, I don't believe she'd had any time to take.

While the nice policeman—who, incidentally, was far too young for me, and yes, I know I'm shallow, but I did notice—got busy righting my chair and undoing the last of the ropes around my ankles and legs, Bert filled me in on what had happened since I'd seen her last.

It sounded to me as if she could've been killed six or seven times over during that damn car chase. Particularly since I've ridden with Bert at the wheel, and I am well aware just how competent a driver she is. I was not a bit surprised to hear that her Festiva now bore a remarkable resemblance to an aluminum can, crushed and ready for recycling. "But it *still* runs!" Bert said. She actually sounded proud. "I'll get to pick it up at the police lot later!"

I tried to look excited that she was going to have the opportunity to drive all around Louisville in a turquoise roller skate that, no doubt, looked as if a giant had stepped on it.

I was, I confess, considerably more excited to hear that Bert had told the policemen arriving at the scene of Glenn's accident all about her appointment tonight at ten on the Belvedere. And that, from what she understood, several

other policemen had been immediately dispatched to inter-
cept this Elliott Sims person, blackmail money and all.

The too-young policeman had at last gotten me free, and
he interrupted us. "I've got orders to bring you two downtown," he said. Having made that little pronouncement, he
asked a few questions, took a few notes, and then he gave me
and Bert a ride in his squad car.

Maybe little kids get a kick out of this sort of thing, but I
believe their enthusiasm must have something to do with
their being too young to notice the numerous dark stains on
the black seat covers. Bert and I spotted the stains the second we got into the back seat. What these stains were I didn't
even want to hazard a guess. If it was blood, the bleeder had
not survived. If it was urine or, say, vomit—like I said, I
didn't want to hazard a guess.

Beside me Bert was clearly getting as big a thrill out of
all this as I was. She'd stopped staring at the mystery stains,
and she was now looking, her mouth pinched, at the large
patch of black duct tape between us on the seat. Its strips
criss-crossed each other and poorly covered a scooped-out
hole in the upholstery. Possibly, this hole had been left by the
previous passenger trying to dig his way out.

Or, it could be that a member of the local canine patrol
needed a few more obedience lessons. This last scenario could
also account for the mystery stains.

The wire mesh between us and our driver was bristly
with rust and, as we passed under street lights, it cast everything around us in thin strips of gray shadow. It felt as if Bert
and I had been packed into an old wire basket.

It didn't help to realize that we really couldn't get out unless our driver chose to release us. There were no handles on
either door back here.

"Oh dear," Bert said. "I hope nobody we know sees us riding around in this thing. They'll think we've been arrested." She started to slide down, so that if anybody passed by and looked in the back windows, they could only see the top of her head. About halfway down, though, she abruptly changed her mind. Bert's decision might've had something to do with the odors I myself caught a whiff of when I reached down to rub my rope-burned ankles. These odors gave strong support to the mystery stains being a combination of those two other things I mentioned earlier, other than blood.

Bert wrinkled her nose, and immediately straightened up.

I think it was as much to give herself something else to think about other than whether anybody we knew could possibly be passing by at any given moment that Bert started to fill me in on everything she'd learned from Glenn while they were waiting for the ambulance. She'd learned a lot. All about how Glenn was blackmailing a guy by the name of Elliott Sims. Who, according to Glenn, was really Les Tennyson, the man who'd killed his parents—and, oh yes, a man who'd been hiding out in Indiana all these years, making a lot of money.

I ran my hand through my hair. "A cold-blooded killer ends up making ice dispensers. Makes sense to me."

I'd expected Bert to at least smile, but she hurried on.

"Dragging you and me into this had been Russell's idea," she said. She explained the whole thing—how Sims had needed convincing that the brothers knew what they were talking about, so Russell had set Bert up. "According to Glenn," Bert went on, "Sims not only murdered the Sandersens, he also murdered Russell and poor Alice."

"You know, I can understand why Sims might've thought he had to kill Russell," I told Bert. Lord knows, now that I'd heard about Russell's little brainstorm, I felt a little homicidal toward him myself. "But why Alice?"

Bert shook her head sadly. "I don't know."

"I mean, unless Alice was lying to us, she didn't know what her husband was up to. So why would Sims have to shut her up?" I reached down and rubbed my ankles again. I didn't want to get another whiff of those memorable odors, so I did it very quick. And I held my breath the entire time. When I straightened up, I had another question for Bert. "How did the two brothers find out who Sims was in the first place?"

Bert shook her head again.

Evidently, when you got to the end of what she'd found out, it was a very sharp drop off.

"I can't believe," I said, "you found out all this, just sitting with the guy a few minutes waiting for an ambulance. I mean, I rode all the way from the Highlands to Jeffersonville with him, and he didn't tell me half what he told you."

Bert shrugged. "I think, when you're trying to get information out of somebody, it helps to have him bleeding all over the place."

I'd certainly remember that.

It was kind of a good thing that Bert and I had gone over everything on the way to the police station. By the time we were pulling up in front of the station entrance, it was all still very clear in our minds. This was a real help when we had to tell it to Goetzmann all over again.

Sitting once again in front of that gray metal desk just inside the door marked *Homicide,* I had a moment of real uneasiness. Particularly when, shortly after we started talking, Goetzmann just sat there, staring at us without blinking. I was actually waiting for him to say something about publicity stunts, but he continued to just sit there and stare. A couple of times he ran his hand over his Marine haircut, and rubbed the spot between his eyes, but mostly, he just listened.

When we were through, he said, abruptly, "Sims hasn't shown up yet. I got the call just before you two came in. Nobody with a package has shown up on the Belvedere."

My stomach twisted. I was sure Goetzmann was going to say that once again we were wasting his time. He paused for a moment, and ran his hand over his Marine haircut one more time.

"Look," he said, "I know you two think I dropped the ball on this one. But, hell, I don't know how anybody could have expected us to know that Russell Moorman's name when he was a kid was Sandersen, and that his murder was connected somehow to a murder committed years and years ago."

Bert and I exchanged a look. The Clod of all Clods actually sounded a little sheepish.

"I mean," Goetzmann went on, "Moorman didn't even have an ID on him when we found him. It took us until almost midnight Friday to even find out that his name was Russell Moorman, and there sure wasn't any reason to go any further than that."

I didn't know about Bert, but I was trying not to smile.

Goetzmann was leaning forward, his meaty hands flat on his desk. "We're going to catch this guy, don't worry. Whether Sims shows up at the Belvedere or not. We've issued an APB on this guy, and we've sent somebody to bring his wife in."

That one brought me up short. *Wife?* Sims was married? I don't know why that surprised me so much. I mean, just because you were a murderer in hiding, it didn't necessarily follow that you couldn't date. Or that, one day, you wouldn't meet somebody who genuinely appreciated you for who you really weren't.

Goetzmann's square jaw was set in an expression of cold determination. "We'll have this Sims character in custody before the night's over."

I nodded and smiled this time. At least, I smiled right up until Goetzmann made Bert and me go over everything we'd just told him one more time. That pretty much wiped any amusement off my face.

Bert had gotten, once again, to the part where she was going through the drive-thru at Mickey D's when the commotion began outside. The door to the Homicide office was not closed all the way so we could hear every word.

"Let go of me, you goon! Let GO!" a female voice shouted. "I said, I'd come in voluntarily and talk to you people, and I'm doing it! So take your grubby paws off me!"

Bert and I immediately turned to look through the glass windows in back of us, and what we saw made us both sit up a little straighter. And lean forward for an even better look.

It was Maxine from the Blueberry Hill Motel. She was easy to recognize even though her hair was now no longer brunette, but strawberry-blond, framing her face in soft, chin-length waves. The hair may have been different, but the face was the same—especially the makeup. She was also once again wearing the tan raincoat. This time it looked as if she'd just grabbed the coat and thrown it around her shoulders as she hurried out the door. Underneath she was wearing a burgundy sweatshirt with a Panda bear stenciled on the front, stone washed jeans, and heels. Have I mentioned that the heels-with-jeans look is not one of my favorites?

Maxine's heels were metallic gold sandals with at least a

four-inch heel. In deference to the cold weather, she also put on hose. You could tell this right away because she wasn't wearing the sandal kind of hose that had a nude toe. No, these had dark toes sticking out of the end of each sandal. It looked as if Maxine had dipped each foot in milk chocolate.

"I *said*, let go!" she shouted, as she jerked her arm away from the uniformed policeman at her side. "You don't have to act like you've just brought in Ma Barker!"

Bert turned back to Goetzmann. "You located Mrs. Ledford?"

I glanced over at Bert. Had I told her on the way over here that Glenn had said he wasn't married? I couldn't remember. If I had, apparently, it had gone in one ear and out the other.

Goetzmann frowned. "That's not Mrs. Ledford. That's Maxine Sims, Elliott's wife."

That little bit of news caused Bert and me to stare at him for a long moment with our mouths open. And then we both turned back around and stared some more at Maxine.

"I mean, I *want* to tell you about Elliott. I *want* to show you this stuff!" Maxine said. I noticed then for the first time that she had a stack of newspaper clippings clutched tightly in one hand. "You're not making me do anything. I *want* you to know who my husband really is. Because I want you to protect me!" She waved her hand around to include every policeman in the outer office. "I want every one of you to protect me!"

Somehow I doubted that the entire Louisville police force was going to be assigned to guard Maxine, but she seemed to be counting on it. "Elliott told me if I ever crossed him, he'd kill me just like he did the others, and even though he was real drunk at the time, I believed him! I mean, why else would I stay with that asshole after he started smacking me around? I was afraid. *That's* why!"

Maxine was waving her clippings around, her eyes traveling all over the room, when she spotted me and Bert through the glass windows.

For a moment, she was struck dumb. She actually tottered backward a little on her gold heels, and then, recovering a little, she said, "Well, I never. Those two really *were* in on it, after all." She turned to the cop still standing next to her. "You better watch them two. They lie like a dog! They had me believing they didn't know diddly squat."

I blinked. Thank you so much, Maxine, for the wonderful character reference. I gave Goetzmann a quick sideways glance to see if anything Maxine had just said had made an impact. He was looking straight at me, his beefy face expressionless.

Uh oh.

When I turned back to look through the windows, Maxine was coming through the door. "They've arrested you two, huh? Well, it serves you right. Blackmail *is* against the law, you know!" Maxine actually sounded self-righteous. Looking over at Goetzmann, she said, "You better be on your toes. Because you can't believe a word these two say!"

Wait a second now. *This* was the woman who'd told us she was Glenn Ledford's wife, that they were getting a divorce, and that he was moving out of the Blueberry Hill Motel. And she said she couldn't believe *us?* I opened my mouth to point out this little oversight to her, but Goetzmann jumped in before I had the chance. "You knew about the blackmail?" he asked Maxine.

Maxine lifted her chin. "Well, I heard about it. From Glenn and Russell, of course. I told them it was a stupid idea, that Elliott wasn't anybody to mess with—I mean, he's got away with murder all these years, for God's sake. Here, just take a look—" She walked over and dropped her handful of newspaper clippings on Goetzmann's desk with a loud smack. "Right after Elliott got drunk one night and threatened me, well, I don't mind telling you, I got a little scared. Wondering, you know, if he was really telling the truth? So I searched all his things the very next day when he was at work. And look—just look what I found!"

I recognized the clippings right away. Of course, I ought to. Bert and I had seen quite a few of them on microfilm during our recent trip to the library. Maxine's clippings were yellowed, and some of them looked as if they were falling apart. But the headlines were the same.

Goetzmann flipped through the newspaper articles, and then—moving a lot faster than you'd expect a man his size to move—he abruptly got to his feet. "We'll need to take your statement," he said, looking directly at Maxine. "Let me go get a stenographer, and I'll be right back."

I noticed that he pulled the door shut all the way when he left.

I could've been wrong, but it seemed to me to be highly likely that Goetzmann could be going somewhere to listen in on us. There was a heavy framed mirror on the wall to my right, and I was sure it had to be two-way. It was my guess that Goetzmann had left Bert and me alone with Maxine just to hear what we all would say.

Maxine didn't disappoint him. The minute Goetzmann was out of sight, she wheeled on Bert and me. "Well, I hope you two are satisfied. If you all hadn't come up with this whole blackmail mess, we wouldn't be sitting here wondering where the hell Elliott is, now would we?"

Bert frowned. "Look, you're making a big—"

Maxine cut Bert off. "Russell and Glenn should've taken care of Elliott just like I told them to." She sat down on the edge of Goetzmann's desk, crossed her legs, and glared at both of us.

"You wanted them to—to—?"

Bert seemed to be stumbling over the word, so I finished for her. "—to get rid of your husband?"

Maxine took a quick look at the door, as if to make sure it was truly closed, and then she leaned toward us, lowering her voice. Apparently, it did not occur to Maxine that there could be anyone listening in on us. "Well, of course!" she said. "Do you really think I spent hours in the damn library, tracking those two down, just so they could hit Elliott up for some money?"

I didn't even blink. What do you know, Maxine here was Tonya Harding.

"I even talked to their stupid aunt," she went on, her tone getting more and more irritated by the minute. "Had to tell her I was from some Kentucky adoption bureau to find out their new names and get their current addresses. God, I was sure all I had to say to those brothers was that Elliott was the one who'd killed their mom and dad, and they'd kill Elliott for me without even thinking twice."

Bert and I exchanged a look. So *this* was how the two brothers had found out who Sims really was. Sims' beloved wife had told them.

"I was finally going to have Elliott out of my life once and for all!" Maxine glared at me and Bert. "But, no-o-o-o, you two had to spoil everything!"

I was really getting tired of being accused of something I didn't do. Particularly by somebody who'd just admitted plotting her own husband's murder. "Maxine," I said, "Glenn and Russell lied to you. Bert and I were never involved in blackmailing anybody."

Maxine's response was less than what I'd hoped for. She laughed right in my face. "Yeah," she said. *"Right.* And I guess the Pope isn't Catholic either, is he?"

"Maxine," I began again, "listen to me, it was Glenn and Russell—"

Once more she interrupted, shaking her blond head regretfully. "Russell!" She said the name contemptuously. "Don't you tell me about Russell! And don't you go blaming me for what happened to him, neither!"

I just looked at her. This did seem to be a sensitive subject with her. Maybe if I pursued it a little, Maxine would tell us more than she meant to. "Well, you know, Maxine," I said slowly, "if you hadn't told Glenn and Russell who Elliott was, Russell might still be alive to—"

Maxine bristled. "Oh, no," she broke in, shaking her head so vigorously, her strawberry-blond curls bounced around her face. "You can't pin that on me. Russell did it to himself. Right off he told me, *What will killing Elliott do for me?* Well, I'll tell you what it would've done—it would've kept Russell from dying, that's what!"

"Not to mention, Alice," Bert put in.

Maxine's face was turning red. "Now, that wasn't my fault, either!" She brushed a strand of hair away from her face. "You both know I tried, I really *tried* to get ahold of

Glenn right after I saw on TV what had happened to Russell. I even followed one of you, hoping you'd lead me to him."

I stared at her. Then Maxine had not only been Tonya Harding, she'd also been the hoarse voice who'd talked to Bert on the phone, and the woman in the tan coat who'd followed Bert. The woman was multitalented.

"Hell," Maxine went on, "You even saw me searching that damn motel room of Glenn's, looking for any clue to where he might've gone. Doesn't that prove I was trying to help? Of course, it wasn't like I had all the time in the world to find him. I did have to get back to Corydon, or else Elliott was going to get suspicious."

Maxine was now kicking her foot nervously. "But I did try to tell Glenn. *I* knew that once Elliott found out that there were people who knew who he really was, he wouldn't stop until he'd eliminated all of them. That's the way Elliott is— he's mean. *Real* mean. I wanted Glenn to know there was no way Elliott would ever give him any money! That now he *had* to get rid of Elliott before Elliott got rid of him!" Maxine crossed her arms across her chest, and gave us a self-satisfied smile. "So, see, your blackmail scheme never would've worked!"

Beside me, Bert took a deep breath. "Maxine," she said through her teeth, "it was not our blackmail scheme. We're not getting arrested. We're just in here giving a statement, the same as you."

Maxine's heavily lipsticked mouth dropped open. "You two really *aren't* getting arrested?"

Goetzmann, oddly enough, showed up right then, walking in and catching the last of what Maxine said.

To my way of thinking, it was Goetzmann who could best

answer Maxine's question. Had he heard what Maxine had just been saying, and decided that Bert and I were involved in this mess, after all?

The moment seemed to stretch on and on, while Bert and I both leaned forward, waiting for what Goetzmann was going to say next.

Chapter 19

•

BERT

I didn't know about Nan, but by the time Detective Goetzmann finally spoke, my stomach felt as if I'd swallowed a few
burning rocks. With everybody in the room more or less
hanging on his next word, you'd have thought Goetzmann
would say something pretty momentous. Instead, without
even looking in our direction, he sort of mumbled, "We're
going to need typed statements from all three of you. The
stenographer will be along in a minute."

Nan and I had leaned forward, our eyes riveted to his
face, and *this* was all he had to say? Of course, the minute
Goetzmann spoke, I did notice that Nan relaxed considerably.
I guess she didn't particularly care what he said as long as it
didn't have the word *arrest* in it.

Neither one of us mentioned that getting a stenographer
had been the reason he'd supposedly left in the first place. I
guess Nan and I decided there was no real reason to bring the
subject up.

Maxine, however, was of a different mind set. She'd been
sitting on the edge of Goetzmann's desk, legs crossed, kicking her foot, but she'd hopped down the second he came
through the door. "Oh, for God's sake," she burst out. "How

long does it take to find a stenographer? Hell, you could've *hired* one in the time you've been gone!"

Goetzmann suddenly got so busy, leafing through the stack of yellowed newspaper clippings that Maxine had left on his desk, he sort of forgot to answer her.

You almost had to admire Maxine. She was not easily ignored. She stood there, hand on one hip, glaring at Goetzmann. "Then, I take it that the Doublemint girls here aren't under arrest? You're going to let them go even though the whole blackmail scheme was their idea?"

My throat tightened up. Had Nan and I relaxed too soon?

Goetzmann just looked at Maxine. "Their story has been corroborated by Glenn Ledford," he said quietly. "He gave a statement just before they took him into surgery."

"And you believe *Glenn?*" Maxine made a scoffing noise in the back of her throat. "He's a liar!"

I didn't say a word, but the phrase, *It takes one to know one,* did cross my mind.

Goetzmann didn't even blink. "We also found written instructions in Mr. Ledford's apartment which seems to verify what we've been told."

I exchanged a look with Nan. The crib notes! The police had found the notes Glenn had used to remember exactly how he was supposed to threaten us. It was all I could do to keep from smiling.

Isn't stupidity a wonderful thing?

Speaking of which, Maxine was stomping her foot. "Well, I hope you don't believe everything Glenn says, because he is a liar, big as anything. He lies like a rug! All the time!"

I knew, of course, why Maxine kept insisting that Glenn couldn't be trusted. Maxine was afraid that Glenn might mention to the police exactly how she'd tried to get Glenn and

Russell to kill her husband. Conspiracy to commit murder, I do believe, *is* against the law.

Goetzmann was still giving Maxine a level look. "If Mr. Ledford lies all the time, why do *you* believe what he said about the blackmail scheme?" Goetzmann asked.

Maxine stared back at him for a long moment, her mouth working, but nothing coming out. Finally, she said, "Isn't that just like a cop? Always twisting your words!" Believe it or not, she directed this last to me and Nan, as if now she actually expected us to come to her support. Fat chance. After all but demanding that Goetzmann place us under arrest, she could hold her breath on that one. "I mean," Maxine was going on, "you try to be helpful, you try to be a concerned citizen, voluntarily coming in to do your civic duty, and what happens? You get treated like dirt!"

For some reason, Goetzmann decided to separate us then— me and Nan remaining where we were, and Maxine being escorted by a uniformed policeman down the hall somewhere.

Eventually, a skinny, sour-faced woman appeared, and while she took it all down on a tiny machine, Nan and I told our tale all over again. After all that talking, I guess Nan and I were finally talked out. On the way home she and I hardly spoke, but just sat like statues in the back seat of the police car, staring straight ahead at nothing. The young cop who'd brought us to the station earlier was the same one who drove us home. He looked a little beat himself.

Once again, of course, Nan and I got another good look at the dark stains and the ripped upholstery in the back seat. And yet, this time I was too tired to care. At five o'clock in the morning, if our neighbors saw me and Nan being brought home by the cops, so be it. Goetzmann could march us home at gun point as long as we got there.

I glanced over at Nan. "Well," I said, "it's all over."

Nan just looked at me. "It won't be over, Bert," she said. "until the police catch Elliott Sims."

"You mean Les Tennyson," I said.

Nan shrugged, her expression bleak as she looked out the window. The halogen street lights suddenly flickered off. "Sims, Tennyson, whoever. The way this guy can change identities, the cops could be looking for Sims for a long time. Or at least, for whoever his alias *du jour* happens to be."

I shrugged. "Well, at least, this whole mess is over for us. The police shouldn't need us anymore—they've got Glenn Ledford and Maxine Sims to give them all the information they need to get a line on Sims. They should catch him soon enough."

I sounded a lot more positive than I really felt. Actually, the idea of a murderer on the loose, who just happened to think that Nan and I had tried to blackmail him for a half million dollars wasn't exactly upbeat. It seemed to me that, wherever this Sims character was, he might not be in his best mood.

"Oh, yeah, he'll be in custody in no time," I added.

I waited for Nan to agree with me, but she didn't say a word. She just sat there, staring out the window on her side.

You could see lights going on in several of the houses we passed, and around us suddenly there seemed to be a few more cars. Louisville was waking up.

"I'm sure of it," I said. "Sims can't get far." I tried for non-chalant confidence as I leaned against the passenger door to put my elbow on the armrest.

Only there was no armrest.

My arm immediately slipped, and I lurched forward. I

managed to stop my fall just in time, or I'd have rammed my ear against the window frame.

In the front, the young cop shot me a worried look in the rearview window. Oh, great. He probably thought I'd fainted from stress. I thought about giving the guy a friendly wave— just to show him there were no hard feelings. I certainly didn't mind that there were no arm rests or door handles back here. I decided, however, that waving at him right after I'd slid down the inside of his car door might be attracting too much attention.

As it was, I already had Nan staring at me. As if trying to figure out what in the world I'd just been doing.

I turned immediately to look out the window.

Fortunately, we were turning onto Napoleon Boulevard right then, and Nan's attention was directed down the street. I heard her soft sigh when the lights of her own front porch came into view.

When the cop opened the car door for us moments later, he said, "You two be careful, now."

"We plan to," Nan said.

We both said our thank yous, and then, without even pausing, we turned and headed for my apartment.

"I think we'll both sleep a little better if we aren't alone just yet, don't you?" Nan said.

She didn't have to convince me. The last time I'd been here, I'd run through both apartments, looking for her. I wasn't sure I was ready to let her out of my sight.

As I moved up my sidewalk, I glanced over at Nan's doorstep, at the two cocoa cups still sitting there where I'd left them looking sort of forlorn. My throat tightened up.

Oh my yes, if I was getting emotional over *cups*, I wasn't

at all prepared to let Nan out of my sight just yet. And I certainly didn't want to be out of her sight, either. That was for sure.

I looked over at Nan's doorstep again. Those cocoa cups would really need washing by now.

I started for her porch, but Nan caught my arm. "How about we get those later today?" she said. "Like maybe at noon, when it's fully light?" Her tone was lighthearted, but it didn't fool me.

I unlocked my door, switching on the living room lights. All of my things in my living room and in the dining area beyond looked absolutely wonderful to me. I was *home*.

Once safely inside, Nan and I stood at my front door, mutely watching the cop car pull slowly out of sight. I wasn't sure what Nan was feeling, but I had a vast sense of relief. As much as I'd wanted to see a policeman earlier tonight, I wouldn't mind now if I never saw another one again. I wanted things back to normal.

I think Nan and I were so tired, we couldn't sleep. Instead of immediately going to bed, she and I headed for my couch. We'd no sooner plopped down, slipping our shoes off, when my phone rang.

"Maybe they've already caught Sims," I said, padding in my bare feet over to the hutch to pick up my phone.

"Miss Bert Tatum?" The voice was male, loud, and enunciated every word.

"Yes?"

"This is WROL-FM News, and we—"

"WROL radio?" I asked. Over on the couch, Nan perked up at that one. She got to her feet and moved toward me.

"Yes," the voice continued, "we just learned about the part you and your sister played in helping to solve the recent murder in the Galleria. We wondered if we could just roll the tape and interview—"

Oh, for God's sake. The guy intended to record our conversation and play it on the air.

The guy was talking so loud, Nan must've heard every word. She took the phone out of my hand and dropped it back in its cradle. "If any radio station gets an interview, I think it ought to be mine," she said.

Made sense to me. I nodded and started to follow her back to the couch.

The phone rang before we'd taken three steps. Another radio station.

Then a TV station called, and a weekly newspaper.

The last time I took the receiver off the hook. Then I sank down onto the sofa next to Nan, wiggled my toes in the plush carpeting, and put my feet up on my coffee table.

Naturally, the doorbell rang.

Nan and I looked at each other. Lord. Could there actually be reporters coming to my door to talk to us?

The doorbell rang again. And again. I took a deep breath and got to my feet.

"If you see a television camera, don't open the door," Nan said. "And if it's Goetzmann again, or anybody in a blue uniform, tell him we don't want to see any more cops for a long, long time. Tell him to put what he wants to tell us in a letter."

Nan was still giving me instructions when I reached the door. Right away, I realized I was doing things differently now. Without even thinking about it, I very carefully peeked out my peephole and squinted to see who was out there, leaning on my doorbell one more time.

When I saw who it was standing there, I almost did a double take. Quickly I undid the lock and opened the door. Behind me, Nan shifted position on the couch, clearly trying to look past me at whoever it was on my porch.

It was Trent Marksberry.

OK, I admit it. I was surprised to see him. In fact, I was *very* surprised to see him. By now, I had it all figured out. Trent's whole play for me had just been an act. Trent had obviously thought that the closer he got to me, the more likely he'd learn something to help his investigation. He'd hoped I'd help him clear up Russell Moorman's death for the insurance company he was working for. After all, I'd been the only one who'd actually talked to Moorman personally.

Quite naturally, I expected that, once Trent's case was pretty much solved—like *now*, for instance—he'd be hitting the road.

But, instead, here he was, throwing a quick smile at Nan and then turning to absolutely beam at me. From behind his back, Trent produced three crystal wine glasses in one hand and a magnum of champagne in the other. The cork for the champagne had already been removed. Ready to pour. At his feet, on the porch, there was a large white paper bag.

I didn't know about Nan, but I was impressed. I'd never in my life had a guy show up carrying wine glasses before. Of course, I hadn't dated hardly any since high school, and back then what few boys I'd gone out with had thought it a big deal to sneak a can of beer out of their parents' refrigerator.

Not exactly romantic.

I eyed the glasses, and t¹ nt. "Is this some kind of celebration?" I asked.

Trent shrugged, grinning that crooked grin of his. "Sure it is, Bert. One bad guy is in custody, the police are on the trail of the other, and, best of all, you're safe." His eyes actually seemed to rest quite fondly on me.

I could feel my cheeks growing warm under his scrutiny. I looked away, and found myself staring at my bare feet. Lord. Was I smooth or what?

"Are you going to let me in?" Trent asked. His tone was amused.

I blinked, and looked back at him, feeling . . . *what?* I wasn't sure. My heart had started to beat a little faster, just looking at the man. And yet, I didn't immediately move away from the door.

Lord. What was wrong with me? After the last Jake episode, could it be that I really had trouble letting any man in my life again?

Or was it something else? I swallowed, still looking straight at Trent, an uneasy something nagging at the back of my mind.

Trent studied me for a moment, and when I didn't immediately move aside, he cocked his head to one side and grinned at me again. Then he easily moved around me, straight over to the coffee table where Nan was sitting. Setting the bottle and the glasses on the coffee table, he headed back out to my porch again. "*And,*" he said, smiling at me as he retrieved the white paper bag, "this is to celebrate you two cracking the case."

He came in, closing the door with his foot, and began unpacking the white bag, spreading its contents on the coffee table. He gestured at both of us with a stack of paper napkins he drew out of the bag. "It's all over the radio, you know," Trent said. "Well, not all over. But there is this kinda nice story about Russell Moorman's killer being sought by the police. And that another man is under armed guard at the hospital. And—" At this point he gave me a wink. "—the news story does happen to mention you two as material witnesses."

"Knowing one particular cop's opinion of us," Nan said, eyeing the cartons Trent was setting out, "I'd have thought we'd have been described as interfering with a police investigation."

Trent grinned. "Anyway, when I heard the news on the radio, I thought we'd just have ourselves a little ol' champagne breakfast. Before all the reporters out there realize you two are out of police custody. And they come here in droves, ready to interview Louisville's newest heroines."

Heroines. I just looked at Trent. There was an odd note in the way Trent had said the word. I found myself studying Trent, that odd nagging feeling back again in full force.

What in the world was wrong with me? I mean, here was a good-looking man who bore a remarkable resemblance to Harrison Ford—who kept giving me smiles that could possibly curl my toes. Not to mention, here was a man who had elevated kissing to an art form.

So what was my problem?

Maybe I was getting more like Nan every day. According to Nan, dating is a whole lot like fishing. Once the catch is in the boat, Nan says, pretty soon it starts to smell.

Was that it? Now that Trent looked interested, I wasn't?

Trent had planted himself on the sofa, and was now pointing at the cartons on the coffee table. "OK, ladies," he said, "I've got your pancakes, your eggs, your bacon and sausage— your you-name-it."

Nan had started opening cartons, and the aroma of bacon made me realize I really was hungry. I stood there, wondering when was the last time Nan and I had eaten. And, incidentally, why was it that I continued to stand over here and not quite join in?

Nan, however, didn't seem to notice. She was already

spreading out a paper napkin on her lap. "You know, this is awfully nice of you, Trent," she said, "particularly since your client is going to have to pay off that insurance policy now."

Trent shrugged, scooping up a handful of butter patties and maple syrup containers from the sack and setting them on the table. "Hey, I get paid whether the insurance company has to pay off or not. Besides, Russell Moorman's little boy is a hundred thousand dollars richer—more or less. More power to the little guy."

Nan smiled and glanced over at me. A questioning look appeared in her eyes. I could see what she was thinking. What on earth was going on with me?

I looked over at Trent again. His mentioning Russell Moorman had almost reminded me of something. What was it? I noticed then that Trent was giving me a concerned look, much like Nan's.

"Are you tired, Bert?" Trent asked. "All of this has got to have been awful for you."

I waved my hand. "No, no, I'm peachy," I said. "Really."

Nan gave me another searching look.

I moved across the room then, and stood next to Trent.

"Before we dig in," Trent said, "let's have a toast." He stood up, as Nan got up and came around the coffee table. Like the time we'd had the little pizza party, Trent positioned himself between us. I noticed that, like that time, too, he chose the spot that kept him from hitting elbows with right-handed me and left-handed Nan.

Now what did that remind me of?

Trent handed one filled glass to Nan and then one to me. "Here's to you, ladies," he said, "Drink up. We've got a whole magnum to finish. It's not every day two amateurs help out the cops *and* a private detective."

Nan smiled. "Yeah, *right*. We're helpful." she said. She glanced over at me, her eyes still a little concerned. "I'm sure, Goetzmann thinks we were unbelievably helpful."

Trent raised an eyebrow. "Who?"

"Goetzmann," Nan said, reaching for a piece of bacon. "You know, the cop in charge of the case." She lifted her glass of champagne to take a sip.

And that's when it all fell together in my mind, like puzzle pieces locking into place.

After that everything seemed to slide into slow motion. I jumped forward, my hand outstretched. I saw Nan staring at me, her eyes wide with surprise. And I saw Trent turning, his hands reaching toward me.

It seemed as if I were moving, not through air, but through water, as I reached toward Nan. With my left hand, I knocked Nan's glass out of her grasp. With my right hand, I grabbed the heavy champagne bottle by its neck.

And I turned and swung the bottle at Trent's head.

When it connected, it made a sickening thunk, and champagne sprayed over all three of us in a foamy fizz.

Chapter 20

•

NAN

According to all the studies I've read over the years, if one identical twin goes nuts, the chances are excellent that the other one will immediately follow suit. As I watched Bert belt Trent with the champagne bottle, it occurred to me that in about an hour tops, a couple of orderlies would probably drop by to outfit me in one of those really chic jackets with the too-long arms that tied in the back.

"Bert!" I yelled. "Are you crazy? What the hell do you think you're doing?"

"Nan," Bert said, "I had to—" Her voice shook as she stared at Trent wide-eyed.

Trent had fallen straight backwards on the couch, and now his limp body was slowly sliding off the couch cushions and onto the floor. As Bert and I stared, Trent ended up, lying face up, sprawled between the sofa and the coffee table.

I started moving. Leaning over him, I put my hand against Trent's chest. "Oh, thank God," I said, "he's still breathing."

I turned to stare at Bert. Who seemed to be in a daze. Taking a deep breath, I began, "Bert—"

She blinked, and started taking deep breaths herself.

"Didn't you see what he'd done?" Bert asked. "He'd already opened the champagne bottle."

I gaped at her. They say you're supposed to humor the insane, so as not to unduly upset them. "That's right," I said slowly and distinctly. "He had already opened the—."

"*Nan*," Bert said, interrupting me. "Trent was trying to kill us!"

My mouth dropped open. "What?"

Bert pointed at Trent. His face was slack now. I stared at him. When he was unconscious, he didn't look nearly so much like Harrison Ford. "Don't you know who this is?" Bert asked.

"A guy about to charge you with assault?" I said.

Bert went right on as if I hadn't said anything. "It's Mr. Sandersen, Nan. *Ted Sandersen.*"

I took an even closer look. "Mr. Sandersen? Bert, Ted Sandersen is dead . . ."

"Oh no, he isn't," Bert said. "He can't be, because *this* is Ted Sandersen. Alias Elliott Sims," Bert said. "Alias Trent Marksberry."

My mouth dropped open again.

It took Bert a little while to explain things to me. While she explained, though, she kept busy. Tying Trent up.

That's right, shortly after clobbering Trent, Bert immediately ran upstairs to her bedroom, and returned about half a minute later with several packages of—what else—panty hose. "I don't think I have any rope, so these are going to have to do," she said. Tearing open the cellophane wrapper of the first package with her teeth, she began winding the legs of the hose around Trent's wrists and then around the inner wood frame of her sofa. Apparently, Bert's plan was, if Trent here woke up and tried to get away, he'd have to do it dragging an Early American couch behind him.

I, of course, didn't start helping Bert with her little panty-hose project until she convinced me that what she now believed was indeed true. Up to that point, I just stood there, watching her wind pantyhose around Trent's ankles and the brace on the sofa leg, and more or less hoping that Trent had a really good sense of humor.

"Just think about it, Nan," Bert said, as she tied a rather large knot that ended with a tan sandalfoot. "What was it that Goetzmann told us? The cops didn't identify Russell Moorman until almost *midnight* Friday. But Trent already knew Russell's identity early Friday evening—when he showed up at my apartment right after it had been trashed."

Oh my God. Could that really be so?

Bert was hurrying on. "I'll bet that Trent was the one who trashed both our apartments—looking, no doubt, for something that would tell him how to locate his blackmailer. Boy, I bet he flipped when, after getting rid of Russell, he got a call from Glenn, and he realized there was somebody else involved in this thing that he didn't know about." Bert looked over at me. "In the case of my apartment, Trent probably searched it, and then, finding nothing, he just went around the building and appeared on my doorstep."

I stared at Bert, feeling a little sick. Good Lord. Could she be right?

"Nan, the only person who could know who Russell was before the police actually did, *had* to be the guy who killed Russell and took his wallet."

I took a deep breath. "Trent told us," I said slowly, "that he'd gotten the victim's identity from the police—and yet, just a second ago he acted as if he'd never even heard of *Goetzmann.*"

Certainly, Goetzmann was a guy you weren't likely to forget. I moved quickly across the room until I was right next to Bert, then I bent down and started winding pantyhose around the interior wood frame of Bert's sofa and Trent's wrists.

"But what makes you think he's Ted Sandersen?" I asked. "And not Les Tennyson—Mrs. Sandersen's lover?"

"Don't you see?" Bert said, pulling a nylon knot tight. "Trent can't be Les Tennyson—he already knew which of us was right-handed and which was left-handed. I don't know why it didn't hit me before. Remember what Trent said when he brought us the pizza? He couldn't sit by southpaw Nan or you'd be hitting elbows. We'd never told him about being mirror twins, so he had to be remembering it from another time." Bert looked over at me, her eyes very round. "Don't you remember how interested *Mr. Sandersen* was in our being mirror twins?"

My mouth went dry. It all made sense. As teenagers at the Sandersens, we'd hardly even met Les Tennyson, but *Mr. Sandersen* had spent some time with us. I looked back down at Trent. "It's the beard," I said, "that makes him look so different."

Bert shrugged. "That and twenty-something years."

Once Trent was pantyhosed to the couch, I hurried to the phone to dial 911. When I returned, I stood, just staring at the man on Bert's floor. "If you're right, this means that he murdered his own son." I swallowed once before I could speak again. "How in hell could he ever bring himself to do such a thing?"

Bert didn't even have to think about it. "Remember what Ted Sandersen's sister said? Once they found out about his wife's affair, Wilma and her brother wondered if the kids really were Ted's." Bert shrugged, and then went over to sit down in the blue upholstered rocker she keeps in front of her bookcase. "And, after all, the brothers were blackmailing their own father, even if they didn't know it—in his new identity as Elliott Sims. Sandersen certainly wouldn't think of them as his sons—just as problems to be rid of."

"He must've killed Alice, too," I went on. "Remember, he showed up at the motel while we were still there." There had been no anonymous caller like Trent had told us. He'd gotten Glenn's address out of poor Alice, just like we did, and, once Alice had seen him, he couldn't let her live.

Bert was now staring at Trent wide-eyed all over again. "Oh my God," she said, covering her mouth.

I thought maybe Trent was coming to, but no, a quick glance told me he was still lying there, out like a light.

I turned to look at Bert. "What is it?" I asked. She really looked pale, all of a sudden.

Bert's eyes got even wider as she turned toward me. "Oh, Nan, I let myself get felt up by somebody who killed four people!"

What could I say? "It happens," I said.

Trent—I would always think of him as Trent—was just beginning to regain consciousness when the cops arrived on my doorstep. For a woman who'd insisted earlier that she didn't want to see any more cops anytime soon, I could have kissed their shoes.

No surprise, the second the police cut him off the couch and hauled him to his feet, Trent started complaining loudly about how Bert had attacked him for no reason. Once again— Lord, what a shock—we all ended up downtown at the police station.

The place was beginning to feel like home.

At the station, in front of Goetzmann, Trent was amazingly convincing. He actually sounded hurt that Bert and I would even think he needed to be tied up. Goetzmann, I noticed, did seem to be listening to what Trent had to say.

It was Maxine who finally clinched it. They brought her in, whining—of course—at the top of her lungs. "I can't believe you've dragged me down here again. I mean, for God's sake, I just got home—" Maxine must've caught sight of Trent at that moment, because she stopped right in the middle of what she was saying. Pointing a lacquered fingertip dramatically at Trent, as he stood in the middle of Goetzmann's office, she said, "That's him! That's my lowlife murdering husband, Elliott!"

It was a touching moment. I mean, don't you love it when a marriage really works?

It occurred to me watching the charming Mr. and Mrs. Sims that it had, no doubt, been Maxine herself who'd shot at us outside of Bert's apartment. Only Maxine hadn't really been shooting at me and Bert. Unable to get the brothers to kill her husband, she'd tried to do it herself.

Once Maxine identified Trent, there were pretty much no surprises after that. We found out eventually that the champagne bottle really did contain rat poison. Apparently, old Trent had been planning to pay us back for the trouble we'd caused him. He was going to kill us, and then go into hiding all over again.

When Goetzmann called me with that little bit of news, I actually shuddered. Bert and I had come appallingly close to having a double funeral. Not to mention, a thing like this could spoil a girl's taste for champagne.

I guess the only other surprising thing that happened was something that occurred on Wednesday of the next week.

Around three o'clock, just as I was finishing my air shift, the receptionist at CKI stuck her head in the control room.

She's about nineteen, and she gets excited easily. "Nan?" she said, her eyes dancing. "There's, um, *someone* here to see you. It must be kind of important." She started to close the door, then rethought it, putting her head back in again. "By the way," she added, "he's a hunk."

The hunk turned out to be Goetzmann. Standing in the lobby, he dwarfed the chairs and tables out there. His hands behind his back, he was studying the posters of country music artists decorating our walls. When he heard my approach, he turned around and gave me an appraising look.

I smiled, trying to look as if I hadn't noticed that his eyes had gone up and down my body twice in the time it took me to cross the room. "Hi," I said. Then I waited.

Goetzmann actually looked ill at ease for once. "I thought you'd want to know what's happened in the investigation."

And he came all the way down here to tell me? In person, no less? When he could've just picked up the phone?

"Yes, I would like to know," I said. I motioned him to one of the chairs, and when he lowered himself into one, he looked like a grizzly bear perching on a foot stool. He ran a hand over his marine haircut, and then he plunged in.

"Well, it was all just like your sister said. Ted Sandersen, alias Elliott Sims, has confessed. He murdered his wife and her lover years ago. And a few days ago, he killed Russell and Alice Moorman to cover up that first murder. Apparently, he assumed the Trent Marksberry identity just to find out what you and your sister knew." Goetzmann shook his massive head. "Actually, the guy was pretty slick. He went into one of those twenty-four-hour printing places and had business cards printed up with his Trent Marksberry alias. Then he rented a cheap office in downtown Louisville, put in an answering machine, and he was all set."

I was stunned. Not about the murders, of course, nor about the multiple aliases. Not even about our being taken in by Trent's charade. What I was surprised about was that he'd actually confessed. The man we'd known as Trent Marksberry didn't seem the type to break down and pour his heart out. "What on earth made him confess?"

"Actually, it was a *who*," Goetzmann said. "I brought in that sister of his that you two told us about—just to see if she could still identify him. And what a lovable person she turned out to be. Wilma Sandersen Cartland marched in, her Bible under one arm. Even after twenty-some years, she didn't seem to have any doubt. She took one look at Sandersen in his cell, and then ordered him to fall down on his knees and pray for God's mercy and forgiveness. Because he sure wasn't going to get any from her!"

I suppressed a smile. Hell hath no fury like a Wilma Cartland.

"She started whooping and hollering at Sandersen about all that he'd put her through. What an imposition it had been clearing up his estate when she'd thought he'd been murdered. Up to and including having to look at a burned up corpse that hadn't even been him, but Les Tennyson wearing Ted's clothes." Goetzmann's eyes had been wandering around the room, stopping for a moment on a poster on the wall of Tanya Tucker in a low-cut black lacy dress. Then he'd turned back at me.

What do you know, his eyes were hazel.

"At this point, even as we speak, Ted Sandersen and his lawyer are no doubt trying to build an insanity defense, based on it running in the family." Goetzmann shrugged. "Of course, after talking to that Cartland woman," he went on, "I was thinking about making up a new identity myself just to get away from her."

I grinned.

He grinned back.

After that, I—the radio announcer with the gift of gab—couldn't think of a damn thing to say. So the two of us just sat there for a few moments, looking at each other. I had no idea what Goetzmann was thinking. What I did know was that—when you didn't think he was about to put you in a jail cell—he was extremely attractive. And probably a lot nicer guy than I'd given him credit for. And, like our receptionist said, he *was* a hunk. I stole a look at the third finger on his left hand. Hmm. *No ring.*

When I looked up, Goetzmann's smile seemed a little bigger. If I had to hazard a guess, I'd say he knew exactly what I'd just been doing.

Goetzmann stood up, reaching down with a big hand to help me up. His grasp was warm and firm, and he stood there for a second holding my hand.

"So," he said.

"So," I said. He was still holding my hand, but I didn't pull away.

"So maybe we could have a cup of coffee together sometime," Goetzmann went on. "We both work downtown."

He made it sound as if everybody working downtown were obligated to get together socially. I smiled, though, looking up into his eyes. I suddenly felt like Sally Field at the Academy Awards. *He liked me. He really liked me.*

"Sure," I said. "Why don't you call me, Goetzmann?"

Goetzmann smiled at me then, finally letting go of my

hand as if he'd just realized he was still holding it. "The name's Hank," he said.

I nodded, as if I'd already remembered without him telling me. I hadn't remembered, though. In fact, I was just standing there, thinking. *Hank?* Could I ever be serious about anybody named Hank?

On the other hand, this was a major improvement over *Tab*.

I stood there until Hank went out the front door, and then I ran back into the office to phone Bert.

Chapter 21

•

BERT

I was right in the middle of typing a letter when Nan phoned—a letter that one of the associate attorneys at Mayer, Krebbs and Gleeson, Attorneys at Law, was waiting for. Once again I was filling in for a secretary on vacation, once again I was working in the Citizens Plaza building, and once again Kentuckiana Temps had placed me at another law office. With said attorney waiting for me, I didn't exactly have a lot of time to talk to Nan.

In fact, I had just enough time to hear Nan's news about Goetzmann; say, "I can't *believe* you want to go out with that guy;" and then pretty much hang up. Nan did laugh and say something vulgar about handcuffs before I put down the receiver, but I didn't quite get it all.

I found myself smiling, though, as I finished the letter, addressed an envelope, and carried it all into the attorney to have the letter signed. Maybe things would work out for Nan this time. It would be very nice if, for once, her catch didn't start to smell.

When I got back to my desk, I just sat there for a minute. A week ago, hearing that Goetzmann had asked Nan out would've made me a little mad. I'd have fumed about how many men Nan always seems to attract. Funniest thing, I didn't feel that way anymore.

Nan and I weren't in some kind of double competition. We were both just trying to find somebody we could be happy with. And, in the meantime, we were very lucky to have been born with our best friend.

Late that very afternoon, I found myself standing on the curb just out of the Citizens Plaza building, waiting for the light to change. It was after five, but the stores in the Galleria were staying open late for something called "Downtown Days." I intended to drop by Laura Ashley's to visit a plaid jumper I'd had my eye on for about three months now. I wanted to check to see if it had been marked down enough, or if I were going to have to wait a little longer for it to get even close to my price range.

At my elbow, a man cleared his throat. I turned to see a man about forty or so, standing at my elbow. Wearing a business suit and a Burberry overcoat, with a scarf matching the trademark inner plaid lining thrown around his neck, he looked quite a bit like William Hurt. He had the same thinning, blond hair, the same intense blue eyes, and the same confident smile. The man was looking straight at me, his eyes on mine.

"I say," he said, with just the trace of a British accent, "could you tell me the time?"

I glanced down to see his wristwatch peeking out of the cuff of his overcoat.

The man saw my look, and then gave me a quick smile. "You know," he said, "I've seen you around here before, and I do believe you are one of the most beautiful—"

The light changed, and I stepped off the curb.

I really didn't mean to be rude.

But I kept right on walking.